SLEEPLESS

ALSO BY ROMY HAUSMANN

Dear Child

SLEEPLESS

ROMY HAUSMANN

Translated from the German by
Jamie Bulloch

FLATIRON
BOOKS
NEW YORK

SLEEPLESS. Copyright © 2020 by Romy Hausmann. Translation copyright © 2020 by Jamie Bulloch. All rights reserved. Printed in the United States of America. For information, address Flatiron Books, 120 Broadway, New York, NY 10271.

www.flatironbooks.com

Library of Congress Cataloging-in-Publication Data

Names: Hausmann, Romy, 1981– author. | Bulloch, Jamie, translator.
Title: Sleepless / Rory Hausmann ; translated from the German
   by Jamie Bulloch.
Other titles: Marta schläft. English
Description: First U.S. edition. | New York : Flatiron Books, 2021. |
   "Originally published in Germany in 2020 as Marta schläft by dtv
   Verlagsgesellschaft mbH & Co. KG. München"
Identifiers: LCCN 2021025637 | ISBN 9781250824790 (hardcover) |
   ISBN 9781250824813 (ebook)
Subjects: GSAFD: Suspense fiction. | LCGFT: Thrillers (Fiction). | Novels.
Classification: LCC PT2708.A96 M3713 2021 | DDC 833/.92—dc23
LC record available at https://lccn.loc.gov/2021025637

Our books may be purchased in bulk for promotional, educational, or business use. Please contact your local bookseller or the Macmillan Corporate and Premium Sales Department at 1-800-221-7945, extension 5442, or by email at MacmillanSpecialMarkets@macmillan.com.

Originally published in Germany in 2020 as *Marta schläft* by dtv Verlagsgesellschaft mbH & Co. KG. München.

First U.S. Edition: 2021

10   9   8   7   6   5   4   3   2   1

For you, Karl.

May your big, colorful heart

always show you the right way.

Thanks for allowing me to be your mama.

Hope is a dangerous thing

for a woman like me to have—

but I have it.

LANA DEL REY

My angel,

I've written you dozens of letters and, now more than ever, regret never having sent a single one of them. I ought to have done. Definitely. You've every right to find out what really happened back then. To find out from me, in my own words, words I always believed to be inadequate. I don't know what you remember, or if hidden somewhere at the back of your mind there's still a fragment of our last meeting. I promised to catch the evil man. I tempted you with the sea, and you must have thought you could rely on me. That everything would turn out fine and that I would be the one to make sure it did.

All words are irrelevant now and I can only write this, perhaps my final letter, in my thoughts.

It's over, my angel.

Today I'm going to die.

Just like her.

He's won.

NADJA

A panic attack is like standing on the cliff edge. *Don't look down*, I tell myself as I put my head back and try to breathe. Above me, slate-gray clouds drift across the sky that's still the color of lavender, but only just. I hear noises. It sounds like the staccato of rain drumming against a windowpane.

It's not rain, I realize. It's rocks crumbling beneath my feet. I try to take a step backward but can't. I teeter, lose my balance and thrash about with my arms because I refuse to believe it's happening. Because every time I believe I've got a chance.

I haven't.

I fall and let out a silent scream.

The water . . .

I blink. Shelves of sweets wash toward me, a freezer glides closer as if carried on the waves. My body lies twisted on a stone floor. It's swaying. I feel seasick and gag on some bile. In the distance I hear voices and a flurry of activity. *What happened?* I want to ask—how stupid is that? I know exactly what happened. I fell from the cliffs, for the fourth time this month. It's Saturday, July 20. Four falls within twenty days. I ought to be thankful—I've had it worse. When I touch the area on my forehead that's throbbing

2

I feel a slight bump and a dampness. Blood. I must have hit my head. My circulation. My eyelids are fluttering like insect wings. Unconsciousness is trying to steal me away. I would cry for help if I hadn't already drowned. In the red water.

Don't worry, she's only sleeping.

I wake up.

The ground beneath me is firm again. I must have drifted ashore. Somebody pulls me up to a seated position and asks, "Are you okay?"

I think I nod. Try to get my bearings. The shelves of sweets, the freezer. The shop of a small, slightly run-down petrol station on the A13. Unleaded at 1.51 euro per liter, diesel at 1.43. I had parked the Land Rover by one of the two pumps, got out and looked around shiftily, like a fugitive.

Nobody. No other vehicle that had followed me into the petrol station and none already there waiting for me. Relief. Through the shop window I had seen the cashier inquisitively craning his neck. So I did something normal, inconspicuous. I filled up the car, locked the doors and went to pay.

"I bet it's just her circulation," I hear a man say. His face is merely a blur at first, but I suspect he's the cashier. I remember a red-and-blue-checked, short-sleeved shirt and the barked laughter coming from beneath his nicotine-stained mustache when he made a joke as he handed me my change. "An old girl like that is a real guzzler, eh?" He meant the Land Rover.

"Not surprising, it's sweltering today," he now says, this time referring to me. The woman who just collapsed by his counter.

Another barking laugh, then he says, "Annelies, go and get a bottle of water!"

My vision slowly starts to clear. I try to get to my feet, but it's a very clumsy attempt. "Don't rush it!" Mustache man grabs my arm to support me. My right knee is shaking as if the joint had been removed and the void filled with jelly. "Oh, you poor thing," he says, fixing his eyes on my bleeding forehead. I open my mouth to tell him I'm okay. That I'm just a very sensitive, nervous individual, that apart from yesterday evening I haven't been behind the wheel of a car since I took my test, and that the drive here was sheer hell—every time the road narrowed spelled an accident, every car behind me meant I was being followed, and that it was probably just a matter of time before my anxiety peaked in a full-blown panic attack. Toppling over the cliff edge and plummeting straight into the red water.

From Letter #9

The new therapist has recommended I should write down my dreams. I don't know what good that will do, especially as I keep on having the same one. It's always the salt marshes of Aigues-Mortes, again and again . . . Do you remember it at all, this image? Aigues-Mortes as it appeared on the June page of the calendar. Everything in the photo looked fake, as if it had been recolored in the most disturbing way possible. An intensely white salt mound rising above bloodred water beneath a lavender sky. You asked me how water could be red. "Looks like blood," you thought. "An entire lake full of blood."

"No, no," I said, and explained to you that this strange color was the result of certain halophile bacteria, and that "halophile" came from the Greek word for salt: "halos." What I didn't tell you was that "Aigues-Mortes" in French means something like "dead water." I didn't want you to be afraid.

NADJA

I shut my mouth without having said anything. I want to allay mustache man's concerns with a smile. Of course it was just the—as he called it—*sweltering* heat that triggered my collapse. There's no reason to suspect me of anything.

My smile falters when, at that very moment, fear shoots through my body like an electric shock. On the floor in front of me is my handbag that I'd dropped and beside it, fanned out like the frayed ends of an old mop, is the blond wig. I instinctively throw my hands up, touch my head and feel tightly bound hair—my own. Attentive mustache man bends down, hands me the wig and turns away politely when I put it on with trembling fingers. In the past I often imagined myself as a blonde and thus a completely different person. Now that the precisely trimmed, light-blond fringe is hanging diagonally over my right eye I just feel incredibly stupid.

"Water!" A woman in a colorful flowery apron comes scuttling over from the fridge with a bottle. Her fat body shakes with her excited, rapid footsteps. I could weep. Instead of taking the bottle I ask for my handbag. I open it and rummage inside. Wallet, house keys, car keys, the piece of paper with the directions, mobile phone and chewing gum. Finally I find what I am looking for:

the foil pack with my pills. The cashier is watching me. Under his inquisitive gaze I scrap the idea of taking my medicine. I don't want him to think I'm ill, and in any case it wouldn't be a good idea to take something now. I need to be able to drive; I haven't got to my destination yet.

"Come on, have a sip at least!" the woman in the apron insists. She's still holding the bottle of water in one hand, while the other is stroking my cheek. When she moves her arms I can smell sweat and frying oil. "She's deathly white, Herbert," she says to the man.

"Maybe we ought to ring for an ambulance," he replies.

"No, please don't," I beg them.

Herbert and his wife, Annelies. She reminds me of Aunt Evelyn, who I only ever remember in one of her various housecoats. With her hands perched on her wide hips and that expression on her otherwise cheerful, squashy face: *My God, child, what have you done this time?* Abandoning the water, they decide that I could do with a schnapps instead. Plum schnapps, homemade. Much better, apparently, than the industrial swill that Herbert sells in little bottles from his counter.

"I don't need an ambulance, I'm feeling better," I assert, which must sound odd to the couple that run the petrol station as neither has mentioned the ambulance again.

All the same, Herbert says, "Okay, as you like."

They escort me into a room at the back of the shop, which smells of stale smoke. It's barely large enough to fit us all in, especially as almost half of the room is taken up by a desk. Behind it, sitting on a swivel chair, is a young boy. I reckon he's about six or seven. Thin, red-blond hair, narrow, pale face, pointed chin.

A delicate little creature struggling to thrive in the haze of nicotine. In front of the boy are drawing things: a pad of paper and a box of colored pencils. He's completely absorbed in what he's doing and doesn't pay any attention to us until Annelies says, "Up you get, Timmy. We need the chair for this poor woman." The boy stands up without saying anything. He stares with his large, piercingly blue eyes. I sheepishly fiddle with my wig, then my T-shirt. I feel like a clown. Herbert wheels the chair around the desk and gestures to me to sit: "Please."

I sit down and turn to avoid Timmy's gaze. Which I fail to do. Now he steps forward, his eyes still staring at me. Her grandson, Annelies says, patting his head. They look after him while their daughter, Timmy's mother, completes her training at a Plasticine factory in Zossen. I nod eagerly, even though I don't want to hear anything about their family. And I certainly don't want the boy to look at me as he's doing now. In his eyes I can see hundreds of broken promises. As well as death.

APRIL 2014

FIVE YEARS EARLIER

Nelly Schütt loves films. She always has. Her parents ran an inn, the third generation in the family to do so, in the flat countryside of Mecklenburg. It was nothing special—four rooms, adequate food and a decent level of cleanliness. The guests who ended up here were either passing through or too stingy to fork out for a hotel. On the buckhorn coatrack behind the leaded glass door that led to the dining room hung the dreams of her mother— there was always enough space among the coats of the few guests. Sometimes Nelly heard her crying. Her father enjoyed his life as the innkeeper. The moment he finished washing the tankards he would sit at the head of the regulars' table and join in the rants about the depravity of city types. In her parents' film Nelly only ever appeared as an extra. Even as a small child she was always in the way. She ran between their legs at the most inopportune moments—*For heaven's sake, Nelly!*—causing beer and sticky brown sauce to rain down, slices of meat to land with a slap on the floor, and glass and crockery to smash. So for a while she was shifted from place to place like one of the little vases with artificial roses or the salt and pepper shakers, until they finally found the perfect place for her behind reception, away from the kitchen and dining room. There she would sit with her grandfather, who dealt with the room bookings—on his knees when she was really small, then on her own chair. They used to pass the time with Grandfather's beloved old black-and-white films that played on an endless loop via a VHS recorder on a small television set. Nelly was a fast learner. Grandfather would say, "*The Woman in the Window*," and she—six years of age—would reply as fast as a pistol shot, "1944, directed by Fritz Lang, starring Edward G. Robinson and Joan Bennett." Grandfather would laugh and give her a caramel from the glass bowl on the reception counter, which first stuck to her teeth and then her gums.

In *The Woman in the Window*, university professor Richard (Edward G. Robinson) falls in love with a beautiful young woman whose portrait is exhibited in the window of an art gallery. Soon afterward he meets the woman, Alice (Joan Bennett), in real life after visiting a gentlemen's club. Richard, whose wife and children are away visiting relatives, and who probably feels unappreciated, accompanies beautiful Alice back to her flat. They are having a drink when Alice's lover Claude suddenly appears and launches into a furious attack on Richard. Richard kills Claude in self-defense with a pair of scissors. Frenetically, he and Alice decide to cover up the murder, Richard promising to sort it all out.

Grandfather said, "*The Woman in the Window*," and the fifteen-year-old Nelly replied, "That Richard is such an idiot. How can someone make so many mistakes?"

Richard does indeed make lots of them. First he transports Claude's dead body on the back seat of his car, his plan being to take the corpse to the woods and hide it there. But on the way he crosses a toll bridge, where his nervousness attracts the guard's attention—he actually drops the toll money, almost allowing the guard a glimpse of the body through the side window. In the woods Richard leaves tire marks and footprints, and gets caught on barbed wire, ripping his suit and even injuring himself. A scrap of material and his blood—evidence that the police will find soon after discovering Claude's body. Then he won't stop blabbing to his best friend, who, as district attorney, is involved in the police investigation.

Her grandfather shrugged and said, "Richard is a university professor, my girl. A perfectly normal chap who never intended to kill anyone and who's now in a panic. Not some hardened criminal who commits murder all the time and makes bodies disappear."

Although Nelly thought Grandfather was right, for some inexplicable reason Richard made her cross. Just as everything else now made her cross. Life trapped in the village. Her mother who went around howling pointlessly. Her father and the regulars who bad-mouthed the city without ever having been there. Her own film, this sluggish, tedious, ineffectual drama. The guests who came and knew when they would leave. Were *able* to leave. And sometimes even her grandfather, who did nothing but waste his time on those stupid old films.

Grandfather didn't say "*The Woman in the Window*" anymore; he'd since died. Twenty-two-year-old Nelly could only think of his voice when she pressed the "play" button on the video recorder. And she would sigh deeply. Because she missed her grandfather so much. Because sitting at reception without him was lonely.

And because of Richard. He was a good man. He'd somehow got himself mixed up in that mess with Alice and Claude. Now Nelly knew for herself what it was to get mixed up in something without intending to or harboring any wicked intent. How she'd have loved to say this to the woman who'd driven up in her car this morning and come to reception. Not wanting a room, but to talk. Set something straight. And to warn Nelly.

The right phrases danced in Nelly's head. The explanations, the excuses, but also the things she could have offered in her defense. A counterattack. Instead she said nothing, not a word. She remained as silent as a fish. Just nodded, felt ashamed and hoped that this woman would never, ever come back.

From: Letter #11

I measured the hallway with the rule that the previous tenant left on the kitchen windowsill when he moved out. I'd love to buy a carpet. My feet are always so freezing when I come out of the bedroom in the morning and go down the hallway to the bathroom. The tiles are so cold that they hurt the soles of my feet; the cold works its way into every bone, even if I've got two pairs of socks on. I made a note of the dimensions then scrunched up the piece of paper. No carpet. I think it's right if it hurts. In fact, it can't be painful enough.

I wonder how your life is. Have you got a large flat? Is it nicely furnished? I can count the items of furniture I own on the fingers of one hand. A table and chair in the kitchen, a bed, wardrobe, cupboard and television in the bedroom. The living room is empty; I always keep the door shut. Only sometimes, when I wake at night with a start, do I get up and go in. In my pajamas I'll sit in the middle of the room on the bare parquet floor and breathe to counter the darkness. From time to time a car drives past outside, its headlights casting shapes on the ceiling. I see lots of things in these: butterflies, fish with stunted tail fins, lightning flashes, battle-axes or the miniature outline of Africa.

My therapist says I probably just need more time. But how much more? How do you become normal? I mean, I am trying. I've got a flat and a job. "You should mix with people," is what she also says, my therapist. "You become normal by doing normal things."

Normal . . . *I can't even buy a carpet.*

NADJA

Timmy is still gawping at me so I close my eyes. A story comes to mind, the story of the woman who could look through walls and doors, even through all the layers of a person right to their very core. One day a girl asked the woman to look through her, as she was desperate to know what she looked like beneath her skin, skeleton and the mass of blood vessels. I hear Timmy shuffling his feet impatiently as if he were able to read my mind and was urging me to tell him the rest of the story. My brother Janek was just like this too. The moment I started telling him something he would pester me with his constant refrain: "What happened next?"

I blink and establish that Timmy's eyes are not looking through me anymore, but up into the air. He's squeezing his little hands in front of his tummy. Clearly he's uncomfortable in my presence. I want to say to him, "Don't feel bad. Your being here makes me equally uncomfortable."

Herbert and Annelies have left us alone to fetch the schnapps and the first aid box. The latter is a lie because the first aid box is hanging on the wood-paneled wall in here, beside a yellowed calendar featuring girls in bikinis, which is two years out of date.

Besides, I can hear them whispering on the other side of the closed office door. Annelies says there's something fishy going on. She asks Herbert if he noticed how nervous I was when I was rummaging through my handbag, and then there was the thing with the wig—all very strange. Herbert doesn't say anything in reply; I imagine him giving an apathetic shrug. But Annelies isn't going to let this go, it seems. She saw pills in my handbag, she says, possibly drugs that might explain my strange behavior. "Maybe she's dangerous."

"So what are you going to do now? Ring the police?" Herbert sounds amused, which ought to come as a relief to me, but this time Annelies says nothing. Maybe she nodded. My breathing is fast and shallow. The police will want to see my papers. I'll claim I left them at home, but in the end a brief inquiry over the radio will establish without doubt that I'm not the owner of the Land Rover.

I feel sick. I shouldn't be here. I ought to be at home on a Saturday like any other. I ought to be cleaning my flat, inhaling the relaxing aroma of Ajax. Later I'd make myself go to the little grocery shop in Charlottenburg. Having paid for a cauliflower, grapefruit, apples and a bag of mirabelles, I would turn my head away and laugh at the owner's tiresome attempts to find out my name. I was the only regular, he once said, who he couldn't greet personally; now he simply invents new names for me on my weekly visits to the shop. Last Saturday I was Frau Schmidt, the week before Fräulein Wagner.

"Just leave it, Anne," I hear Herbert say before the door opens and he comes back with a bottle of clear liquid. Annelies waddles behind him carrying a washcloth, which she gives to me so I can clean the wound on my forehead. Her gaze is penetrating; I can practically feel her sucking up every detail so that later she can give the most accurate possible description if necessary.

She was about 1.65 meters tall, Inspector. She was wearing one of those cheap wigs and a garish T-shirt with a parrot on it, which had neon green, thumbnail-sized rhinestones for eyes.

My wound smarting, I put the washcloth down and thank Annelies. She nods and cuts a length of bandage from the first aid box. As she comes over to me I turn my head away and say, "I'd rather not have a bandage, thank you. It's better if it's open to the air." That's what Aunt Evelyn always said when we grazed our knees playing outside.

Annelies doesn't look convinced.

"But it might need stitches."

I nod a little too forcefully. The pain continues to throb in my head.

"I'll go straight from here to the nearest emergency clinic and have it looked at."

She cocks her head and studies me closely.

"For heaven's sake, calm down, Anne," Herbert says, who's unscrewed the bottle of schnapps and is laughing. "Can't you see she's fine?" He offers me the bottle and I take it. The plum schnapps bites my throat. I think of yesterday evening, the expensive bottle of Chardonnay with Laura. I was happy—I must be mad.

Annelies clicks her tongue.

"Well, I'm not happy about letting you drive off in this state—"

"Come off it," Herbert interrupts. "Just look at her; some of the color has returned to her face."

"You're no doctor," his wife hisses. "What if she's got a concussion? We'd be accused of failure to render assistance. Or just imagine we let her go and she causes an accident. We'd be partly responsible then."

"Anne, please!" Herbert protests, making a hand gesture in my direction. Interpreting it correctly, I give him the bottle back; he smiles, then immediately puts it to his lips.

"Where are you from?" Annelies asks next.

"Berlin."

"Berlin?" Herbert says, drawing out the word and looking in wonder, as if it were some enchanted city in an exotic country, far, far away. But Berlin is barely an hour from here, even for me who drove below the speed limit the whole way.

"And where are you heading?"

"The Spreewald," I reply. "A weekend trip."

"I see," Annelies says. "The Spreewald. Nice place."

"The Spreewald," Herbert echoes after another large sip, sounding momentous. "Do you know the history of how the Spreewald came about?"

I shake my head circumspectly.

"All I know is what Fontane said about the place. That it's like Venice fifteen hundred years ago when the first fishing families settled there."

Herbert raises a bushy eyebrow, the right one.

"Fontane," I tell him. "The writer."

There is silence apart from the hum of the ceiling fan.

"Well," Herbert says, "according to legend, the Spreewald was created by the devil himself. But by accident." A schnapps-fueled giggle quakes beneath his mustache. "Supposedly he yoked two hell-oxen to a plow to break up the riverbed of the Spree. But the beasts went right through it, running every which way like crazy. The plow made thousands of deep furrows, which eventually filled with water. And there you have it: the Spreewald with its intricate network of streams and canals." He gives me a sly wink. "Are you really sure you want to go there?"

"Herbert," Annelies grumbles, reaching for the bottle that he's just about to bring to his lips again. "That's enough. It's Saturday morning, not even half ten yet."

Broad daylight—she's right. Another stupid move. I was all for waiting until it was dark, but Laura said we didn't have that much time. I can't help burping and taste the plum schnapps. Herbert takes it as a compliment and laughs again. I don't like the expression on Annelies's face.

"I think I'll be fine to drive now," I say. "I really do feel better. Thanks so much for your help." Pointing to my forehead, I add with a smile, "Don't worry, I'll get that looked at."

Annelies shakes her head.

"No way, dear. You're staying right here."

I'm suddenly standing on the cliff edge again. Below me lurks the water, and the rocks are crumbling. The wind drives gray clouds across the lavender sky as if they're being fast-forwarded. I hear it whisper, the wind. It whispers: *You!* I put one foot backward, but now Annelies is standing behind me, her arms outstretched, ready to give me a shove. *You're staying right here*, she repeats, and bursts into wicked laughter. I blink furiously, blink myself back into reality. I'm still sitting in the office of the petrol station. I have to get away from here, urgently.

But first Annelies insists I've got to eat something—apparently there are some fried potatoes left over from yesterday evening. She smiles; I retch. I can't help thinking that she's trying to distract me with her potatoes while secretly contacting the police. Who would come and question me. Who would come, question me and take me away. Who would lock me in a cell where there's no bed, just a bare, saggy mattress. Dirty concrete walls, a thin layer of gray cement dust and flakes of paint on the floor, with cement dust and paint under my fingernails too.

Something snaps inside me and I yell, "Leave me in peace!"

Annelies flinches, while a frightened Timmy scurries behind Herbert's legs. I leap up from the chair and grab my handbag—time to get out. Out of the office, through the shop, out of the glass door, across the forecourt to the car. I slip behind the wheel, speed away and feel relieved for a moment. Until in the rearview mirror I glimpse Annelies standing beneath the sign displaying the petrol prices, watching me. In one hand she has a piece of paper or a little notebook, in the other a pen. *The license plate*, I think, and smash my fist into the steering wheel.

What the hell have you done, my girl?

From: Letter #12

Anniversary.

So much blood, everywhere.

On the floor. On the rug. On the wall. It even sprayed on the ceiling.

The water is red. Dead water.

MAY 2014

Nelly Schütt had been feeling nervous for days. At least as nervous as Richard in *The Woman in the Window*, when he and Alice suddenly find themselves blackmailed. Claude has been shadowed by a man who's followed him several times to Alice's place and now rightly suspects that she has something to do with the murder. Particularly when this man, searching for evidence in Alice's flat, finds Claude's watch, which unequivocally links Alice to Claude. Scared and eager to avoid any future attempts at blackmail, Alice and Richard plan to kill him too. Alice will poison him. When this fails and all the evidence in the police investigation points toward Richard, he can no longer see any way out and he tries to kill himself by taking an overdose of sleeping pills.

Unlike Richard, Nelly would never give up, no matter how hopeless everything seemed at times. Falling in love wasn't a crime, as she kept telling herself whenever the phone rang and the woman who'd made a brief appearance at reception was on the line to remind her of their conversation. Nelly was to keep her hands off him, as she was destroying a family. Nelly was to keep her hands off him or she'd regret it. Nelly hung up, every time.

She guessed straightaway that Paul was married when he

booked a room at the inn not quite six months earlier. He was a friendly, charming man whose looks reminded her of Victor Mature (*Kiss of Death*, 1947, directed by Henry Hathaway), someone who at first glance looked too good to be true or single. From the guest registration form she learned that he was forty-one and came from Berlin. She gave him room four, as she thought it had the nicest curtains. Cream with a flowery pattern, unlike the three other rooms that had ochre corduroy curtains, which must have been there before Nelly was born.

Paul ate in the dining room, then after dinner she joined him as he was lighting a cigarette outside. She didn't know for sure what made her leave her place at reception and go out at this particular moment; it must have been some instinct. One that grew stronger and wilder the longer she chatted to Paul. He was on a business trip, he told her, from Berlin to Lübeck. He was married with one daughter, and he envied Nelly for living here—so wonderfully peaceful and idyllic. Life in Berlin was so exhausting sometimes, so completely crazy, like an out-of-control carousel. Nelly said she wouldn't be so averse to the occasional wild ride as there were times when she got really bored here. Paul replied that boredom had nothing to do with the place where you lived, but with the people around you.

Paul seemed to know what he was talking about; he gave the impression of being bored too. When he stayed at Nelly's parents' inn again on the way back, they kissed for the first time. It was exciting. He was no longer happy with his wife, he told Nelly later on in the bed of room four with its flowery curtains. She was so possessive, so controlling, so bossy. Nelly thought of Gene Tierney as Ellen Harland in *Leave Her to Heaven* (1945, directed by John M.

Stahl)—Paul's wife must be like that, a really vicious, mean creature. Only no longer quite as pretty as Gene Tierney, obviously
not. Nelly imagined her as plain; she had to be unattractive. After
all, there must be a reason why their sex life had fizzled out years
ago, according to Paul. At least Gene Tierney, alias Ellen Harland,
kills herself at the end of the film and her poor husband can be
happy with his new love.

Nelly waited, waited in vain.

He was going to stay with his wife for a bit because of his
daughter. He was going to stay with her for a bit because they
hadn't yet paid off the mortgage. Then she lost her job, she suddenly fell ill, and in such circumstances of course he couldn't
leave her now. Nelly had heard a lot over the past few months
when she met Paul halfway in a hotel on the A24. When she lay in
his arms in bed, her cheek pressed to his hot chest, or when they
took a walk through the woods close to the hotel, her hand firmly
in his. And she believed Paul, she refrained from hassling him.

Until that day when his wife turned up at the inn, looking
perfectly healthy, terribly determined and, most strikingly, at
least as pretty as Gene Tierney. Perhaps this was what disturbed
Nelly most of all.

Now she wanted clarity. Paul had to decide. And he promised
to sort everything out: this time he really would. That was almost
a month ago.

Nelly decided to lend a hand.

From: Letter #13

My dreams are now black. That's probably down to the new pills.
They allow me to sleep deeply and peacefully. But they're so strong
and work so quickly—I mean, immediately—that the whole process
of falling asleep is bypassed. You know, that phase where you're lying
in bed and feel your body and thoughts growing heavier. Where
you gently slide into sleep. I don't have that. One moment I'm wide
awake and the next I simply pass out. Recently I made the mistake of
taking my pills in the kitchen while I was sitting at the table, writing.
I was writing to you. It wasn't until I woke up the following morning
that I realized my face had smashed into the tabletop. The doctor
established that it was just a simple fracture of the nasal bone, and it
healed quickly. All the same I found it significant that my blood had
dripped on this very part of the letter. Right on your name.

"But I told you quite clearly what the correct dosage is," my ther-
apist said at our next session. "Half a tablet at the onset of a panic
attack and a whole one if you can't sleep at night." She looked at me
with that strange expression. As if I'd deliberately ignored the dosage
instructions. Perhaps she was right. My dreams may be black, but

25

the questions still remain, they refuse to fall silent. What were her feelings at the end? Was she scared?

I don't want to consider the possibility that she was scared. I'd rather imagine the pain sparking a firework in front of her. Colorful flashes and beautiful stars, as if she'd carelessly looked at the blazing sun. I want to persuade myself that she was happy in her final hours.

I can't.

NADJA

I blink; the world is dazzling, and in the heat, invisible fires are shimmering on the road. I flip down the sun visor. It was precisely twelve minutes ago that I made my hasty getaway from the petrol station. I feel cold—even though the heater is on full blast it makes no impression on me. The air inside the car is stuffy, stale and strangely sweet. As if over the years dust had caught in the air-con vents and is now burning. My eyes keep flitting to the rearview mirror. The red Golf, which was behind me for several kilometers, has turned off. Now I'm being followed by a dark blue MPV, but not for long because I'm driving too slowly and it overtakes me. I reach for the mirror to adjust it by a few millimeters for the hundredth time, and in doing so catch a fleeting glimpse of myself: goggle eyes, and beneath them, dry, black lines where my mascara has run. To the left of my forehead is a laceration like a precise knife cut, three or four centimeters long. I note to my relief that it has already started to scab, so I don't need to see a doctor. When I concentrate back on the road, however, I decide to stop again at the next opportunity. I need some fresh air or I'll suffocate.

I drive until a sign indicates a turnoff to a car park. No café, no kiosk, no petrol pumps, not even one of those makeshift plastic

27

loos. Just a few parking bays and beyond them a dustbin and three tables, each with two benches fixed to them, on an arid, trampled-down meadow. I picture a lonely trucker sitting here, a cigarette hanging from the corner of his mouth and a thermos of bland coffee out of a machine. Or a family. Mother, father, two children—a little boy and an older girl. Sitting there with Tupperware boxes full of apple slices and vegetable sticks, and the crackle of aluminum foil as they unwrap their lovingly made sandwiches. They're going on holiday to the coast. A soft voice asks, "What's it like, breathing in salty air? Do the grains of salt make you cough?" To which another voice replies, "There aren't any grains of salt, you silly Billy. It's just air." My mind switches back to the trucker; I'd rather think of him.

In truth I'm very glad that nobody else is stopping here. All the parking bays and picnic tables are empty. I drive the Land Rover to the end of the car park and get out. As if the fresh air had given them a secret order, my legs double up. With one hand I grab the handle of the driver's door for support, with the other I rub the back of my neck, where the seam of my T-shirt is already clammy with cold sweat. I need to calm down, compose myself, order my thoughts. I mustn't have any doubts or cave in, like my legs are trying to do. I have to be strong. Think of Laura. Remember that all this is happening for the best and that there's simply no other way. So I summon an image: Laura turning up shortly after work yesterday evening. Standing in the door to my office, swaying and pale, clutching the straps of her handbag. Laura, formerly Laura Brehme, used to be an assistant at the law firm where I work. Now she was Laura van Hoven, married to my boss. I hadn't seen her in years.

"Hey, Nadja."

Her mouth formed a dreadfully fake smile, while mine merely opened silently as I sat behind my desk as if paralyzed, trying to get over how she looked. The deathly white face. The tiny, sad eyes. The blond hair kept back with a black Alice band and tied into a plait, making her face look flatter than usual and her head almost gigantic on her thin neck and slim body. I was immediately reminded of how I'd almost dyed my hair once, blond like her, how I'd even made an appointment with the hairdresser, and how in the end only an acute panic attack had prevented me from going to the salon. At a stroke, the prospect of sitting for two hours or more in front of a mirror and having to put up with my face, not to mention the dreadful noises—whining hair dryers, rushing water, the cold clatter of scissors hurriedly being put down on the edge of a ceramic basin—had seemed impossible.

I'd always considered Laura to be the second-most beautiful woman in the world. Now she just looked like a matchstick figure in a child's picture, a sad matchstick figure with yellow hair.

"Isn't Gero back yet? I've been trying to get hold of him all day, but he's not answering his mobile."

It struck me that even after all these years I still hadn't got used to her calling the man who I knew as Herr van Hoven by his first name. Something about this hurt me. It wasn't a bad pain—it felt more like a scratch, like a needle scraping a sensitive area of skin—bearable but unpleasant. From somewhere deep inside me I dug out an overdue greeting and finally got up. We had a brief, stiff hug. That too used to be different.

"So, is he here?"

I shake my head. Herr van Hoven left yesterday for a two-day conference of lawyers in Magdeburg and wouldn't be getting back till later. I was surprised that Laura was unaware of his schedule.

"According to the conference program, the last talk ends at seven." I lifted the sleeve of my blouse to check the time. "So in about an hour."

"Oh, right."

"Can I help you at all?"

Her ghostly white face looked as if it were about to burst into tears.

"Is there something wrong with Vivi?" I asked, feeling my heartbeat accelerate. Vivi, the van Hovens' daughter, who'd just turned four. Laura gave me a look I found hard to bear.

"She's fine," she answered coolly. "She's with her grandparents." I smiled uneasily.

"Okay, that's nice." Unable to think of anything else to say, I stared at my shoes. They urgently needed polishing.

I could hear Laura breathing.

"Could . . . could I have a coffee, perhaps? Would that be too much trouble?"

I hastily shook my head.

"No, not at all. Coming up."

Coffee with Laura, like in the past. Although she hadn't explicitly asked me to join her, I would make use of the opportunity. Like a rain dance, I shifted about in front of the automatic coffee machine at the end of the corridor, as if my restlessness might remedy the inertia of the droning machine, from which brown liquid dribbled into the two cups.

"Hurry up!" I hissed at the machine. I was worried that Laura might change her mind and leave if it took any longer. I fetched milk from the fridge, spilling some on the work surface when I filled up our cups. Instinctively I reached for the cloth in the sink to wipe it up, but then left it. Laura was waiting for me.

When I came back from the kitchenette, the connecting door between my office and Herr van Hoven's was open. Laura was sitting in his chair, gazing at the ceiling. I essayed a poor joke.

"Two coffees to stay, for Laura and Laura's friend."

She gave a start and looked at me as if seeing me for the first time. She was surprised, shocked; these were a stranger's eyes gazing at me. Laura opened her mouth and her lips moved silently. I was about to ask her again what was wrong when she did come out with something. "Thanks. But another time, perhaps." Within seconds she'd leaped to her feet and rushed past me. I stayed where I was like an idiot, still holding the two coffee cups.

I put them down and caught up with her by the lifts.

"Laura, please talk to me!" *Insult me. Tell me where I can stick my coffee and that we haven't been friends for ages. Remind me what I did. But for God's sake, say something.*

And she did. She said it after collapsing into my arms. "I've got a problem, Nadja."

Now that problem is in my trunk.

MAY 2014

Nelly Schütt was prepared. She'd booked a train ticket for a Sunday because she didn't trust the Berlin traffic in her little old Twingo. She'd made a note of the address and washed her hair specially the night before so that she could wear it down. People had often complimented her on her hair, at least on those good days when it looked like the hazelnut locks of angels. She had spent a long time wondering what to put on, ultimately deciding against her favorite summer dress because she was worried about looking too girly. Which she wasn't anymore. She wasn't a clueless, naïve village girl, she was a woman who got along in the world and Berlin, and knew precisely what she wanted. So she plumped for a tight-fitting black skirt, a white, short-sleeved blouse and the black peep-toes she'd ordered online a few years ago, but had only worn a few times when practicing strutting around her room. These were the shoes worn by the women she worshipped: Joan Bennett, Ava Gardner, Rita Hayworth, *Gene Tierney*. When she arrived at the station, Nelly took a taxi and was dropped off one street before her destination so she could collect herself and reapply her red lipstick. As she wandered down the street, she focused on her gait, making sure she extended her back, kept her shoulders up straight and swayed her hips. Her gaze swept this residential area and she imagined living here. It wasn't the Berlin she'd pictured as she read the registration form Paul had filled out when staying at their inn. Not the Berlin of modern sky-scrapers that looked as if the architects were just a few oversized boys who'd gone crazy with their likewise-oversized LEGO bricks, or of period buildings whose ornate façades spiraled upward. No shops, no bars, just neatly mown lawns divided by garden fences and strewn with toys, behind which stood terraced or detached houses, all of them seemingly from the same catalog. Nelly found this area slightly dull and she decided that Paul and she would move as soon as they could. Preferably to one of those gorgeous period blocks in a more central part of Berlin. A two-bedroom flat with tall, stuccoed ceilings and a small wrought-iron balcony for Paul, who was a smoker—which didn't bother Nelly, as all the men smoked in her beloved black-and-white films—but also so they could have breakfast there in the summer months. Kitchen, bathroom, bedroom, living room and a study for Paul, which they would also use as a guest room. They would meet new people in Berlin, suave individuals—artists, doctors, high society and old money—and the guest room would allow someone to stay the night when Nelly threw cocktail parties for her new friends. The only thing they wouldn't need was a children's room as Nelly had no plans in this regard. She didn't want children and thus to have to give up her newly discovered autonomy. She wanted to look for a job, something in catering, and then, in a few years' time, open her own little 1950s-style café. But most of all she wanted Paul, and when everything had been sorted out at the end of today, the world could finally find out about him. The promise to keep their relationship secret, which Paul had solemnly insisted Nelly make, would then be obsolete. This very evening she would reveal to her parents who the guest in room four really was; she could hardly wait. Sure, her father would grumble. He'd rather she got together with a boy from the village. And her mother would cry. Not out of anger or disappointment, no. For the first time that Nelly could remember, she would see her mother cry tears of joy because her daughter was showing the courage to live the big life, which she herself had only ever been able to dream of.

By now Nelly had arrived at the right address. Swinging her hips, she took the concrete path through the front garden and climbed the three steps to the front door. Taking another deep breath, she squared her shoulders and pressed the bell, beside which a fired clay sign displayed the name of the family engraved in wonky, childish letters.

Paul's face fell when he opened the door. His mouth opened, but no sounds came out. Nelly smiled more shyly than she'd intended and was just about to say something herself when at that moment she heard a woman's voice—"Paul? Who is it?" Seconds later *she* appeared at his back: Paul's wife, who, unlike him, immediately thought of something to say.

"How dare you turn up here!" She spun around. Her daughter must be there, assumed Nelly, who had inadvertently flinched at the wife's harsh tone, but then recovered rapidly.

"I'm here because I'd like to sort this out once and for all." She gave her rival a penetrating look and tried not to blink. "Paul loves me and there's nothing you can do about it. Let him go."

"What are you talking about? Paul?"

Paul began fidgeting.

"Paul?" Nelly said.

"Please go, Nelly," he said, shaking his head. "It's over. I made a mistake."

"What?" It sounded soft, almost little more than a sigh. "What are you saying?"

"He's telling you to get out of here," his wife said, pulling Paul back into the house by the sleeve of his shirt. Then the door closed and Nelly fell into a deep, black hole.

Afterward she could barely recall how she'd got home that day. There were just scraps of memory: pavement stones beneath her rapid footsteps and her heels clack-clack-clacking on them; her body slumped limply in the back seat of a taxi; people standing around her on the platform, pushing and shoving; the soporific rocking of the carriage and the houses flying past the window, which at some point became countryside.

Then she was back home.

Nelly spent the next few days as if a thick glass bell had been placed over her head. She pushed keys across the counter at reception and filed away registration forms. She fluffed up pillows and filled the soap dispensers in the bathrooms. She watched her favorite films without taking in a word. She met up with Hannes, who'd had a soft spot for her even at primary school, and let him do as he pleased. A few times she considered ringing Paul. Confronting him. Having a go at him. Begging him to come back to her. But she abandoned the idea because she was afraid he would repeat his words: *It's over. I made a mistake.*

Nelly wanted to die in that clichéd way people long to when

their heart has been broken. But then, as if fate finally showed some understanding, Paul texted Nelly requesting a meeting. Where they'd always met, at the hotel halfway between them on the A24. *Tomorrow, my darling, 4 p.m. I miss you.*

Nelly Schütt wanted to die, but this time for joy.

From: Letter #15

The sales assistant in the department store said I had a good body, definitely a size thirty-six. And that I should try something a bit colorful. I said that in my profession it was all about looking respectable. White blouse, gray suit. I even said it was an instruction from my boss. She kept plucking at the shoulder seams of the blazer I was trying on and said, "Well, you should at least try a thirty-six. You're disappearing in this." I tried to control myself, I really did. I didn't want to shout at her, but that's precisely what happened. I screamed for her to leave me in peace and that I didn't need any help. I wriggled out of the blazer and stormed back into the booth to get changed and leave the department store as fast as possible. I ran. Ever since, I've been imagining her explaining to her husband that evening what a crazy customer she'd had to deal with. A mentally ill woman.

You are what you are.

NADJA

I don't know how, but I keep driving. There was a point when I almost gave up. I'd dragged myself to one of the benches, fiddled with my mobile and resisted the temptation to switch it on and call Laura. I wouldn't have told her about the incident at the petrol station, but I'd have loved to hear her voice. It was only when another vehicle turned into the car park that I hurried back to the car and set off again.

Take the A13 toward Dresden/Cottbus (about sixty kilometers), keep left on the A15, after about four kilometers take exit two—Boblitz, then right onto the L55. From there follow the signs to Lübbenau/Lehde. That's what it says on the piece of paper with the directions. The Land Rover does have a GPS, but the police would be able to access the information just as they could the data on my mobile.

Music.

I turn the radio right up. I want the music to drown out the chaos in my head and distract me, for a while at least. It always worked for my mother. When she put on old Johnny Hallyday records she could forget everything around her. She forgot who she was, who she would rather be, she forgot herself until absolutely nothing remained of her for a brief, curative moment. Like a trundling aircraft, she would move with arms outstretched and eyes closed against the light of the summer sun that poured in through our living room window. I can still see the rapturous smile on her face, individual hairs standing up indecently from her head and even the tiny dust particles floating around her as if eager to join in her insane dance. I can hear the crackling on "Retiens la nuit" and her voice that kept breaking into low notes because she was a hopelessly untalented singer. But that didn't matter when Johnny Hallyday was playing, for then she was a happy woman . . .

It doesn't work—the music just drives me mad. I turn the volume down and think of Laura.

All she said when we were standing by the lifts yesterday evening was: *I've got a problem, Nadja.* A second later she sped toward the lavatories. I followed her. Through the locked cubicle door, I heard retching noises and suffered along with her with each new surge. This is how it had been five and a half years ago, only the roles were reversed. My first day at Abramczyk & van Hoven, my new beginning. I'd been sitting at my desk and everything was fine. Then, a moment later, I was seized by panic, accompanied by the feeling of a huge mistake, a brazen injustice. It dragged me from my chair, lashed me and spat in my face. I tore myself away and sped down the corridor to the loos, where I locked myself in and cowered there, howling in my misery. It was Laura who knocked on the door and asked if she could help me. A total stranger, whose warm, friendly voice enticed me out of the cubicle and who soon afterward was cooling my face, swollen from crying, with a damp paper towel, as if it were something she did every day. That's how we met.

"Laura," I now said, taking her approach. The noises I could hear coming from the other side of the locked door sounded deep and hollow; her stomach must be empty. "Please come out, Laura." I don't know how many times I had to say it before the lock finally clicked and she staggered out, so feeble that I had to support her.

"Would you drive me home, Nadja? Please, I have to go home."

"Maybe I ought to call you a taxi instead."

She shook her head vigorously.

"No, not a taxi. Forget it, I'll manage somehow."

"But a taxi would be here in five minutes. I could wait outside with you."

"No, really, it's fine. Don't worry, I'll be okay." There it was again, this dreadfully fake smile, and there was I, holding out my hand and saying, "Give me the car key."

The van Hovens' enormous bungalow is in Westend, supposedly the most beautiful part of Charlottenburg, a chunk of luxury: proof that some people really can have it all. Beyond the terrace lay the inimitable peace of the Grunewald, which allows you to forget that you're part of a bustling global city of three and a half million people with all its frenzy, din and heightened collective pulse. And outside the front door, just a few minutes' walk away, is Reichsstrasse with its shops, restaurants and cafés, as well as that frenzy, din and pulse, which people always claim make them feel alive. The house was designed and built by a well-known architect in the late 1980s on this incredible patch of land in Berlin. After the wedding, Herr van Hoven bought it off him and modernized it. A beautiful house, an expensive house. A house in which everything had its place and family life went on. A house in truth I didn't want to enter.

And yet all Laura had to say was, "Come with me." She went on ahead; I followed. Through the hallway, which was quiet and cool, then three wide, white marble steps up to the living room, where she sat on a sofa and buried her face in her hands. The first thing I noticed was the dusky light that felt strange on a sunny day like this, then the curtains which were drawn across all the windows that gave on to the terrace. But I suspected that Laura was merely trying to keep the heat out. The next thing that caught my eye was a Barbie doll lying on the coffee table, which Vivi must have given a new haircut. The doll reminded me of the pink fluffy dog I'd once bought to apologize for what happened with the little girl. Which was still in the top drawer of my bedroom chest, and which I occasionally took out and caressed wistfully. Only then was I ready to look at what I must have already registered out of the corner of my eye. On the left-hand side of the room, right in front of the open fireplace and directly below the happy family photographs on the mantelpiece, there it lay—the body.

I give a start. The car has jolted over some bump or other. I let go of the steering wheel in shock then grab it again just in time. To be on the safe side I reduce my speed. The roads are narrow and only partially paved. I see some of the markers that Laura mentioned in her directions. The gable end of a village church, hidden behind some trees to the left; to the right, about ten meters farther on, the sign for a boat jetty. Through some clear patches on the embankment I can see a barge of tourists gliding its way along the warren of streams. I imagine it proceeding in silence, the only sound a gentle ripple as the ferryman takes the pole out of the water, then pushes it once more against the boggy ground. An unchanging movement, so fluid and monotonous that it must hypnotize the passengers. Then the alders along the bank, soaring gigantically upward and probably leaving no more than a narrow strip of sky above the streams. Like a tunnel, an endless tunnel in a beautifully green nothingness. I'd love to stop briefly, get out, stand beneath this sky and take a few deep breaths. I've never been anywhere like this before. I know the sky of my hometown, which was always slightly hazy with the metal dust that poured from the chimneys of the steel factory, and the sky above Berlin, with the vapor trails from the aircraft by day and the flashing lights at night. How absurd, the thoughts the human mind tries to plug its gaps with in certain situations. As if a sky could help me. I don't suppose even God can.

I turn up the volume again. The woman on the radio bellows the weather forecast at me. A dreamy summer weekend awaits. People will go to the seashore or lie on blankets in the park and squint in the bright sun. People will arrange picnics and barbecues. While others will drive to the Spreewald to dispose of a dead body.

From: Letter #17

Maybe you were too little to notice how different things were in our home. Or like me you just pretended not to notice. I even said to the woman from the child welfare office, "I don't know what you're on about," at which she plainly drew my attention to the pile of washing, to the fact that children ought to have clean clothes, to the dust and balls of fluff, to the bottles of beer that our guests had drunk when they came round then just left, and to the toys that were lying around and which were clearly not made for children. I tapped the side of my head and shoved her out of the flat. Then I sat on our bed and bawled. I knew she was right, of course, and I'd promised myself a thousand times to do something about it. Every time I went into the kitchen and smelled the stink coming from the drain I decided that as soon as I could I'd borrow some money from my friend Aniela to buy cleaning fluid, detergent, really strong stuff that would properly work its way through the old pipes. And paint for the walls, I'd buy paint too so we could decorate. First, of course, I'd have to tear down the old wallpaper, though that couldn't be too difficult a job as most of the sheets were peeling away from the concrete of their own accord. And when I'd finished we would put up some pictures, posters of

43

French landscapes or your own drawings. I bet you'd be proud if your mama stuck up your pictures rather than just scrunching them up and chucking them into the recycling.

But sitting there as I was, on our bed, I realized yet again that even if I had the money and the energy to realize all my plans, these would always end up as short-term solutions. At some point the fridge would be empty again, the drain would stink again, and the new paint would be stained by nicotine and peel from the walls. I'd never manage to offer you a normal childhood, not in this flat, not in this city, not in this life. In moments like this—yes, I admit it's true—in moments like this I hated her . . .

MAY 2014

Nelly Schütt was lying comfortably; it almost felt soft, apart from the tree root digging into the back of her neck—or it might be a stone—something hard, at any rate, which caused a flaring pain. In the distance the traffic roared along the motorway, which also bothered her slightly, but in compensation she had the most gorgeous view. Above her the sky was driving snow-white clouds across its cobalt-blue canvas, with the tips of a few spruces edging their way into the picture, appearing black against the afternoon sun, almost like paper cutouts.

Nelly thought about the end of *The Woman in the Window*, when the case centered on Richard and Alice takes a surprise turn. The man blackmailing them is shot dead by police in an incident and, when they find the dead Claude's watch at his place, is assumed to be his killer. Richard is unaware of any of this, however, as he's dying after his overdose of sleeping pills. But because his death isn't a good way for the film to end—not the ending that ought to happen, because dying isn't real, it can't be true, not here and not now—it's nothing more than a rhetorical device to flog the story to its climax—Richard wakes up and finds out it was all a dream. Just a really bad dream.

Yes, Nelly thought. *I'm dreaming, that's all.* She smiled at the cobalt-blue sky, a smile that was as much exhaustion as it was relief. All of a sudden the pain had gone from the back of her neck and not even the hands that were now around her throat mattered. The only thing of importance was her grandfather's voice that sounded warm as it asked, "Shall we watch a film together, my girl?" Before she could answer in her head, she already heard the click of a videocassette being drawn into the slot of the recorder, then the screen lit up and Nelly saw herself. She was Lizabeth Scott as Coral Chandler lying seriously injured in hospital following a car accident in *Dead Reckoning* (1947, directed by John Cromwell).

"Everything's slipping," Coral says in a delirium to her lover Warren Murdock, alias Humphrey Bogart. And: "Inside I'm falling."

"It's like going out the jump door," Warren tells her gently. "Hold your breath and just let go."

Nelly closed her eyes. And fell.

Paul Heger slumped on the bed of room 231. Thoughts shot through his head like bombs detonating and leaving large craters. Within barely six months his whole life had turned inside out. Seventeen years of marriage, all those promises and convictions, had just gone up in smoke. His friends would have described him as *solid* before the thing with Nelly. Paul, who had only existed as one half of a pair with Simone. He remembered invitations to birthday parties, weddings, christenings and events at the rowing club, of which he'd been a member for a good ten years. Invitations that read "Paul and Simone," so inseparable, as if they were really a single word: *Paulandsimone*. Are you coming,

Paulandsimone? Paulandsimone, will you be at the barbecue this weekend?

Was this what had driven him into Nelly's arms? The fact that he no longer existed as an individual? That he'd disintegrated as a person and was now only viable in symbiosis with Simone?

Paul shock his head sluggishly and got up. What a fool he'd been to believe he could simply turn his life inside out and start again from scratch. Damage limitation was all he could hope for now.

He went over to the window that could only be tilted open, probably for safety reasons, and peered down at the A24. At the stream of cars, in which drivers fiddled with their radio knobs, hummed along to well-known songs or even sang along at the top of their voice. People who kept looking at their GPS every minute because they couldn't wait to get there. People who hadn't pro-grammed their GPS in the first place because they knew the way off by heart. Because they knew where they belonged. Paul took a scrunched packet of cigarettes from his trouser pocket and lit one. A few last drags through the slit of open window, then he'd go. Back to his old life in which he was an inseparable part of *Paulandsimone.*

NADJA

Kaupen. I know the term from a TV documentary about the Spreewald. Tiny, isolated sand islands, emerging from the water like the backs of diving aquatic animals. The *Kaupen* support the houses of the settlers who've lived there since the seventeenth century. Some of these islands are still unconnected to the network of paths and can only be accessed by boat. Not this one, thank goodness, given what I've transported here in the trunk of the car. I keep driving until the house is in sight, but according to Laura I'll have to walk the last few meters across a narrow, weather-worn bridge that leads directly to my destination: a small, old log cabin, surrounded by greenery. It used to belong to Laura's grandmother, but has stood empty for several years now.

As I park, my heart is pounding. Laura can't be here yet, because she would have had to park by the bridge too. We'd decided to drive separately—me in her Land Rover and her in her husband's Porsche—to avoid any potential witnesses seeing us together en route. *Witnesses.* People who see something and make up even more.

I remove the key from the ignition and get out of the car. The air is clear and I take a deep breath. But it doesn't help; I still feel sick. The trees sway all around me, and inside my head Aunt Evelyn says: *What on earth have you done, child?*

I haven't done anything, I want to reply, but she doesn't believe me. *You've been nothing but trouble, Nadja, from day one. Even when you were learning how to walk I knew you'd be the ruin of the lot of us one day.*

But I was only a child, I protest silently. *And even if I did do the odd silly thing, didn't I get better after Janek was born because I wanted to be a role model for my baby brother?*

Huh! Aunt Evelyn says and her laughter sounds bitter. *You were just pretending. Everybody knows what you're really like, Nadja Kulka.* Her words are blows to my stomach; I pant. I shake my head and curse at the bridge a few paces away. Bracing my arms against the rail, I look down. Beneath me the water cuts a swathe through the rampant greenery. The devil's furrow, if you believe the legend the petrol station cashier told me. Aunt Evelyn isn't giving me any peace—*You are what you are, Nadja.* She's making me angry and I'm going to defend myself.

Oh really? Then tell me what you would have done in my place, Aunt Evelyn. In my mind I run through what awaited me in the van Hovens' house yesterday evening. The dead body, lying there on the expensive white marble in the living room. The expensive marble that wasn't white anymore, but red, red all over, and even more red, the deep-red stains that had worked their way through the material of a gray T-shirt. A sight that switched off my reason and sucked all feeling out of me. I approached the body as if being controlled remotely and was shaking as I lifted the T-shirt and saw four stab wounds.

"I don't know how that could have happened," I heard Laura say. "It was like I blacked out. All of a sudden I was standing there

49

with the knife in my hand and my nightie soaked with blood." She swallowed. "What am I going to do now, Nadja? My life is ruined."

Yes, it was.

"Vivi . . . I'm going to lose Vivi."

Yes, she would.

"Please, Nadja, say something!" Her hand touched my shoulder; I said nothing.

The dead body, the eyes.

"Nadja!"

Laura clutched me from behind; I gasped for breath. I couldn't escape those eyes. I imagined they would now pursue Laura for the rest of her life. She would see them in her dreams and even when she was awake. Every person who looked at her in the future would do so with these very same eyes.

"You're right," a voice said. It was mine, though it sounded unfamiliar. "You're going to lose everything. Your daughter, your husband, your home. You'll be left with nothing, nothing at all."

Like me.

So—what would you have done in my place, Aunt Evelyn?

Aunt Evelyn doesn't say anything. Obviously she doesn't because she's not here. I'm alone. Just me and the body in the trunk of the car.

MAY 2014

Paul Heger lay in his bed, tossing and turning. He felt hot, he was burning. Beneath his pajamas blisters were starting to form on his skin. He felt someone touching him. A pleasantly cool hand pushing its way under his top and carefully stroking the painful areas. Something else was there too. A weight on his body. Paul blinked. At first she was just a blur. She was sitting on top of him, now bending her torso forward. He felt her breath on his face. Then her lips on his as her soft brown hair tickled his nose. Now he realized.

Nelly.

Nelly, whose face he barely recognized because it was totally blurred. It looked like a mask, an encrusted mask of old, brown blood. Sheer disgust overcame him. He reached for her wrists and pulled her hands out from under his top. They were covered in dried blood too and for a moment he wondered whether it might be his. Nelly giggled.

Paul wrenched open his eyes and sat bolt upright. Somebody was gasping for air—it was him. *Just a dream*, he realized, sinking back exhausted. He felt his brow. The heat was for real. Perhaps he had a temperature. He stared at the ceiling and tried to regulate his breathing. Simone had already got up; the other side of the bed was empty. He was pleased about that as he couldn't have shared his dream with her. She wouldn't have stopped pestering him with questions, she would have gone on and on, annoying him, and again his only option would have been to concoct some sort of horror story. As he had every night this week when he'd woken with a start because of Nelly.

Paul closed his eyes. Perhaps he could doze a while longer until Simone came to get him for breakfast; it was Sunday, after all. It had also been a Sunday when Nelly appeared unannounced at their door and destroyed everything. Simone had already found out about the affair a month earlier; she'd got hold of his mobile and read the messages he and Nelly had exchanged. But he'd sworn he would end it and after a while she'd believed him. Just like Nelly, who he went on seeing. But then came that Sunday three weeks ago. Nelly really ought not to have come. Paul buried his head in the pillow and begged God for half an hour of deep, dreamless sleep.

"Paul?" A distant voice. He must indeed have fallen asleep again.

"Paul?" Simone's voice.

He opened his eyes. Simone was standing beside the bed. He knew at once that something was wrong.

"What is it?"

He could hear her swallow before she told him. "The police are here, Paul. They've got some questions to ask you."

I can't find the right words. It's so hard . . . I really want to write you a letter that I don't tear up afterward. That finds its way to you and explains everything. Yes, I did hate her—sometimes. And yes, a lot of bad things happened to her in my imagination. She slipped on the freshly polished steps, fell and broke her neck. She fell out of the window, ran in front of a car or died from being beaten up, playing the choking game or as a result of the obsessions of a sinister guest. Her death never formed the climax of my fantasies, however, only the lead-up. She died and then . . . cake. I know it sounds crazy, but that's what this was all about: cake. I thought of tray bakes with lemon glaze and colorful sprinkles, yeast pastries and cream gateaux, fried angel wings dusted with icing sugar and all those delicacies that the women in the neighborhood would bring round to comfort the bereaved when somebody died. They baked for heart attacks, death from old age and crib death. I imagined them rushing into our flat and laying so many cakes on our kitchen table that you couldn't see anything of the torn oilcloth beneath. I imagine my heaped plate, a feeling of satiation, long arms around me and words of encouragement. Cakes and consolation. The feeling of community, warmth. And sometimes . . . I was on our old sofa in the living room, surrounded by neighbors, with my plate on my knees, when my father appeared. It could have been one of the men from the city finally revealing himself or a total stranger who by chance had heard about her death and had immediately jumped into his car to come here. He crouched and held my hand. He begged me for forgiveness for never having played a part in his daughter's life, never having been around and not even having left a photograph. And he said, "You're not on your own anymore. I will look after you."

Yes, I liked these fantasies; I wasn't ashamed of them, not back then. Because they were just fantasies, the fantasies of a child, silly, extravagant trains of thought that never did anyone any harm. Because I didn't really want anything to happen to her. I loved her, in spite of everything. When she danced, looking so beautiful and oblivious of everything around her. Or when she was ill and needed me.

Once, when I'd just turned ten, she had a bad case of the flu. Or at least I thought it was the flu, as that's what she and everyone else told me: she just had the flu. So I made her tea to combat the cold and water bottles for her cramps. I borrowed milk and oats to make porridge. I dabbed her brow with a cold flannel when a fever replaced the cold, and held her hand when she gasped with pain. In the end I even managed to make the vital cut, helped by my unbelievably strong willpower, bags of energy and our kitchen scissors. Blood hasn't always been something terrible, you know . . .

NADJA

Yesterday evening at the van Hovens' house.

"Who is that?"

No answer.

"Who *is* that, I said?"

Still nothing. Laura looked completely apathetic.

"We have to call the police."

Only then did she open her eyes.

"What? No, no way! They'll come and take me away. They'll lock me up!" She was breathing rapidly. "I need to talk to Gero first. He'll have to think of something, I can't go to prison!"

I looked down at the dead body. I couldn't stomach it for long. The wide eyes, the lips slightly apart, keen to say something but unable to. No last words. No farewell. My gaze returned to Laura.

"If you had an argument, then it happened in the heat of the moment. That's it, isn't it?"

She nodded so keenly that for one ridiculous moment I was worried the movement might break her thin stick-figure neck.

"Maybe even a case of self-defense?" I went on. She nodded

again. I grabbed her by the upper arms. "Your husband will sort it out. He's a good lawyer, maybe even the best. He'll manage, somehow."

"You're talking crap, you know you are!" She jerked; I let go of her arms and turned away.

"I'm sorry. I wasn't trying to—"

"No," Laura said softly. "I'm the one who's sorry. It's not your fault. It's just . . ." Out of the corner of my eye I saw her gesturing to the body. "For Christ's sake, Nadja! Manslaughter! Five years if I'm lucky. Maybe even ten!"

Seven, if the judge is having a good day and feeling sympathetic to you for some reason.

"But Vivi's still so little." She started sobbing again. "There'll come a time when she doesn't remember me anymore. Then it'll all be gone. All those hours I spent on the floor of her room, playing with her. All the puddles we jumped over, hand in hand. Or when she had measles and I put little red dots on my face with lipstick so she didn't have to be sick on her own."

I turned around. Saw Laura. A mother who was going to lose her child. A child who would grow up without a mother. Vivi, sweet little Vivi, would forever have a pain that no medicine could help against.

"What's my daughter going to think of me when she finds out I'm a murderer?"

Vivi's eyes, the disappointment in her face. I tried to banish the image from my mind, but in vain; the past was already floating on the surface like a rotten old piece of wood. The pain and all those broken promises . . .

One day we'll go to the seaside.

Is it nice there, the seaside?

Oh yes, very nice. There's no shouting, just the squawking of the gulls. And the wind whispering stories from other times.

Stories with Vikings in them?

Yes, those too. Lots of different stories, but they all have good endings.

What about the air?

What do you mean?

Is it true that the air by the sea is salty?

I don't know; yes, probably. That's what they say, anyway.

What's it like, breathing in salty air? Do the grains of salt make you cough?

There aren't any grains of salt, you silly Billy. It's just air. That's enough now, otherwise you won't get out of bed tomorrow morning.

What does a gull sound like when it squawks?

It goes *kwakwakwa*. Like that. At least I think so.

Sounds more like the crowing of a jackdaw.

A jackdaw doesn't crow. A cock crows. A jackdaw does more of a caw. Anyway, it doesn't matter. I've no idea what gulls sound like. But we'll soon find out. Have you taken your asthma spray?

Yes.

Okay, then go to sleep now.

Good night. Love you, Mama.

You shouldn't call me "Mama."

. . .

"Shall I try ringing your husband? Perhaps he'll take my call—I mean, it might be something important to do with work and . . ." I faltered when I noticed Laura, who'd been nodding at first, now shaking her head in short, twitchy movements. Her pupils were huge and shimmering; she was staring past me toward the body. Panting.

I spun around, expecting to see movement, the body angrily rearing up, like in a film, one of those moments designed to shock, when the person everyone has presumed dead rises to their feet again, with the sole aim of wreaking revenge for what was done to them. But the body was still lying there as before—of course it was. It's only in films that the dead come back to life. Or in dreams.

"Oh God, I thought . . ." I sighed with relief.

Laura was still staring.

"Laura?" I cautiously touched her arm. She whimpered.

"I know now."

"What do you know?"

"It's going to be quite different."

"What do you mean?"

"Of course it will be."

"Laura, I really don't know what you're on about."

She wasn't whimpering anymore. She said his name in a firm voice; it almost sounded hard: "Gero."

"What?"

"Gero," she repeated. "He's not going to get me out of this. He won't defend me. He won't do a thing for me." Laura made a sound, a plaintive sound, then rolled her eyes as if she were about to pass out. "And if he takes on the case for my defense, it'll only be because he wants to make sure I get the maximum sentence."

I still didn't understand.

"What are you talking about?"

"He'll manipulate the judge. You don't know what he's capable of. He'll only pretend to help me. In reality—"

"Come off it, Laura, that's nonsense. He's your husband." And my boss, who I considered to be one of the friendliest people around. He could have sacked me at any time, and with good reason. Instead he would occasionally let me see photos of Vivi on his mobile. I loved it when his face lit up, when he talked about how she was developing. *Vivi can write her name now. That's Vivi on stage playing the wind. Vivi laughing, Vivi crying, Vivi building a sandcastle.*

No, I really didn't understand.

"Why would he do that?"

Laura flapped a hand in the direction of the body and cried, "Because of him, for God's sake!"

MAY 2014

The only thing Paul Heger could be sure of was this: the moment Simone stood by his bed and told him the police were there, he knew something serious had happened, something he might not have much influence over. As if dumbstruck, he put on his dressing gown, a Christmas present from his wife—thick, dark-green toweling. She'd wanted to get him something cozy in his favorite color and she'd even had his initials embroidered on it. The police officers were waiting for him in the dining room, and he walked down the stairs to the ground floor as if on the way to the gallows, dragging his heels, one stair at a time. Each seemed to represent an anecdote, and together these made up his story as a husband and father over the years.

The third stair from the top, which creaked so treacherously. In the past, when Simone and he still used to go out occasionally, they would always avoid this step when they got back home—giggling, tipsy on wine, in love and horny for each other—so as not to wake the little one.

Another stair halfway down, the one with the tiny spot of blood on the edge, which you wouldn't notice unless you knew it was there. That's where Julia had fallen and hit her head when she was three years old. Whenever he recalled the episode he at once felt her small, limp body in his arms, heard her whimpering and himself comforting her. He saw his wife, shaking and as white as a sheet, a reflection of his own feelings in a moment when he'd realized how quickly things could happen, how fragile life was.

The entire staircase which his daughter, now fourteen, stormed up in a pubescent rage when Paul forbade her from meeting her friends during the week, or when Simone refused to buy her the jeans you had to wear to be part of the "in" crowd in her class.

His stairs, his house, his family, his life.

Paul trudged to the dining room, where he stopped in the doorway. Two men sat at the table, both in plain clothes. Paul didn't know whether this was a good sign. Simone stood by the window at the far side of the room. She had her back turned to him, which momentarily made him more nervous than the presence of the two men. He wanted to be able to read her face.

"Banzbach," the elder of the policemen said, getting to his feet.

Paul nodded.

"And this is my colleague, Hartwig. Please sit down, Herr Heger. We'd like to talk to you about an incident near Suckow. Does the name ring a bell?"

"Yes," he replied hesitantly, staying standing in the doorway. "It's somewhere on the A24. I pass it on my route when I drive from my firm's offices to Lübeck."

Banzbach nodded.

"Correct."

He looked at Simone, then back to Paul.

"If you'd prefer, we could continue this conversation in private."

Simone turned around, her arms crossed and face devoid of

expression. Paul cleared his throat. "That's not necessary. I don't have any secrets from my wife."

"All the better," Banzbach said, gesturing to Paul. "So, please take a seat now."

Obeying, Paul sat down and clasped his hands on the table. Now it was Hartwig's turn. He reached into the inside pocket of his denim jacket and took out a small notebook.

"Do you know a Nelly Schütt?"

Simone's eyes narrowed.

Paul stared at his hands, which had done so many bad things. These hands had touched Nelly, these fingers had typed messages to her, the same fingers he'd crossed when swearing to Simone he'd never see Nelly again.

"Yes."

Hartwig leafed through his notebook.

"Three days ago Nelly Schütt was found dead, Herr Heger. On a woodland slope bordering the A24 at Suckow. We're assuming that she fell down the slope, seriously injuring herself in the process." Hartwig cleared his throat. "But she ended up being strangled."

Paul stared at his hands, which swam before his eyes.

Nelly. Dead.

The room started spinning, faster and faster. The centrifugal force tore him from his chair and dashed him against the wall. From somewhere far away he could hear Simone sobbing.

"What have you done, Paul? What the hell have you done?"

From: Letter #20

Happy Birthday, my darling!

My God, you were such a little miracle, I couldn't believe it. Your sweet little feet, those tiny toes. The little fingers that grabbed on tight to my thumbs. Your wonderful, big, round blue eyes. I held you in my arms wherever I went, I carried you around like Bella the doll, which I was given on my fifth or sixth birthday. I loved Bella even when she no longer had a head, and for ages I wondered if it was painful for her to lose it. To have it ripped off. They said it was me who did it, but that's not true. It was my punishment for having disturbed them at an inappropriate moment. But I took my revenge. I dragged Bella around relentlessly, like an accusation, a headless, hard plastic memorial in a poorly stitched flowery dress, and would place her head in different places in the flat, where for a while it provided plenty of shocks, until one morning it disappeared. As did Bella's body. For days I wept in anger at myself. I hadn't looked after Bella well enough.

But now you'd arrived and I would protect you. Nothing bad would ever happen to you so long as I was around. That's what I swore to you on my life, my angel.

NADJA

Crazy laughter rings out above the woods. *A green woodpecker*, I think. They're very common in the Spreewald, I remember from the television. A green woodpecker or some other bird blatantly reveling in my stress. I creep around Laura's grandmother's house and try to peer through the low windows, but they're so filthy that all I see is my own face. A sight I can hardly bear. I turn away and take the ridiculous wig off my head. I look up at the sky in an attempt to find it beautiful. It doesn't work. Laura ought to be here by now. What if she doesn't come? What if something's gone wrong?

Then I would be guilty.

Again.

But Aunt Evelyn said you need to let the air get to them!

She meant grazes. They heal better when they're open to the air.

Maybe bruises too.

No. Anyway, you know that nobody must see them. Otherwise people will think things aren't right at home and then we'll have to leave and might never see each other again. So put your sweater on now, please.

Yes, Mama.

Don't call me that.

Sorry . . .

No, my darling, I'm the one who's sorry . . .

I suggested repeatedly to Laura that she ought to call her husband, but she just kept staring into space. I was worried she might fall into a state of shock, and I called out her name several times as if trying to keep her with me, in the real world. Her eyelids fluttered briefly, then she turned away, went back to the sofa and slumped onto it.

"As you said," she gasped, "I'm going to lose everything anyway. Ring the police or Gero, whatever you think's right. It doesn't matter now."

I swallowed a few times and glanced again at the body on the floor. Which was dead. Which was dead whatever happened, and wouldn't come back to life again if a mother was locked up, if her freedom and child were taken away.

Manslaughter. Ten years.

Seven, if the judge is having a good day and feeling sympathetic to you for some reason.

Afterward nothing would be the same again. Never. I pictured Laura, alone and lost. In a barren prison cell to begin with. Unable to bear the sight of the dirty walls, scraping the paint from the concrete with her bare fingers because there was nothing else to do in her timeless universe. Then the time, those many years, eventually passed and I saw her released into something they grandiosely referred to as "freedom," although ultimately freedom was no more than another room with dirty walls. Laura, now sitting at the kitchen table of a tiny, sparsely furnished flat, writing letters to Vivi to explain what happened back then, i.e. *today*. I saw her struggling to work out what to write, becoming increasingly desperate, because all words, all reasoning, all excuses paled against the fact that in one brief, rash moment Laura had destroyed everything. Swallowing her like a deep, black sadness and never spitting her out again.

I hauled myself over to the sofa too, collapsed beside her and promised, "I won't abandon you. Whatever happens, I'm here for you."

Laura sighed, then nodded at the corpse.

"His name is Aron Bruckstätt . . . *was* Aron Bruckstätt. He played the occasional game of tennis with Gero. He was an artist, a photographer. We met at the tennis club Christmas party." She smiled. "He was nice and I found him interesting. All Gero ever thinks about is the firm and since Vivi was born . . . Gero's different, Nadja. Everything has changed, including, well, you know, in bed."

I nodded as if I knew what she was talking about, but secretly I felt like a little child.

"Didn't your husband suspect anything?"

"No," she said, shaking her head. "Of course not. He would have killed me." She gave me a piercing look. "Do you understand? That's why he won't help me. I cheated on him and he'll never forgive me. He'll want me to pay."

"Laura . . ."

"No, Nadja, that's what he'll be like, I'm absolutely sure. You only know one side of him. He had a girlfriend once, when he was a student, who cheated on him. He completely lost it." She buried her face in her hands again and her shoulders shuddered as she sobbed gently. I thought of how she knocked at the door to the lavatory cubicle on the day we met, as if she'd heard my silent begging, as if we were unwittingly and invisibly connected to each other. How after work that same day she turned up unexpectedly in my office and took me to the coffee shop around the corner. How she ordered two cappuccinos to go, *for me and my friend*, and when she was asked what names were to go on our cups, she just said *Laura*, with the result that hers said *Laura* and mine *Laura's friend*. I didn't want to think that she'd only done it out of pity, or how pathetic it was of me to take the cup home, wash it out and keep it. I preferred to remember the lunchtimes we spent together after that and how Laura was the reason I even dared enter the staff canteen, something I would never have done on my own. Too many strangers, too many eyes. But when I was with her, nobody seemed to take any notice of me. They had eyes only for her. In her long, colorful hippy clothes, with all that jewelry and blond hair, she stood out from the mass of suits like a flash of lightning on a dark night. How wonderfully relaxing it was to hide anonymously in her shadow. I wanted to think of how she'd once asked me whether I'd like to go with her to the new club in Kreuzberg, and that I almost said yes. That one day perhaps I would have said yes if we'd had more time. But then she met Herr van Hoven and suddenly everything happened very fast. Now when she spoke about him, she called him Gero.

And Gero thought she should focus on the wedding preparations rather than spend eight hours sorting files in the office. At her going-away party I sat in the same toilet cubicle, knees pulled up to my chin, trying to contact her via our invisible connection. She didn't come. Surrounded by colleagues, she raised a toast to her new life, and I resigned myself to the fact that some things in life were just not meant to be.

But now that I saw her sitting here so forlorn, so lonely, so sad that it almost broke my heart, I was certain of one thing: I'd do anything for her. For Laura, who'd restored life to me in such an unexpected, horrific and magical way.

"We have to get rid of the body."

Laura lowered her hands and looked at me in surprise.

"What did you say?"

I hesitated. What had I said? . . . Probably the only thing that sounded right.

"I said we have to get rid of the body."

Laura shook her head.

"Gero once told me that ninety-five percent of all corpses eventually turn up again somewhere. Often not for decades, but they do reappear. Ninety-five percent! And when they've got the body . . ."

". . . they'll work out what happened," I said, finishing her sentence. I recalled a television documentary I'd seen recently about John Haigh, an English serial killer in the 1940s who'd also realized the fundamental importance of the dead body to the police investigation. When Haigh looked for a way to get rid of his victims, and thereby the most incriminating piece of evidence, he came across the idea of dissolving the corpses in sulfuric acid. The only problem with sulfuric acid is that it doesn't break down fat, and so Haigh ended up with liters of body fat, which he simply poured down the drain. I was shocked by the idea that so little could remain of a human life if someone put their mind to it. Just a few buckets of fat.

"Then we'll have to do all we can to ensure that our corpse is one of the other five percent."

Something approaching a smile twitched at the corners of Laura's mouth.

"You said *our*."

I nodded, took her hand and squeezed it as hard as I could so she would realize how serious I was. I didn't have access to any chemicals that might allow us to simply sluice away the problem that was Aron Bruckstätt. I didn't even have the faintest idea how to set about the problem. But I was utterly determined to help Laura, no matter what it entailed.

"If there's no body, then officially nothing ever happened."

"But it did happen!" She wrested her hand from mine and kept gesticulating. "Look at him, Nadja! He's dead, I killed him!"

"Yes, you did."

"How am I going to come to terms with that? How can I go on living knowing what I did?"

"It's not something you'll find any easier in a prison cell." I shook my head. "No, you'll never forget what you did, but you've got plenty of years to make up for it in other ways. You'll be the best mum to Vivi that a child could possibly hope for. You'll be there for her as she grows up and you'll always protect her. You'll sit in the front row when she performs in the school play and clap louder than the other parents. You'll hug and comfort her when she feels the whole world's against her. You're needed here, Laura. And for that reason, yes, you're right, you can't go to prison." I wiped my nose with the sleeve of my blouse. "So, if you really want to do it, if you want to get rid of the body, you can count on me."

Laura smiled briefly, then leaped up so abruptly that I flinched.

"Oh God!" she cried, her eyes as wide as saucers. "We've got to get rid of him before Gero comes home!"

I check the time again. A quarter to one. I have to call her, there's no other way. I have to know where she is. If she's okay. I head back to the car to fetch my mobile. All thoughts of the police and the possibilities they have of tracing the call—telephone records and that sort of thing—have shrunk beneath a nasty feeling. A feeling that has taken hold of my body and is tugging at its every fiber. It's not fear—or not only that—I know fear, I know what it feels like. Sometimes it comes at night, crawling out from under my bed, squatting on my chest, making me gasp beneath its weight and laughing hideously in my face. No, it's something else. The worst feeling after loneliness—the feeling of irreversibility, of having lost control. Like a raised arm poised to strike. Or a word that has fallen from one's lips and can no longer be retrieved. My stomach cramps; wrapping my arms around my torso, I quicken my pace. Beneath me the wooden bridge creaks, above me the crazy green woodpecker cackles.

Something has happened, I just know.

Perhaps I knew the whole time but didn't want to admit it.

Just like before.

I get to the car. The mobile is in my handbag, which is on the passenger seat. I pause. Leave it where it is. Instead I step around the car and push my trembling hand beneath the lever that opens the trunk. What if my mind has twisted this story about Aron Bruckstätt, perhaps even made it up?

A protective mechanism, I hear my therapist say. *You're just play-acting*, I hear Aunt Evelyn say, and then a five-year-old girl screams: *You've got to believe me, it's the truth! He does exist, I didn't make him up!*

I shake my head furiously. *I didn't make him up*, I repeat silently, ready to open the trunk. Ready to find Aron Bruckstätt lying there, just as he lay there yesterday evening, his body wrapped in a dark-blue woolen blanket with only a waxy hand peeping out from beneath. The main thing is that his face is covered, his eyes.

Then I hear it. Another voice. Except this time it's not coming from my head, it's real.

The voice at my back.

The voice that says, "It's one of your biggest problems, isn't it, my dear?"

I'm no longer breathing. It's as if my right hand has frozen around the lever to open the trunk, while my left is clutching the wig.

"One of your biggest problems is that you can't trust yourself. That's right, isn't it? With every breath you take, you doubt your own sanity. No surprise, really, given your history."

JUNE 2014

The suspect Paul Heger met Nelly Elisabeth Schütt while staying at the inn of Bettina and Klaus-Peter Schütt, the victim's parents. A relationship developed between the two of them, as attested by, among other things, text messages found on both devices, the suspect's mobile and the victim's. Hotel reservations and credit card bills seized at Paul Heger's home (desk in study, bottom-left drawer) as well as concurrent statements made by hotel staff also show that between November 2013 and May 2014 Herr Heger and Frau Schütt met thirteen times at Zervenwald motorway hotel at Suckow on the A24 (witnesses: Heinz Höppner, reception; Caroline Brehbeck, reception; Anatol Bork, room service; Lena Marie Maybach, room service; Simar Bikum, room service). According to Paul Heger's wife, Simone Heger, she learned of the extramarital affair in April and then went to see Nelly Schütt as well as telephoning her on several occasions. Nelly Schütt did not, however, say anything about the relationship. Then Frau Heger insisted her husband end the affair, which he supposedly did. In May, however, Frau Schütt turned up unexpectedly at the Hegers' property and revealed that the relationship was still going on. According to his wife, Herr Heger was "furious" at Frau

Schütt's appearance. There is no evidence of any contact between Herr Heger and Frau Schütt over the following two weeks, but according to his wife, Herr Heger seemed "tense and stressed" during this time.

On the day before Frau Schütt's death there was contact between her and Herr Heger in the form of a text message, found on both the victim's and Herr Heger's mobile phones, in which he asked to meet Frau Schütt. It is not known how, on the day the crime took place, he lured her into the woods near Hotel Zervenwald, but the assumption is that he intercepted her as she was driving into the hotel, got into her car and directed her to the woods. After Frau Schütt parked in the car park at the edge of the woods, she went on a walk with Herr Heger, during which he assaulted her and pushed her down a slope. When the body was later examined by Professor Ansgar Littmann from the Institute of Forensic Medicine at the Charité hospital, he found that the base of the skull had been separated from the cervical spine (atlanto-occipital dislocation). It was believed that without immediate assistance Frau Schütt would not have survived the effects of her fall for long. The coroner recorded asphyxiation, however, as the direct cause of death.

After committing the crime Herr Heger walked back to the hotel, where he was recognized by staff members, and spent around half an hour in the room, which had been booked in advance. Afterward he went down to reception and checked out. When the duty receptionist, Caroline Brehbeck, inquired as to the reason for his premature departure, Herr Heger claimed that there was an emergency at home and he had to leave straightaway.

Afterward Herr Heger drove back to Berlin, where he arrived

home around 7 p.m. and, according to his wife and their daughter, Julia Estelle Heger, they had dinner together: spaghetti bolognese and cucumber salad.

Paul Heger sat slumped on a chair in interrogation room two. The recap Inspector Banzbach had just read out was like a foreign language he didn't even have a smattering of. The words had been present, they'd flown around the room and there was something definitely impressive about how they sounded. But they meant nothing to Paul. Banzbach, who'd been sitting opposite, got up, placed his hands on the desktop and leaned toward him slightly.

"Motive: sheer rage. As far as you were concerned, Nelly Schütt had made a mistake when she turned up at your home that Sunday. In your eyes she'd crossed a boundary, especially as your whole life was now unraveling. All of a sudden your wife was now threatening to divorce you. You were worried you'd lose everything. Your marriage, your daughter, the house, your reputation. Over the next few weeks you probably tried to talk your wife around; you made an effort to smooth things over. But she no longer believed you. You were in a really tight spot, Herr Heger. Things had got too difficult." Banzbach's head twitched. "Perhaps you thought you could solve all your troubles by going to the root of the problem: Nelly Schütt. If she were out of the way, everything could be all right again."

Paul gaped; his head was buzzing. What Banzbach had just stated sounded like a logic that was horrific and yet somehow comprehensible. He tried to remember, but hearing the news that Nelly had been found dead had done something to his head, completely addled his brain. Nothing had been clear since; a peculiar veil lay over everything.

"I wasn't in the woods." He looked at his hands. "I waited for her in the hotel room, but she never came, so I thought she must've changed her mind. I could hardly hold it against her, given everything that had happened over the past few weeks."

"You didn't leave your hotel room between 3:45 p.m., when you checked in, and your departure at 6 p.m.?"

Paul gave an energetic shake of the head.

"No. I was in the room. Which surely means I've got an alibi."

"Think carefully, Herr Heger," Banzbach said, but Paul just looked bewildered. "Strange," the inspector said. "The lady at reception says she saw you three times that day: checking in and out, and at about 5 p.m., when you came into the reception area from outside and went to the lift."

Paul rummaged through his memory, but found nothing.

"I was in the room," he affirmed, at which Banzbach merely growled and looked him in the eye for a moment, before waving to the back of the room, where Hartwig was waiting by the door, holding Paul's mobile in a transparent plastic bag. Hartwig handed it to Banzbach.

"What would you normally do if someone failed to turn up for an appointment, Herr Heger? Wouldn't you call and ask what had happened?" He brandished the bag. "But you didn't call Frau Schütt. We were unable to find an outgoing call. You didn't call her because you knew full well that she couldn't answer the phone anymore."

Paul cast a desperate glance to his left, where beside him sat his lawyer, Tabea Lenggries, who'd been recommended because she was a tough cookie and pedantic. He wasn't reassured to see her chew her bottom lip for several seconds before she finally seemed to get engaged.

"My client didn't ring Frau Schütt because he didn't want to be spurned on the phone too," she then said. "By not showing up, Frau Schütt had instinctively told him everything he needed to know. Besides, you checked my client for traces of a struggle. He doesn't have a single scratch. Do you really believe that Nelly Schütt would allow herself to be strangled without offering the slightest resistance?"

Banzbach sighed.

"It sounds like you're poorly briefed, Frau Lenggries. As it says in the coroner's report, Frau Schütt broke her neck in the fall. She couldn't offer any resistance—from a purely physiological point of view, it wasn't possible any longer."

Paul winced internally.

"I didn't lure her into the woods."

Banzbach gave Hartwig the wrapped-up mobile phone back without taking his eyes off Paul. Eyes that glinted with satisfaction.

"I didn't mention earlier that we discovered a lighter close to where the body was found. Now, Herr Heger, guess whose finger-prints we found on it?"

NADJA

I'm trembling. I wish I were on the edge of my white cliffs. Gazing down into the depths, feeling rocks crumbling, abandoning myself to gravity and allowing myself to fall voluntarily. Even if the water was red down below. And then, then I would wake from my unconsciousness, right by the till in the petrol station shop and I'd know: this here, this moment, didn't really happen, it's just a perverse joke my mind has permitted itself to play while I was helplessly at its mercy.

I blink. The panic doesn't set in and the moment is as it is. Real. Just like the voice behind me. Still standing at the back of the Land Rover, I carefully take my hand away from the lever that opens the trunk and try to understand something even though I know I won't be able to.

The voice laughs.

"It's all right, Nadja. Don't mind me. You go ahead and check to see whether he's still in there. And that you didn't just imagine the whole thing."

I slowly turn around. There's about thirty meters between us. I don't know how he got here; there's no other vehicle to be seen for miles around.

"It must be terrible when you doubt your own sanity. I thought you were taking medicines for that?" Dry leaves rustle beneath his shoes as he approaches. I try to take a step backward, but in vain—the tailgate of the Land Rover is pressing into my hip.

"Where's Laura?" I splutter.

"Laura? Oh, I'm afraid she's busy at the moment. But I'm here instead."

"What is—"

"I know exactly what your little game is," he says, his voice now a hiss. "Laura has told me everything."

"I don't believe you."

"You don't believe me? Well, that's a pity." He cocks his head and again I hear the sound of leaves rustling under his shoes. My eyes dart right, left, he'll be facing me soon, so close he'll be able to grab me.

"Please . . ."

"Please," he repeats in a high-pitched voice, pretending to be plaintive. "You sound like Laura. *Please*," he says again, now imitating her.

"Where is she?" I ask. "What's happened to her?"

"Oh, my dear, who knows, who knows? Let's play a game."

I shake my head.

"I don't want to play any games. I just want to know where Laura is."

He just laughs. Takes a leap forward. I wrench myself from my paralysis and start running. Rapid footsteps pound the wooden bridge: my own, and his behind me. A wild beating in my chest too. I know I've gone the wrong way; before me is nothing but the house on the tiny island. Too late to turn around; I have to keep running. The branch of an overgrown bush lashes my cheek like a slap. I stumble and behind me his voice drones, "There's no point, Nadja! You won't get away from here!" The voice is right, as I know before his hand grabs my hair and yanks back my head. I scream, I fall, the skin on my head burns like fire. I hit the ground hard and he lands on top of me. In my ear his breathing and a whisper: "I've got you. Now we're going to play a game."

I writhe and gasp beneath his weight.

"What are we going to play?"

"We're going to play courtroom."

From: Letter #21

What was I to do? I had to help her! She'd fainted in the bath, or at least that's what it looked like to me. She was lying unconscious in the tub, her right arm hanging limply over the side. The water must have been too hot, made her light-headed and dragged her down into the depths of unconsciousness. I was glad you were at kindergarten and didn't have to see me grab her weak, naked body under her slippery armpits, haul her out of the tub and across the hallway to the bedroom. Her awkward wooden arms dangled uncomfortably against my knee, while her heels scraped noisily across the yellowed linoleum. I tried to think of Milosz Nowak, a classmate who I'd got into an argument with in the playground the week before when he'd claimed she'd given his father chlamydia. I told myself that if I could deck Milosz Nowak, a boy built like a massive tree trunk, with a single blow, then I'd bloody well manage to get her to bed, seeing how delicate and elf-like she was. Hadn't she often told me that I was unbelievably strong-willed? Sometimes this impressed her and sometimes it made her angry. Perhaps it took me hours, perhaps just minutes, before she was finally in bed. Time no longer existed in our universe. I pulled the nightie over her stubborn body, arranged the pillow beneath her head and covered her, tightly and up to her chin. I even hummed the melody of her favorite song. I hummed until I thought I saw a faint smile on her lips, then I went into the kitchen to boil some water for the hot water bottle. As I waited by the stove I looked around. The burn holes in the oilcloth. The cold butts in the ashtray with the raspberry-red traces of lipstick on the filters. The wall calendar that hung beside the fridge with its pictures that always made us dream. "The most beautiful French landscapes 1999." I thought of the rose gardens of Alès on the page for April and Montmartre in May. Now it was June and the calendar showed the salt marshes of Aigues-Mortes. "Dead water." I reached forward, ripped off the page, tore it into pieces and threw them into the bin. Among more cigarette butts I noticed the scrunched-up silver foil of a bar of chocolate, yesterday's paper, in which I'd looked in vain for jobs, and one of your drawings. I took it out and smoothed it flat. You'd painted the three of us. A stick-figure family, walking hand in hand along a beach. Above our heads I could make out tiny black shapes—gulls, I guessed. Looking at your drawing gave me the determination I needed. I would nurse her back to health as I'd done when she had the flu. As I'd always done when she wasn't well. I'd nurse her back to health and put everything back in order.

JUNE 2014

To begin with, Paul Heger just felt empty, hollowed out. But now he was absolutely furious. He was furious with his wife Simone who, from what Inspector Banzbach had told him, seemed to regard the constant questioning as a course of personal therapy. Paul had always had an eye for other women, she'd said, and flirted a lot, maybe more too, which had been difficult for her. But she tried to understand him. After all, his mother had died when he was young and so he'd struggled all his life with the fear of loss and also for the recognition which he'd lacked as a boy with only one parent. He was like a squirrel, she'd said, who hoarded love and attention rather than nuts. He'd been a good father, at least when his daughter's needs had fitted in with his schedule as a pharmaceutical rep. The day after Julia had hit her head on the stairs he'd gone straight back to work as if nothing had happened. And yes, she could imagine Paul doing what he was accused of. Especially as—*She should be ashamed of herself!*—he liked to be a bit rougher in bed these days and—*Shame on you! Shame on you! Shame on you!*—he had put his hands around her neck on occasion before. Besides, she added, he had a tendency to angry outbursts when he felt under pressure and, let's face it, Nelly Schütt definitely put him under pressure.

Then there was Banzbach, that idiot with his boozer's nose and grubby leather jacket, who had nothing but a handful of clues and yet he still believed that Paul had lured Nelly into the woods, pushed her down a slope and strangled her when she didn't die quickly enough of her broken neck.

And finally he was furious with Tabea Lenggries, his lawyer, who clearly wasn't fit to handle his case. She hadn't even managed to get him bail. This morning, though, she was sitting opposite him in the meeting room in Moabit, looking immaculate, which only raised Paul's hackles even further. The time she must have spent in front of the bathroom mirror with her makeup and complicated updo could have been put to better use studying his file.

"Have the police got anything else relating to the day of the crime?" he asked.

Lenggries leafed through the papers in a folder. Paul slid his hands beneath his thighs when he felt the urge to grab this woman by the collar of her smart, fitted blazer and drag her across the table to spell out the seriousness of the situation.

"They've got the text message in which you arranged to meet Nelly Schütt on the day of the crime, the booking confirmation for room 231 at the hotel, the witness statements made by the employees, affirming that you were there that day and when, as well as the lighter found at the top of the slope."

"Anything else, I asked," he said acidly. Lenggries flapped her pink eyelids upward and looked at him in bafflement. "I know all that already," he said. "Something new. DNA, that sort of thing."

The lawyer kept looking through the documents.

"No. In terms of flakes of skin, hair or bodily fluids, nothing yet—" she said after a while.

"Come on," Paul interrupted her. "I mean, seriously, that can't be enough for them to charge me." He pulled his hands out from under his thighs, clasped them on the table in front of him and leaned toward Lenggries. "If I'd strangled Nelly Schütt, there must have been some sort of trace left behind, no?"

"Well, you see, Banzbach's argument is that three days passed between the established time of death and the discovery of the body. And during those three days it evidently rained hard several times. Moreover, the water collected in the hollow where Frau Schütt lay. The body was terribly muddy."

Paul closed his eyes briefly when the image of Nelly's brown-crusted face flashed before him. The image from his nightmare. "Which means most traces were washed away," his lawyer continued.

Paul blinked. She'd said *most*.

"Apart from a few fibers that must have got caught in the wool of Frau Schütt's cardigan."

"What sort of fibers?"

"They're being analyzed at the moment. So far all they've established is that these didn't come from Frau Schütt's clothing."

Paul shook his head and sighed.

"Then let them do the analysis, for all I care. Just get me out of this place."

Lenggries shut the folder.

"That's not so simple, Herr Heger. Your wife has told the police that she's afraid of you."

Paul felt his eyeballs push their way out of their sockets.

"She said . . . *what*?"

A sharp pain had bitten its way into the back of Tabea Lenggries's neck. She hoped she could ease it by removing the tight hair clip from her red locks and making a few circular movements with her head.

"Are you tense?"

"No idea," Tabea said, rubbing the back of her neck. "That Heger guy is really getting on my nerves."

"Why don't you sit down?"

She nodded, sat on the chair in front of Gero van Hoven's desk and stretched out her legs. The heels of her new shoes were without doubt a centimeter too tall for a day like this when she wanted one thing only: to get out of here. On the journey back from the prison, her eyes irritated by the constant switching between the shadows of passing houses and the sun dazzling through the gaps in buildings, she'd scrolled through her playlists until she found the right one. Listening to the Mamas and the Papas, she inhabited her fantasy world of a little house in the country. In the mornings, still in her underwear, she would put on her rubber boots and shuffle through the garden overgrown with wildflowers to the chicken hut to fetch fresh eggs for breakfast, while her beloved made coffee in the old-fashioned way, with coffee grinder and porcelain filter.

"Would you like to join me for a coffee?"

"That would be lovely," Tabea said, unable to suppress a smile. Gero had already picked up the phone to pass on the order to his PA when she suggested they get the coffee themselves and go up onto the roof of the offices. "I think I could do with some fresh air."

"And you shall have it," Gero said, getting up.

In the summer months, the flat roof of the legal practice, which had been a boiler works until the early twentieth century, was used as a terrace where staff spent their lunch breaks. They'd even put some furniture up there: a few pub benches, tables and umbrellas. It had only just turned eleven o'clock and so they had the place to themselves.

"You're gnawing at this case," Gero said once they'd sat down with their coffees at one of the tables.

Tabea shrugged.

"Heger's right, they haven't got much on him. But what they do have seems to paint a perfect picture. On top of that, Inspector Banzbach is on good terms with that new public prosecutor—what's his name again?"

"Mertens."

"Mertens, that's it. And even before he was appointed, he kept commenting on how Berlin was much too lax at prosecuting criminals."

Gero smiled over the rim of his coffee cup.

"I like him."

"No, Gero. What you like is the game. If you like getting into the ring with Mertens, then bully for you."

"Do you really not know me?" He winked at her. "It's all about justice, not my ego. And that's what I like about Mertens. It's all he's concerned about too. He refuses to compromise, which basically I consider to be a positive character trait."

"If you say so. To be honest, I've no desire to compete with him." Tabea took a sip of her coffee. "He and his bootlicker Banzbach are dead set on getting the charge through."

"So? Surely you're not worried that you're not up to handling this case? You're a bloody good lawyer, one of the best we've got."

"I know that. And of course I'm up to the case. Till now I've managed to get all my clients off."

"What is it, then?"

"I simply don't care—that's it. I'm sure I could play Mertens's game with ease, if I wanted to. But I don't, that's the point. It just doesn't appeal anymore. I'm not like you." Tabea tried to smile, but it didn't work. The corners of her mouth turned down and from somewhere her eyes had gathered tears. She turned to look at the Kreuzberg skyline, hoping that Gero wouldn't notice. In vain.

"Hey . . ." he said, reaching for her hand. His grip was warm and firm. Tabea still couldn't understand how something that felt so good could suddenly be wrong.

"Things will change. You're just going through a difficult patch at the moment."

Now Tabea was smiling—a faint smile.

"Do you remember how we used to fantasize about chucking it all in and doing a runner? Just you and me, our little house in the country, the clucking of happy hens, fresh coffee and the Mamas and the Papas playing all the time?"

"Tabea . . ." Gero said.

"No, leave it." She sniffed, taking her hand out of his and leaving the terrace as quickly as her too-high heels would allow.

NADJA

I don't know much. I don't know about the sea, the salty air or gulls. I don't know what it's like to wander calmly down the pavement without turning my head back every few steps. What it's like as a regular customer in a grocer's to be called by my real name and feel comfortable with this, rather than thinking that I've been rumbled or caught. What it's like to stand in the coffee shop without flinching when the beans are ground in the machine or the milk frother hisses. I don't know how to take the subway. Every morning I've forgotten again how to do it, take that first step on the escalator. I can't do it until I'm jostled from behind by someone who's in a hurry. Sometimes it's the going down itself that brings me out into a cold sweat. Down, down, ever farther, below ground where the arched roof seems like a huge brick tomb. As tightly as I grip the handrail, as far as I stand to the right, keeping absolutely still, while people push past to my left, there are all these bodies that keep knocking into me, with briefcases and rucksacks that strike out. I can see myself losing my balance at any minute, falling headfirst and lying at the foot of the escalator with my head split open and limbs dislocated. On other days it's waiting for the train that runs me ragged. Standing underground on the platform, where the people, those pushers and shovers, suddenly have nothing else to do but to wait too. And stare. Looks from strangers that penetrate my skin all the way to the slate-gray insides. The fear that they can see my past like a suppurating rash right in the middle of my face. The train, screeching a high-pitched scream as it brakes. The yellow safety line, all blurry. More pushing, shoving, knocking, the cramped carriage, the shrill beeping before the doors close, being shut in, stares, sometimes from children too. I was in a subway car with a school group recently. Thirty or more children. Thirty or more broken promises, death thirty times over.

I don't know what it's like when the night swallows you and only spits you out again as it's getting light, laughed hoarse, danced off your feet, hungover and sweaty, somewhere unfamiliar beside a person who's loved you for a wonderful, insignificant moment. I'm the woman who sits at the open window of her kitchen when she sees that her neighbor has friends over again on a Saturday night. Who sits there listening to the conversation and laughter that drifts over from the other window, also open, and imagines she's been invited too. I'm the woman who leaps up and scampers to her door when she hears the friends leaving. Who then peers through the spyhole and envies other people's Saturday evenings and their entire easygoing, free lives.

I don't know what it's like to be normal, but I do know one thing. I know what people are capable of. And I'm scared. The past has come to get me and it's shredding me.

We're going to play courtroom.

· · ·

Earlier, outside the house, I screamed and begged—not a chance. He rolled off, pulled me to my feet and dragged me into the house. Through the small hallway, past the kitchen and open living room to a flight of worn wooden stairs, and up all seventeen of them. Now I'm here, alone and locked inside this room—it's Laura's grandmother's bedroom or a guest room. A double bed with turned wooden posts stands with its head against the left-hand wall. There are no bedclothes, just a bare mattress. On the right-hand wall are a wardrobe and chest of drawers, above which hangs a gold-rimmed mirror. Through the window with its beige curtains I can see the stream overgrown with vegetation. My hands are tied behind my back with packing tape that cuts into my skin when I pull at it. I've called out his name at least twenty times and rammed my shoulder pointlessly against the door. I can't get through, neither to him, nor the solid wooden door.

I step over to the window, spy a gray-and-white tabby cat darting under a bush and wish I were in its place. I reckon the window must be about two and a half meters from the ground; I could risk it. Jump. And then run, run, run. I try to move the handle with my shoulder. It's stuck. I look around. I'd have to be higher up, with my back to the window and on a chair—high enough so my hands could grab the handle despite the packing tape around them. There isn't a chair in this room. The next plan is to push the bed beneath the window. The heavy wooden bed that doesn't budge a centimeter. The chest of drawers that scrapes loudly and jarringly across the floorboards as I set my weight against it. I give a start. Impossible—he would hear me and thwart my escape attempt before I'd got the chest of drawers anywhere close to where I want it. I collapse to the floor; my head is thudding and feels as if it's about to burst. I briefly think of the incident at the petrol station, how I injured my head as I fell and the wife of the cashier saying: *What if she's got a concussion?* Then I realize how stupid I am. How selfish. How can I think only of myself right now?

Laura . . . he's killed her.

You don't know that.

Yes, I do.

Because it's the only thing I know for sure. I know what people are capable of. And Laura knew it too. She knew exactly what was in store for us. She even told me; I just didn't listen properly because I was too busy trying to be her friend. Or, more accurately, trying to finally have one again. At any price.

From: Letter #23

Today my therapist asked how the letter was going. The truth would have been to tell her that there still isn't one yet. There are just these pitiful attempts. Barely an evening goes by when I don't sit at my kitchen table, pen in hand and in front of me a fresh sheet of paper. And I do write, I write late into the night. But at the end, when I read through what I've written over the past few hours, I just realize again that the words don't exist for what I really want to say to you.

Only today my therapist looked so expectant, and for some reason I suddenly felt bad about all those hours I'd merely sat silently opposite her, drinking liters of her coffee. So I said, "The letter is almost finished," and smiled. A lie, but so what? Nobody has ever seen me as anything but a liar.

"What happened at your place on June 17, 1999?" they always wanted to know. But what could I have told them apart from the fact that Marta had fallen ill and I stayed home to look after her? I did make an effort, I really did. I mean, I only wanted to do everything right. After she fainted I hauled her out of the bath and took her to bed. After that I went into the kitchen to boil some water for tea and a hot water bottle. I was scared, of course I was, but I also remembered

the flu she'd had a few years earlier and that everything had turned out all right in the end.

When I returned to the bedroom, she was staring at the ceiling. In the flat above ours there had been a leak some years earlier and ever since we'd been able to see brown patterns on the ceiling. A butterfly and a fish with a stunted tail fin floated there, then something that looked like a lightning bolt, a battle-axe and the outline of Africa.

"Chamomile," I whispered, putting the cup on the bedside table. "It's very hot."

She didn't react; she hated tea. She thought it tasted of being ill, and she hated being ill. Unlike me. I had pneumonia when I was in the third year and could still remember two things from that time: her sitting on the edge of my bed, holding my hand, and the strawberry flavor of the penicillin. I'd loved both of them.

"I know, I know," I say with a smile. "But if you want to be back up on your feet soon you've got to hang in there now." I briefly stood wavering by the bed, but then—"Oh yes!"—realized I still had the hot water bottle wrapped in a tea towel beneath my arm. I placed it carefully on her tummy and slipped into the bed. Closeness—people still said this, didn't they?—closeness and love were sometimes more of a help than any medicine. I pointed my right index finger at the ceiling and said, "Do you see that pattern right below Africa? It looks like a heart, what do you think?"

She didn't reply. Her eyes were shut. Surely sleep would also help her recover quickly. I pressed my nose into the hollow between her neck and shoulder. Something about the way she smelled unsettled me, but I didn't think any more of it. I was tired too, so tired and worn out. I closed my eyes and murmured, "Sleep well, Marta."

JUNE 2014

Tabea Lenggries gasped for air before pressing the button that cut the connection. "Van Hoven," the woman on the other end of the line had said. But that wasn't her name. It wasn't even her telephone number. She was Brehme. Laura Brehme. She was a lowly assistant at Abramczyk & van Hoven, someone you got to punch holes in folders, and look up articles. *What on earth was he doing with someone like that?* Tabea thought bitterly. As if in a trance, she put the telephone back into its dock on the chest of drawers in the hallway and went into the living room, where she rolled up on the sofa like a freezing cat. Silent, colorful images flashed up on the television screen; apart from that the room was dark. It was late, gone eleven o'clock, which must mean that the Brehme woman was spending the night with him. Of course she was, she was his girlfriend now. The one he listened to the Mamas and the Papas with and dreamed of moving to the country. She was the one who put on the rubber boots every morning and waded through the wildflowers to collect the eggs for breakfast while he made the coffee indoors.

Tabea couldn't help thinking of a car accident she'd seen when she was eight. She and her parents were on their way to Lido di

Jesolo for their summer holidays. Tabea remembered her father saying, "Uh, oh!" and her mother's sharp intake of breath, and she herself sliding forward and peeking between the two headrests.

All three of them able to see what was about to happen.

The car that had overtaken them in the left-hand lane and the other one up ahead, which swung out at the same moment. Metal on metal, which crumpled like paper as the two forces collided. Parts were sent flying and there was a horrendous bang, followed by this eerie, all-encompassing silence. Her father managed to brake just in time and none of them came to any harm. The car ended up on the hard shoulder, where they did nothing for a while apart from sit there, catching their breath, before Papa undid his seat belt and got out to help.

It was similar with Gero and this Brehme woman, Tabea thought. Two vehicles that had collided at full speed and she'd been the one watching it happen. She could identify the precise moment too—a Friday when she'd arranged to have lunch with Gero in the staff canteen. They were standing side by side in the queue at the counter, right behind Laura Brehme, who turned around, holding the plate that the cook had just passed over the counter, and knocked straight into Gero. The gravy slopped over the rim and within seconds had formed a large brown stain on his smart white shirt. But Gero didn't get annoyed; he didn't even flinch. His eyes moved from the stain on his shirt to Laura Brehme; he just looked at her, saw in her—*whatever*. And Laura Brehme returned his strange, lengthy gaze. That was it, the moment, Tabea knew for sure. They didn't see each other the following weekend; apparently Gero had gone hunting with the senior partner, Ludwig Abramczyk. And when he came to her place on the Monday evening, he told her. He'd been thinking, he said. He'd enjoyed their relationship but he couldn't go on like this anymore. He was going to be honest with her; he'd fallen in love with the woman who'd messed up his shirt. Tabea took this as a joke.

"So that's what you were really doing at the weekend, was it?" she asked when she realized it was no joke. "Hunting, my ass! You were checking out whether she was interested in you too so you'd know if it was worth dumping me."

He shook his head.

"No, that's not what happened. I didn't meet her. I don't know her at all. I couldn't even tell you which department she's in."

Tabea was dumbfounded.

"And despite this, you want to finish with me? For the sake of a woman you don't even know?"

Tabea only knew her by sight too, but she remembered that she'd had a negative impression of Laura even before the incident in the canteen. As if Laura were herself an ugly brown stain on a smart white shirt. An alien entity. Someone who just didn't fit. Who floated around the corridors in colorful dresses—instead of the suits that the female employees of the firm wore without exception—barefoot and with blue toenails. With her long blond hair and all those bangles that jangled with every step, like a cutlery drawer being yanked open, she seemed to Tabea like a girl who'd missed the last bus back to the 1970s, not a woman to be taken seriously. And certainly not one Gero might feel attracted to. He liked impressive women who were elegant and educated, who could compete with him intellectually and only lose by a whisker. Or so Tabea had thought. Clearly she'd been mistaken.

"Whether I know her or not is irrelevant," Gero replied. "This may sound harsh, Tabea, but if you really were the one, then no other woman would be able to beguile me like this. And definitely not by tipping her lunch down my shirt." He grinned, for which she felt like giving him a slap.

"So what now? Are you going to ask her out on a date, or what?"

"That's not why I'm here, Tabea. Yes, I would like to ask her out, but not behind your back."

Tabea laughed.

"I suppose you're expecting me to praise you for your honesty too."

"No, absolutely not. But perhaps you'll be grateful to me one day. There are so many liars in this world who we have to deal with all the time. Cowards merely intent on saving their own necks." He reached for her hand, which she immediately pulled away. "You mustn't lie to people who mean something to you. No matter what the consequences."

"So what are the consequences for me? You're cutting the ground from under my feet!"

"I'm sorry, Tabea. But I can't help it." He left.

That was four months ago. Four months in which she'd hoped he would mull things over and come back to her. In which she spent longer in the bathroom in the mornings, taking particular care with her makeup and hair. In which she bought and wore new clothes and shoes with heels that were too high, so that when he bumped into her at work he'd be able to see what he'd let go. Let him regret it and miss her.

Four months and Laura Brehme was already answering his home telephone.

Four months of pure pain.

Tabea couldn't go on like this, nor did she intend to. She sniffed, sat up and reached for the remote control, to put an end to the crazy flickering of light on the screen. With a sigh of relief, she savored the darkness, in which her thoughts seemed to find an anchor for the first time again. What was it that Gero had said? That he was prepared to take the consequences? *Very well*, Tabea thought. That was exactly what he would start feeling now: the consequences of his actions.

From: Letter #24

Do you recall the story of the woman who could look through walls and doors? I told it to you when you were about four years old and starting to get nosy about what was happening in Marta's bedroom. I understood you so well because I was exactly the same at that age. But of course I wasn't going to tell you what happened to me once, when Marta caught me spying on her. Unlike adult bones, the bones of children don't shatter because a child's skeleton is still growing, and so everything's elastic and heals much quicker. A wrist fracture is painful all the same—I didn't want you to have to go through that. I had to teach you to be careful. So I told you about the woman who could look through everything. Walls, doors, even people.

"I don't believe it," you said.

"The girl in the story didn't want to believe it either at first, which was why she asked the woman for proof of her abilities. The woman screwed up her eyes and looked deeply into the girl: You are dark gray, like an old slab of slate."

You started to giggle.

"That's funny."

99

"No, sweetheart, it's not funny. Little girls should be white inside, not dark gray, almost black."

"Did the girl turn dark gray because she was always so nosy?"

Yes, maybe, I said. Maybe the girl turned dark gray because she interfered in things that didn't concern her. The truth, however, was different: in Marta's eyes, the girl had been dark gray from the day she was born. With her first breath, the girl destroyed Marta's life, for she'd had to give up her career as a dancer.

Because of this girl, she lived in a small, run-down flat in a shabby Polish block instead of an elegant apartment on the Champs-Elysées. This girl had arrived like a punishment. First she'd come for Marta's body, making her tummy fat and etching stretch marks on her firm, slim thighs. Then she'd launched into her dreams, her fridge, her money and her nerves.

Of course I never really believed that Marta had supernatural perception, but sometimes—no, often—I'm haunted by the idea that she might have been afraid of me. Afraid that one day I might cause her even greater misfortune. And unfortunately she wasn't the only one who saw me like that. I was a cheeky brat always spoiling for a fight. Dark gray to everyone who knew me.

Apart from you.

NADJA

Yesterday evening at the van Hovens'.

Laura said she couldn't take him from the *front*. *Front* meant where Aron Bruckstätt's head was. I understood her; it was the eyes. His look, which must be unsettling for her. His entire face, which wasn't hardened with terror and anger, as she might have expected, but looked completely relaxed. I assumed she hadn't had much experience of death before and so didn't know that in the final moments of someone's life, all their muscles, including their facial features, went limp, regardless of what had just gone before. I declined nonetheless to give her a detailed explanation; it seemed inappropriate. Instead I grabbed Aron Bruckstätt under the armpits, Laura took his legs, and together, panting and straining, we dragged him out of the living room, down a narrow corridor and past the open-plan kitchen, until we got to a metal door that connected the living area with the garage. He weighed a ton; his arms knocked against my knees. When Laura sniffed, I hissed, "Pull yourself together!"

We had to put him down by the garage, to unlock the door and wedge it so it didn't shut again immediately. As Laura kicked the wedge beneath the door, I looked down again at Aron Bruckstätt. Something happened; his lifeless body blurred and changed shape. His facial features changed too, became soft like a woman's. I threw my head back and took a deep breath. As soon as we'd loaded him into the trunk of the Land Rover, I'd take one of those pills my therapist had prescribed me for acute panic attacks and which I always carried around in my handbag for emergencies.

"Everything okay?" Laura said, stepping past me and bending over to pick up the legs again.

"Everything's fine," I replied mechanically, putting my hands back beneath his armpits. The Land Rover trunk is at waist height, so we growled like fierce animals under the additional effort it took to heave the body inside. Laura covered him with the blue woolen blanket she'd fetched from the back seat of the car. I wondered when she'd swapped her beloved red Mini Cabrio for this monstrosity of an off-roader, and whether it was her decision or her husband's, just as he'd been the one to decide that she should stop working at the firm. Although Laura had made it out as if they'd taken this step together, I didn't seriously believe her for a second. She loved her job and never once gave me the impression that she was ready to swap it for house and home. Besides, she was particularly fond of an audience. Of being noticed. That was the only explanation I could fathom as to why over all her years at the firm she'd never conformed, never blended in with all those suits. From the corner of my eye, I glanced at what now remained of the lively flower girl with all that jewelry and the long, colorful dresses, and the word "sensible" came to mind. The hair kept under control with an Alice band and a plait, jeans, T-shirt and a mustard-colored knitted shawl that made her appear paler than she already was. I didn't want to see her as a little bird you catch, then bind its wings to keep captive. But that's exactly what happened. Suddenly, that's how I did see her.

"I hate this car," Laura said, as if she'd read my thoughts. "But Gero said we had to think practically, think of Vivi and shopping." She laughed briefly; it sounded like a dry cough. "He didn't actually buy it for me, but for himself and his hunting trips." When the trunk crashed shut we flinched in sync, then just stood there for a moment, our eyes fixed on the tailgate, as if the two of us had been doped. Eventually Laura said, "What now?"

We didn't have a clue; we were just terrified. A few minutes earlier, when Aron Bruckstätt was lying in the living room, nothing had seemed more obvious than the decision to get rid of the body, and with it the entire unfortunate incident. Now not even I—who had persuaded Laura it was the best thing for all concerned—was sure whether we could really go through with this. There was a soft cracking sound in my ear. Laura was gnawing at her thumbnail, while a bad feeling was gnawing at me.

"We need a plan," I said firmly. "The slightest mistake and we'll end up behind bars."

"I know."

"Which means we would have only made everything worse."

"Yes."

"Do you really want to do this?"

She nodded.

"You've got to be absolutely sure."

She nodded a second time.

"Okay."

We left the garage, having decided that Laura should try calling her husband again. This time he answered immediately. She had to find out how much time we had before he arrived home.

None. Herr van Hoven was already on the way back from Magdeburg and had got as far as Brandenburg, only an hour or so away. She told him not to be surprised to see they had a visitor. "Your assistant." She giggled inanely. Yes, dinner would still be punctual. "Nadja's eating with us this evening." She took the mobile away from her ear and looked at it in puzzlement.

"Either he's hit a dead zone or he hung up."

"Doesn't seem thrilled that I'm here."

"Right now I think that's the least of our problems," Laura replied. She was right. If Herr van Hoven was already on the way back, it would be impossible for us to take Aron Bruchstätt's body away this evening. And where would we go, anyway?

"Shit!" Laura cried. "We've got to clean the living room."

Ajax and several buckets of red water and painful knees. She sobbed and shook as her cloth described uncoordinated circles across the marble. I told her she ought to sort out dinner instead; I would continue cleaning without her—an offer she readily accepted. At the same time, I wished she'd stayed with me. Squatting in the middle of Aron Bruckstätt's blood gave me the peculiar feeling that I was responsible for his death. *I've got nothing to do with it*, I repeated mantra-like in my head. *I'm just helping.* But the feeling was persistent. I focused on the clattering coming from the kitchen, wiping the floor with my sponge in jerky, hectic movements, wringing it out and reminding myself: *I'm just helping.* It didn't work. All I could see was more red water, red water and streaks on the marble, ever-present streaks and traces, as if new ones kept appearing, as if I'd never manage to get the floor clean again, as if it were a hopeless enterprise.

"Nadja?" Laura came in from the kitchen. I paused and turned my head toward her. "I just wanted to say thank you." I nodded and kept scrubbing, more determined now; I was going to do this. The floor was clean. I emptied the last bucket into the guest loo, flushed several times, lifted the seat in search of telltale red splashes, flushed one last time and washed out the bucket. I was just about to put the sponge and cloth into a plastic bag that Laura had given me when I noticed that there was already something in it. White material smeared with blood. I flinched.

"That's the nightie I was wearing when . . ." she said, unable to get any further with her explanation. I nodded knowingly and stuffed the cleaning things in with it.

"Could you take the bag to the car, maybe? I don't think I can open the trunk again."

I nodded once more. We would dispose of the contents of the bag along with Aron Bruckstätt, even if we still had no idea where we were going to do it. So I entered the garage for a second time. Went to the back of the Land Rover. Put my hand beneath the lever and opened the trunk.

There he lay, wrapped in his blue blanket, two waxen fingers poking out. I held my breath. Stretched out my arm. Carefully moved the blanket.

Those eyes. Those eyes that were staring at me. No longer Laura and me, just *me*, all on my own. That look which was saying: *I know who you are. I know you.* As if on autopilot, my body lunged forward; my right hand thrust itself into the trunk again, put the blanket back to how it was, and my left hand threw the plastic bag in. My arm reached for the tailgate and slammed it shut with a crash, and in my head I heard Aunt Evelyn, who could only say a feeble *Oh, child*. Then I returned to the kitchen, where Laura had been peeling the potatoes while I was scrubbing the floor; now she was busy preparing the salad. As I watched her cut out the stem of a tomato, it occurred to me to ask her about the knife.

"You know which one."

She nodded vaguely in the direction of the sink. "I washed it and then hid it in the garden shed beneath a bag of compost."

"It's got to vanish completely," I insisted. "Just like the nightie and especially . . ."

". . . *him*, I know," she said, biting her lower lip thoughtfully. "Maybe we should sink him in some lake."

"Not a good idea," I replied. "Although bodies decay faster in water, gases are produced that bring them back up to the surface. Burial would be better."

"I don't know. It would have to be an enormous hole. Do you remember the Witzleff case?"

I shook my head.

"Must have been before my time."

"I suppose. Anyway, there was this Witzleff guy, a dodgy property dealer who killed his business partner and then buried him in Spandau Forest. But there's a game reserve nearby, and a few wild boars broke out and promptly unearthed the body. They can easily dig down half a meter, you see." She looked at her watch. "Gero's going to be here soon. Could you maybe give the meat a wash? It's at the bottom of the fridge. Well, wherever we take him, it can't be anywhere near here."

"No, absolutely not." I opened the fridge and bent down to a vacuum pack of meat. When I shut the fridge door again and turned around, Laura was standing before me, clutching the steel handle of the tomato knife so tightly that her knuckles stood out white. For a brief second I thought it would only take a few centimeters, a short movement, and she could ram it into my stomach.

"I know, Nadja! We'll go to the Spreewald."

Her dead grandmother's house stood empty there, she said. A nice area if you knew how to get away from the tourist spots. We'd head there first thing tomorrow morning and look for a suitable place for Aron Bruckstätt. For somewhere to bury him.

"Wouldn't it be better to leave in the evening so nobody sees us?"

"No, we can't leave him in the trunk that long because it's going to be eighty-six degrees tomorrow, they say. Besides, Gero would get suspicious."

"Okay, we'll go to the Spreewald in the morning, then."

"And we can always decide once we're there whether we should sink the body in one of the smaller, unknown watercourses or bury him in the woods," she said as I was patting dry with a paper towel the meat I'd just washed. She looked at her watch again, muttered, "Shit!" and asked me now to cut up the meat. I felt slightly uneasy as I took the knife Laura had pointed at from its slot in the block. And then I noticed another empty slot, which must have housed the knife she'd attacked Aron Bruckstätt with. I'd have loved to ask her what they'd been arguing about, what he'd said or done to cause her to storm into the kitchen and grab the knife. But I left it; this wasn't the right moment. I didn't want to risk her breaking out into hysterics again just because of my curiosity. Not when her husband could come home at any moment.

"Thanks," she said, when I pushed the chopping board with the cubes of meat across the work surface. "You're discharged from duty, take a seat."

I did. I sat at the wonderful large wooden table in Laura's kitchen, listening to the hissing of the meat as it browned in the pan. Drank the glass of Chardonnay that she'd given me, traced with my fingertip the grain of the wood. I'd been invited to dinner. I inhaled everything. The aroma of the meat. The feeling of a close bond. And I almost forgot what was actually happening here. For a moment, as inside my brain the wine mingled with the effects of the pill I'd secretly taken when we got back from the garage, I was even—*happy*. I watched Laura in a flurry of activity at the stove and wished time could simply stand still at that moment. Then we heard the drone of an engine in the drive and the moment passed.

He's coming. I hear his footsteps on the creaking wood, then the metal scraping in the lock. I breathe fitfully and try to get to my feet before he enters the room. I succeed.

"Have you calmed down?" he says with a smile.

My jaw is clenched.

"I said, have you calmed down?"

"Is Laura dead?"

"Oh, for goodness' sake, Nadja!" Now he's laughing. He comes closer. The edge of the windowsill digs into my back. "Why do you think we're here, you and I, hmm? Who deserves to appear in court, if not Laura? You?"

I swallow, he shrugs.

"As far as you're concerned, I would call it aiding the cover-up of a crime. Okay, let's just say: aiding and abetting. Do you mind if we call each other by our first names, Nadja? I thought this would be the perfect opportunity, seeing as we've known each other for so long. And a murder creates a certain intimacy, wouldn't you say?"

I don't answer, not this question. I also try to ignore the smug look on his face. There's only one thing I'm interested in: "What's happened to Laura?" Laura, who told me right at the outset: *You don't know what he's capable of.* I just failed to listen.

"She's fine. Whether she stays that way depends on you."

He grabs my shoulders, turns me around roughly so I have my back to him, and starts untying me. I bite my lower lip as the packing tape rips at my skin and the tiny hairs.

"What do you mean, it depends on me?"

"What ultimately happens to her is going to be a matter of negotiation between you and me," he replies, as if that's perfectly normal. "The fact is, Laura has committed a crime. One which in certain parts of the world is punishable by death."

"But not here. Here there is no death sentence."

There's a rasping noise as he pulls the last strip of packing tape from my skin. I turn around. He's just smiling, not saying anything, still not. I feel sick. I shake my head.

"I don't understand any of this."

Gero van Hoven, who I'd thought was one of the friendliest people I'd met. Who'd had every reason to sack me on multiple occasions, but instead showed me the pictures of Vivi on his mobile. Who was now standing facing me like a stranger. A monster.

"But that didn't stop you getting involved, did it? I gave you a chance to rethink the idea. You could have turned around, Nadja."

I look at him in bewilderment.

"I followed you to the petrol station," he explains. "I thought you'd spotted me when you were at the counter and your gaze fell on the surveillance mirror in the corner. You turned as white as a sheet and then fainted. In the confusion that followed I left the shop straightaway and waited behind the building until you came out again. I could scarcely believe that you were going to continue the journey. But that's precisely what you did, Nadja. You took that decision and now you have to face the consequences. Such is life."

I think back, trawl through my mind. I took the turn-off for the petrol station. Up till then I'd been constantly checking the rear-view mirror, nagged at by a strange feeling the whole time. I got out and looked around, but couldn't see another vehicle. I filled up with petrol and went to pay. Then came the moment when my legs gave way, falling over the edge of the cliffs . . . No, stop, something else must have happened in between. I delve deeper until I unearth something. An image that flashes in my mind. The image of a man, distorted by the convex mirror, entering the shop. The reason for my panic attack. The man who pushed me over the edge of the white cliffs.

"But I didn't recognize you."

"And yet you must have sensed something, otherwise you wouldn't have fainted, would you?" He points to his forehead. "Does it still hurt?"

I shake my head as if numbed.

"Something bad is going to happen now, isn't it?"

He strokes my upper arm in a nauseating gesture of comfort and says with a smile, "Yes, Nadja. I'm afraid something bad is going to happen now."

From: Letter #27

*The night before last I dreamed for the first time in ages. Of Marta,
floating on her back in the red salt lake of Aigues-Mortes. She was
wearing a long white dress that was almost see-through in the water
and shimmered pink. Suddenly her blue eyes opened wide and she
stared at me. I was awoken by my screaming. At least I thought I
was awake until I saw the man standing beside my bed. His face
was blurred, but I could see his uniform in perfect clarity. Only now
did I really wake up, not screaming, just panting and with a feeling
of resignation. I told my therapist about this at yesterday's session.*

*"What do you feel when you think about this man?" she asked.
"Are you afraid of him?"*

*"Afraid," I repeated and nodded in confirmation, only to shake
my head immediately afterward. "Angry. I hate him."*

*"For what he did to Marta?" Her expression, which until then
had been sympathetic, now changed; she looked suspicious. I had an
inkling of where all this was heading. If I gave a wrong answer now,
the next thing I would hear would be "protective function," a term
that I hated almost as much as the man in my dream.*

To be on the safe side, therefore, I said, "She wasn't all bad," hoping to steer the conversation in a different direction. "Far from it." I remembered once kneeling by my bed as a small girl, praying. I'd even strewn grains of rice on the floor, because I didn't think I could offer God any other sacrifice apart from my own willingness to suffer, and it was indeed painful—the hard grains digging into my knees, leaving deep imprints in my skin, and in some places drawing blood too. So I kneeled there, begging God to take me back so that Marta would be rid of me and could finally live the life she deserved. I said my prayer out loud and didn't notice her come into my room.

"Nadja!" she exclaimed in genuine horror, scooping me up from the pool of rice to her chest. "You must never think anything like that, let alone pray for it! What would I do without you?" She rocked me in her arms, kissed my brow and the top of my head and said she loved me.

"And is that how you felt?" my therapist asked. "Loved?"

"She did love me," I said, batting back her stupid question. "She loved me as much as she could."

"And yet she hurt you."

I shrugged and avoided her gaze by staring at the ceiling of her office. "It's probably very difficult to love somebody if you hate yourself. Damaged people damage other people. Can you blame them?"

I gave a start when the therapist took my hand and gave it a firm squeeze.

"Yes, Nadja. You absolutely can. You can be critical of Marta. In fact, you should be critical if you feel that way. Don't suppress it."

I took my hand away and clamped it between my crossed legs.

"I think I'd like to try out some new medicine," I said in my thoughts to the man in the uniform. I don't want him in my dreams.

How is it with you, my angel? Are you able to sleep? Do you have good or bad dreams, or do you not dream at all? It's something I often wonder. Do you know what? Tonight I'm going to send you a dream of the sea.

Sleep well, my angel.

JULY 2014

When Tabea Langgries turned up to work that morning, she was wearing jeans, a plain jumper and an unusually careless pony-tail. She didn't have a handbag on her either; her car keys and key card were in the back pocket of her jeans. In her hand was an envelope. Old Herr Kohn at reception, who was just signing for the receipt of some legal documents, looked confused as he watched her walk past. By her standards she was late.

Tabea took the lift to the second floor. Her destination was Gero van Hoven's office. She'd called his phone on the drive to work, withholding her number, just to make sure he was there. She explained to the gray mouse in his outer office—who tried to put her off because he was apparently preparing for a trial— that it was urgent, and before the assistant could raise another objection, Tabea was already knocking at his door.

"Tabea." He looked surprised.

Without being invited, she sat in the chair in front of his desk and said, "Just listen to what I've got to say."

Gero van Hoven had gone up to the roof terrace to have a cup of coffee. Now the coffee stood untouched on one of the tables, while he was on the edge of the roof, his forearms leaning on the railings, looking out over the city. In the past few years he'd been used to things running smoothly, as if by themselves. And if not, then they could be ironed, pulled, stretched smooth. He'd been used to being the one in control of things.

In his mid-twenties he'd come to Abramczyk as an intern fresh out of college. Even then it was one of the most prestigious and, with over a hundred members of staff, largest law firms in Berlin. A place that offered opportunities and where, depending on your commitment and determination, you could become either an insignificant screw or irreplaceable wheel in Ludwig Abramczyk's machine. To begin with, Gero did no more than fetch his coffee, look up articles and carry his briefcase. But Ludwig had always been a fair man. He gave everyone a chance, especially those who proved to be good listeners. After work, over a glass of whiskey, he loved to recount his heroic deeds until his cheeks were glowing and he became drowsy. Gero had proved to be patient and even went on listening when the stories became increasingly repetitive. For five years now, his name had been engraved on the golden sign at the entrance to the offices. He was forty-two, he was a partner and he'd made it.

And yet, at that moment on the roof, he felt once more like the gangly young man who was only good for making coffee and carrying a briefcase. And all this because of Tabea. Tabea, who'd always worshipped him. Tabea, who he'd always been able to rely on. Tabea, who'd simply gone.

When, downstairs in his office, she'd handed him the key card and envelope with her resignation letter, his first reaction had been to laugh.

"Come on, Tabs," he said. "You can't be serious. I mean, I can understand you're pissed off with me. But this shouldn't be the reason for a decision that you're very soon going to come to regret."

"I realize that you see this as a knee-jerk reaction," she retorted. "But it's not. It's the only right thing to do."

"It's stupid. And truculent." He got up, wandered around his desk and began massaging her shoulders. Tabea gave a satisfied sigh. "This isn't like you at all."

Most of all, it wasn't like Gero's image of her. Tabea had always been reliable, consistent in what she said and did, and considerate, and always put him and his well-being before her own needs. It was as if he'd carved her in the image of his perfect partner. He felt as if the two of them together were as one. Both of them against the rest of the world. Not like his parents, who he'd never seen as an indissoluble unit. If Tabea could be considered his work and he'd carved her to his own requirements, there was one thing he'd have to admit he'd forgotten to correct. A rough patch of stubborn splinters that couldn't be sanded smooth afterward: due to an endometrial disorder, she was unable to have children. When, about nine months earlier, he told her he felt ready to take the next big step and start a proper family, and she revealed this couldn't happen with her, he realized his search for the right partner wasn't over yet. Nonetheless, he would stay with Tabea until he'd found a suitable replacement for her, and after that they'd simply be friends, the best of friends. That's how it would go, he was sure of it. Tabea had never disappointed him in the past. She would always be his refuge, his safety net.

He abruptly let go of her shoulders.

"I can't let this happen."

"You don't have a choice," she said, getting up and going over to the window. "You know, Gero, this isn't just about Laura Brehme and the last four months. That was the trigger, perhaps." She turned around. "But I've been asking myself when I was last really happy, and no matter how hard I rack my brains, I simply can't remember. I come close to happiness when I sit in my car and listen to music that lets me dream of another life. And in this other life I'm not a lawyer. There's no suit fastened around my body like a corset that barely allows me to breathe. And the point of my existence is no longer to justify crimes that I actually condemn myself." She shrugged. "Maybe I just went astray at some point. Made a mistake."

"Are you talking about me?"

"You too. Everything. This here isn't my life anymore. I crave something simpler, something . . . I don't know . . . something genuine. I'm toying with the idea of taking some time out and really moving to the country for a while, where I can look after a garden and a few fractious chickens."

Gero laughed again.

"Look, this is how I see it. You've had your pride dented and the only response you can come up with is to punish the man who left you, but who's also your boss, by plonking your resignation letter on his desk." He shook his head. "I can't accept that."

"You don't understand."

"And you're not leaving. Full stop. The firm needs you. You know we have far more cases than lawyers at the moment. You're going to at least see the Heger case through to its conclusion. After that, you can take a bit of holiday until you're right in the head again and then—"

"I'm leaving, Gero, and I'm leaving today. I've accumulated plenty of overtime and I have holiday left. So that covers my notice period, as you know."

"Forget it, Tabea."

"Fine, then I'll get a doctor to sign me off work. Chronic fatigue syndrome, burnout." She crossed her arms. "I'll find someone who'll attest to it."

"Are you threatening me? Is that where we've got to? Just because of the thing with Laura?"

Tabea sighed, walked over to him, put out a hand and laid it on his cheek.

"Once again, this isn't just about Laura."

"But it's mostly about her."

"Okay, yes," she admitted. "You know, I . . ." She faltered and her lips formed a crooked smile. "You were everything to me. And I would have done anything for you. For that reason alone, I can't stay here. How do you expect me to put up with seeing you every day? Seeing *both* of you? I don't want to become like so many of our clients, like that Heger, for example. I don't want to be driven mad by love, only to one day do something that would make all of us unhappy."

"Then bloody well pull yourself together," Gero hissed. "You're a grown woman, for Christ's sake. Not everybody turns into a psychopath the minute their heart is broken."

"All the best," she said softly, and was about to give him a farewell hug. But he'd already turned away. Tabea had stabbed him in the back, left him in the lurch. As if at the flick of a switch, he felt lonely—a feeling he'd found hard to cope with ever since childhood. Because loneliness made you vulnerable. And weak.

Gero stepped back from the railings and sat at the table. Although his coffee was now cold, he drank it all the same. He needed a bit more time here, on his own, up on the roof. He had to think.

It was always easier for the person who left than the one who was left behind. Gero wasn't the type to have affairs, but that wasn't the only reason he'd finished with Tabea rather than cheat on her with Laura. Tabea would have noticed sooner or later; after all, the three of them worked under the same roof. She would have found out and dumped him—he just got there first. And it had felt right, even good. It always felt good to be the one making the decisions. He just hadn't expected Tabea to follow suit.

Gero rubbed his brow. There were two things he had to do now. First, he needed to find a replacement for Tabea in the Heger case. Second, he was going to propose to Laura.

NADJA

We leave Laura's grandmother's bedroom and go downstairs to the ground floor. He makes me go in front, as if I were his protective shield. I feel his firm grip around my right arm and his breath on my neck, which covers my skin with a film of dampness. I'm still waiting for the panic to come, to find myself back on the edge of the white cliffs, but nothing happens. I walk slowly to stall for time and go easy on my head, which hurts and throbs with every step. I'm certain that Herr van Hoven has prepared something; I just know he has. Why else would he have kept me locked up in the bedroom for so long? From the last few steps I can glance into the living room via the hallway. I briefly make out the back of a leather sofa, a standard lamp with a semi-circular metal shade and a curved arm that looks like an oversized flower stem, a bookcase that's empty apart from one section, and a wood-burning stove. Apart from that, there are at least a dozen moving boxes.

"Turn right, Nadja."

I obey. To the right, where the kitchen is. A table with turned wooden legs, a corner bench, and two chairs that look like they came from an old pub. All that remains of the galley kitchen are base cabinets, a sink and a gas stove. The wall cabinets have been removed; brownish stains on the white wall testify to where they hung for years. Beneath the window are more moving boxes that suggest Laura or other family members had at some point begun to liquidate the grandmother's household.

"Sit down." I look at him. "On the bench, please," he adds with a gesture. "Oh yes, I've got something for you. I don't want you to think we're playing under unequal conditions." He leaves the kitchen, but there's not enough time to make constructive use of this other than to look around. At the window, which could be an escape route. For a weapon, or object that could be used as such. I don't want to hurt him; I just want him to let me go.

"I asked you to sit down."

I nod and slide my way into the middle of the bench. He hands me a thick book and smiles. "Criminal code, latest edition."

I don't know why I thank him for this; I don't know anything anymore. Apart from the fact that this can't be the same man I worked under for five and a half years. This isn't the Gero van Hoven I know. Thinking back, I suspect this occurred to me yesterday evening, but I ignored my gut feeling just as I ignored what Laura had said. *Gero's different, Nadja.*

Yes, he was different, strange and cool somehow when he came home yesterday, wandered into the kitchen and greeted me with a curt, "I've heard you're joining us for dinner." "Yes," I replied, adding that Laura had invited me. "You're very welcome, then," he said, although it sounded anything but. To Laura, who was just setting the table, all he said was, "I thought dinner was ready."

"Almost, darling." She smiled coyly. "Another ten minutes,

tops." I immediately thought of my mother, who'd often smiled like that when she wasn't sad enough for tears.

"Good," Herr van Hoven said, adding that he was going to get changed. I didn't dare take another breath until he'd left the kitchen.

"Oh God," Laura whispered. I nodded knowingly. Neither of us had any idea how we'd get through the evening without giving anything away.

"What if he goes into the garage?" I asked in a hushed voice as she arranged the cutlery around the plates.

She shook her head.

"There's no reason for him to go to the car."

I hoped she was right.

Then came dinner.

The cutlery clattered above the oppressive silence, I found the meat tough, and every time anyone swallowed it sounded too loud. At one point Herr van Hoven raised his wineglass and proposed a toast to my visit.

"How come you're here, actually?" he asked, giving me a penetrating look. I pretended to chew even though I'd already swallowed the last mouthful.

"Nadja is in the middle of having her flat renovated," Laura spluttered. "Total disaster, isn't it, Nadja?"

"Disaster," I confirmed.

"That's why she's going to spend the night here too." We hadn't spoken about that, but I nodded anyway, realizing that it was reassuring for Laura to have me close by.

"Oh," Herr van Hoven remarked. "Is she now?"

I essayed a smile. "Only if it's all right, of course."

"It is," Laura affirmed, before turning to her husband and asking, "isn't it, darling?"

Herr van Hoven muttered something.

"Anyway, I've promised Nadja I'd help her," Laura explained. "We're going to get started early tomorrow morning. We need to go to the DIY store, so I was going to ask you if I could borrow your car."

"But you've got your own car. Why do you need mine?"

"Yes, but we thought that Nadja might borrow the Land Rover for the weekend as she wants to take some things to the recycling depot. Don't you, Nadja?"

"Yes, that's right," I said hesitantly, rubbing my brow as I realized that Laura was planning to drive to the Spreewald in separate cars. I understood her point—she wanted to make sure we weren't seen together. On the other hand, I didn't want to think about how I was supposed to manage the journey on my own, especially with Aron Bruckstätt's body in the trunk. I mean, most days I couldn't even take the underground, let alone drive a strange car—together with corpse—a hundred kilometers down the motorway. As I felt my face starting to glow, I just hoped I wasn't turning red, which might raise Herr van Hoven's suspicions. I reassured myself, told myself that I'd driven Laura home this evening through the Berlin traffic, and that I'd cope with the trip tomorrow too, so long as I kept focused on why I was doing all of this. I was doing it for her.

"The thing is," Laura now told her husband, "if I had your car, I'd be flexible."

"If you like."

"Or do you need it tomorrow?"

"No, it's fine. I'm planning to play tennis tomorrow morning but I can get picked up, it's not a problem."

"Oh," Laura said. Her attempt at a smile ended in a crooked grimace. "Who are you playing?"

"Why do you ask?"

"No reason . . . Aron Bruckstätt?"

Herr van Hoven said no. He hadn't been able to get hold of Aron all day, so he'd arranged to play Fred Mertens, the public prosecutor; she knew who he was.

"I'll send him a message later asking him to pick me up and then you can take the Porsche. But, as you know, if it comes back with a dent, you're dead." It was meant to be a joke and we stammered a laugh. I was relieved when he said good night after dinner. He wanted to take a shower and go straight to sleep; it had been a tiring day. Laura and I did the washing up.

"Right," she said quietly when we could hear the jet of water from the rear of the house. "We'll wait until Gero has gone in the morning, then you'll set off for my grandmother's house. I'll give you the precise directions; I'll write it all down so you don't have to switch on the GPS. We mustn't phone each other either, because the police could use that as evidence later."

"What about you?"

"I'll drive to Aron's flat and see whether any of my things are there. Then I'll head for the Spreewald. I might even be quicker than you, as I know the area and all the roads by heart."

"Maybe you ought to clean the flat, or at least wipe down the surfaces so they don't find your fingerprints there if it comes to that. Did you always meet there?"

"Yes." She lowered her gaze. "Well, mostly. Apart from the last time, obviously."

"Never at a hotel or anywhere else?"

"No, just . . ." She paused.

"Laura?"

"Once we went to a pub on the federal highway. But that's thirty kilometers away from here and the people that go there . . . well, I don't think they're the sort who would talk to the police." I tried to imagine Laura in a place where there were people who wouldn't talk to the police—without success. It must be a really grubby place, with really grubby people.

"How about his neighbors?"

"Are you talking about potential witnesses?" She shook her head. "It's a huge apartment complex on Potsdamer Platz. More than two hundred people live there, nobody sticks out."

"Okay."

Suddenly she looked pensive.

"What?"

"I was just thinking . . . maybe we should disguise ourselves. I mean . . ."

"I understand," I said. "We shouldn't look like we normally do. That way nobody will be able to identify us later."

"Exactly. Do you think you could do without your mouse outfit for a day?"

I smooth the parrot T-shirt she gave me this morning with the words, "I wanted to get rid of this anyway as it's so horribly ugly." She laughed without the laughter ever making it as far as her eyes. She must have realized that I heard them last night, even though I tried not to let it show.

Herr van Hoven has started making coffee. It's going to be a long day for both of us, he said. I watch his back as he spoons the ground coffee, which he took from the fridge, into the filter, and think about last night. Me lying in bed in the guest room, which is next door to the van Hovens' bedroom, my eyes screwed up and a pillow over my head.

She screamed, he grunted.

Is he hurting her?

No, my sweetheart. She's fine, don't worry. Go to sleep now.

Why's she screaming then?

She's not really screaming. It's just because she's stressed. Now, come on, close your eyes and go to sleep.

What's that creaking?

It's the bed.

I can't sleep if it's so loud.

But you've got to, darling. Both of us have to go to sleep, otherwise we won't hear the alarm clock in the morning again. And then you'll be late for kindergarten and I'll be late for school.

Why does he say such bad things to her?

He doesn't mean it. It's more like a game.

It's not a nice game.

Shall I sing you something before you sleep?

Yes.

What would you like me to sing?

"The Royal Children."

Oh no, darling, that's such a sad song.

But I want to hear it.

Okay, then . . . *There were once two royal children / who made each other's heart leap / but they couldn't be together / for the water was far too deep / the water was far too deep.*

I clear my throat.

"Herr van Hoven?"

He turns around, holding the coffee spoon.

"We were going to use *first* names, Nadja. Call me Gero."

I look down at my lap. I don't want to look at him, not after I heard him pounce on Laura like an animal last night. But also because I'd continue to search in his eyes for the man I thought I knew as my boss for over five years. A good man.

"I just want to know where Laura is."

"I told you she's fine. That's all you need to know."

I nod apprehensively, hear the coffee spoon clatter on the work surface, then a chair scrape across the floor tiles. Once he has sat down opposite me, he extends his hand, palm facing upward, across the table. His fingers wiggle.

"Come on," he says. Even though I don't want to, I put my hand in his and put up with him clasping it. "Look at me." I do. "I'm not a liar, Nadja. Okay? Nobody is so determined to get to the bottom of the truth as I am. That's why we're here. I told you Laura is fine and that's the truth. Everything else is on trial, with you and me battling it out. I'm representing the prosecution and you the defense."

I shake my head.

"You've got to be joking."

"As I told you"—he responds with a shrug—"we're playing courtroom."

"Who's going to pronounce judgment?"

"Me." He grins. "But let me promise you this: I'm a fair man."

With a noise of disbelief I wrench my hand from his and wipe it on my jeans.

"What's going on right here is anything but fair."

"What Laura did wasn't fair either." He leans back in his chair and crosses his arms. "And neither were you, Nadja. I'd have thought you'd be more loyal. I mean, I am your boss. And you know full well what I could have done after the incident with Vivi." I pursed my lips. The incident with Vivi took place just a few weeks after she was born, when Laura came into the office to introduce the baby to her colleagues. Most days I manage to suppress the memory, but sometimes, when I spy the pink fluffy dog in my chest of drawers, it surfaces again and I feel ashamed. "You know I could have sacked you on the spot. And worse than that, I could have sued you."

"But you didn't," I respond quickly, before he feels obliged to go into the episode in more detail. "Because you're a good man, Herr van Hoven. And because that's the case, we have to finish this here and now before you end up doing something you'll regret for the rest of your life. Think of your daughter."

He smiles.

"Nice try, Nadja. But I've made my decision. Today the two of us are going to try the case of Laura van Hoven, adulteress and murderess."

It takes me a while. I can't do it right away. First I have to really chew on the tough word and become aware of my cowardice. Just as every morning I wait at the underground station for someone to come and jostle me from behind so I can take the first ludicrous step onto the escalator. Just as I sit at my open kitchen window on Saturday evenings, imagining I've been invited to dinner, rather than ringing my neighbor's doorbell and introducing myself. Just as I keep writing letters to my brother, but never send them. How cowardly I was, how cowardly I am. And then I simply say it, I say it as loud and with as much determination as I can: "No."

Herr van Hoven looks confused.

"It's not as if you have a choice, Nadja."

"Oh yes, yes, I do," I say, pushing the wooden table right into his stomach. I leap up, run out of the kitchen and across the hallway to the front door. The handle. I push it, once, twice, lots of times at ever-decreasing intervals. The door. The door which is locked. No key in it. And finally the shadow towering behind me and the metallic rattling of a bunch of keys.

"Are you sure you want to leave already, Nadja?"

I tentatively turn my head over my shoulder. The bunch of keys rattles again.

"You see, it's like this: if you decide to give up your client's case prematurely, my judgment will be pronounced without a trial."

"What does that mean?"

He shrugs.

"It means that Laura will die."

Haven't I told you? I'm in urgent need of a different drug! At my last session, after the last dream, I asked my therapist for it. But she didn't want to prescribe me anything new and said I should stick with my old medicine. After all, she said, one single dream in months didn't represent a pattern. I suspected at once that she was going to be wrong, but I gave in.

And now? The dreams are piling up again. Last night I saw Marta, her head bowed, standing in our old bathroom. Her hair was a wet curtain covering her face. Her white dress was wet too, dripping water onto the floor tiles. Dripping red. All of a sudden she raised her head and stared at me with her big blue eyes. I ought to have woken up at this point, but it didn't happen. When Marta now stretched out her hand, I realized that I was standing facing her, with less than half a meter between us. I sensed my breathing getting faster and yet I also felt as if I were suffocating. I shook my head in panic. She mustn't touch me, I didn't want that, so I stumbled a pace backward—and promptly crashed into something hard. I turned around and in front of me stood the man in uniform. I tried to make out his face, but he didn't have any eyes or nose, just a mouth which he now opened. At a stroke I turned cold, I started shivering.

"Poor little girl," he said. "Nobody believes you."

It was only at that point that I woke with a start, awake in a flash. In the echo of my dream I could still hear him laughing, the man in the uniform. He was making fun of me.

JULY 2014

Forty-eight lawyers, thirty-two of them who specialized in criminal law, all up to their eyes in work and none as good as Gero van Hoven. So he had to take on the Heger case himself. Another good reason for a few silent but sharp curses he aimed at Tabea on the way to the firm's underground garage. They weren't finished yet, he resolved—*not this way, Fräulein.*

Once upon a time there had been another woman who'd tried to take him for a fool: Lilian Kössling. Lilly, as he called her, who he'd met at university. Lilly, who studied literature and wrote the loveliest poems. Lilly, who was so special, so pretty, so uncomplicated and so fun-loving. Lilly, his first great love, his first serious this-is-forever. But then, after almost two years, came that winter's evening when they met on Savignyplatz. *How wonderful,* he thought at first. As if they were part of one of Lilly's poems. The glittering lights of the Christmas market and the thick white snowflakes dancing around them as they held each other like two figures in a snow globe, blissfully isolated from the noise and chaos of the world. Until he noticed that Lilly was quivering and getting stiffer all the time. He put it down to the weather, the bitterly cold winter. But then she lifted her head from his shoulder and looked at him with an expression he'd never seen on her face before. And her voice, which sounded completely different from usual. *Gero, there's something I've got to tell you . . .* That was when the first crack appeared in the snow globe, a crack that grew bigger and bigger as Lilly now confessed that she'd been seeing someone else for several weeks. It had just happened, she couldn't say why, and of course it had nothing to do with him, Gero. Love, that wild, unpredictable creature, didn't ask permission; it stumbled, lacking all coordination, on unforeseeable paths; it fell and just lay prostrate like a drunk. *I'm really sorry, Gero.* With those words she went away, without even turning around again, and he was left standing there like an idiot, alone in the snow globe, its glass walls cracking and creaking until it burst and shattered, just like his silly, silly heart. Ever since he could remember, he'd longed for that indestructible togetherness you usually only found in films and love songs—but it must exist or it wouldn't be possible to make films and songs about it, would it? And even if the entertainment industry was guilty of exaggeration, surely there must be something different from what he'd experienced at home, with his parents. His mother and father, who seemed to have done nothing but fight for decades, which even as a child Gero had thought was a criminal waste of one's life. No, he would never have a relationship like that. And in Lilly he'd believed he'd found his other half. Until that evening when she destroyed the snow globe. How could he have got her so wrong? Let her do to him what she did? For weeks he locked himself away in his student room, missing lectures, licking his wounds, tasting blood and salty tears. He didn't eat, only drank, drank too much, just beer. He was also holding a bottle of it when he finally braced himself to leave his room again. It was late, and outside the night was cold and dark. The frozen asphalt rumbled beneath his heavy footsteps, and ahead of him the gloomy light from the street-lamps cast absurdly long shadows of his body. He no longer had to think, just follow the shadow that seemed to know the way: to the hall of residence where Lilly lived. He stood there for a long while, raising the bottle to his lips and staring up at the window of her bedroom on the fourth floor, one of the few where a light was still on. Not the harsh ceiling light, but a warmer, more muted light from her bedside lamp. Gero knew precisely what occasions Lilly used that for. In its glow they'd often lain in her bed, bodies entwined, her lips on his, his hands on her body. *So you've got a visitor, Lilly*, he said inside his head, sensing his teeth grinding. The other man was there . . .

Gero thrust the car into reverse and jerked out of the parking bay with his name on it. Surprised by the roughness of its han-dler, the Porsche howled like a wounded animal. On hearing the sound, Gero's thoughts turned away from Lilly and to his father. *Only people with hang-ups drive cars like that*, the old man would have sniped now. *That's also what people say who'd never be able to afford one*, Gero would have retorted, just as when he'd visited his parents in his new car for the first time, intending to take his father for a spin. He would have lifted him carefully from his wheelchair, hauled him into the car, put down the hood, played with the gears and his speed and heard his father say: *I'm proud of you, my boy*. Instead the old man had just blurted out his usual poison and wheeled back into the house.

That's quite enough, Gero told himself as he drove up the ramp leading out of the underground car park. He had better things to do than aggravate old wounds as a result of Tabea's behavior. Wasn't this always his strength? The ability to focus on the important things, set priorities and work through them one by one, unbending steel while everyone else melted in the heat like cheap plastic?

He made his way to the prison to meet Herr Heger. The limp handshake and one look into his watery eyes told Gero all he needed to know: *actor—coward—guilty*. He made a mental note. Earlier in the office he'd studied the photographs from the crime scene and those taken by the forensics department.

"I'm going to be honest with you, Herr Heger," he said, gesturing to his new client to take a seat. Heger, who appeared relieved that his case had been passed from Tabea to Gero, nodded keenly and did as he was told.

"We've got a rather big problem."

Heger blinked nervously.

"What do you mean?"

It took Gero almost an hour to explain it to him, over and over again, as if Heger were a dim-witted child. It wasn't just the clues lined up like a pearl necklace strung too tight: far more problematic was the popular misconception that justice was blind. It wasn't.

At most it was slightly myopic, and it was also a woman. As such it was easy to influence. It would look at the photographs, just as Gero had done, and see exactly what he had seen. A doll-like face, ghostly white in death, but otherwise beautiful, like everything about that young girl, who had her whole life ahead of her till she met Heger. Who, with her closed eyelids, looked almost peaceful, as if she'd surrendered to the whole thing, like someone who was unbelievably tired but knew she'd wake up again after falling asleep. Hearts would burst with a painful din, every heart, that of the judge and the associate judges. Then her slim neck with the strangulation marks that had turned brown, and that beautiful, delicate body, in the first set of pictures lying there in the muddy hollow, and in the second set on the cold mortuary slab in forensics. It would be a cinch for the public prosecutor. All Mertens had to do was persuade the dead girl's parents to give him a few pictures of their enchanting daughter while she was still alive and hard at work at their inn, laughing, beaming and full of confidence, pass these on to the press and the die would already be cast, sympathies fixed. With public opinion unanimous in its condemnation, no judge in the world would allow Heger to escape unpunished.

"And the wheels of the press are already rolling," Gero explained. "Right now the girl is still an anonymous body found in some woods by the motorway. But what do you think is going to happen when they publish a picture of her face? When her parents have recovered from the initial shock and decide to share their suffering with the world?"

Heger was weeping now, and Gero despised him even more for this.

"But I'm innocent!"

"Okay." Gero sighed. "Would you then care to explain to me how a lighter with your fingerprints on it turned up at the crime scene?"

"Maybe I gave it to Nelly at some point."

"Was she a smoker?"

"No, but . . . in the hotel rooms we sometimes lit tea lights, to make it a bit more romantic. Maybe . . ."

Gero raised an eyebrow; Heger fell silent.

"Then there's the receptionist's statement," Gero went on. "At some point between checking in and 5 p.m., you left the hotel for a short period of time. Or at least the receptionist says she saw you come back in. Where were you, Herr Heger?"

Heger started fidgeting.

"She must be mistaken. I was in the room the whole time."

"She sounds like a credible witness." Gero leaned across the table. "There's an old rule in criminal prosecution that says if a person has a motive—which in your case is beyond question—second, has the means to commit the crime"—he pointed to Heger's hands—"and third, the opportunity to carry it out, then they're guilty. So, if you left the hotel between checking in and 5 p.m., you had the opportunity, too."

"Oh yes!" Now Heger slapped his forehead. "I did in fact leave the hotel briefly! To get cigarettes! There's a machine in the car park and that's where I went!" He beamed—*what an idiot*.

"You remember this only now?" Gero asked. "After the police asked you a dozen times about this window of time?"

"I'm innocent!" Heger's voice was cracking.

"It's just that the pieces of evidence are saying something completely different, Herr Heger. What about the fibers, for example, that were found on the victim's cardigan? They're from your sweater. The sweater which, according to your wife, you were wearing on the day of the crime."

Heger swallowed loudly, but still seemed unwilling to give up.

"I expect I wore the sweater another time when I met Nelly. The fibers could have got stuck to her cardigan on that occasion too."

"That's true," Gero admitted. "Just like everything that points to you as the killer could be a chain of unfortunate events. Only—and you should be aware of this—I suspect nobody's going to believe you."

Heger's face had turned red.

"It's your job to get me out of this mess! You're my lawyer!"

"The best you could wish for."

"And as my lawyer you should—"

"—believe you?" Gero shook his head. "I can only advise you to the best of my knowledge. And my advice—to spare you and me from wasting unnecessary energy and effort—is quite clear: make a confession so we can negotiate a reduced sentence with the public prosecution department."

"But it wasn't me!" Heger had leaped to his feet. The anger oozed from his reddened brow like the sweat from every pore. Gero didn't move a muscle; he merely felt his suspicions had been confirmed.

"You told Lilly to come to the scene of the crime, Herr Heger. You were seen at the scene of the crime. You had a motive, the means and the opportunity. Don't be a fool, man. You left too much evidence behind."

Heger's lips were quivering. Everything about him seemed to

switch off, like a kitchen gadget that has the plug pulled while in operation.

"Nelly," he whimpered.

"Hmm?" Gero raised an eyebrow.

"You called her *Lilly*, Herr van Hoven. Her name was *Nelly* and I loved her."

NADJA

Yes, the front door. Beyond which lay the Spreewald, freedom. Just three or four centimeters of stupid wood and yet impenetrable. Locked, and the keys were jangling in Herr van Hoven's hand. A choice which wasn't a choice: *if you decide to give up your client's case prematurely, my judgment will be pronounced without a trial.*

He would kill Laura.

So I turned around. Walked past him without saying a word and went back into the kitchen. Sat down in my place, my head bowed, while he resumed making the coffee.

"I get the slight feeling that you're not taking me particularly seriously," he says, filling the reservoir of the coffee machine with water. "And, you know, I can sort of understand you. This situation really is—how shall we put it?—unusual. I can also understand that you're trying to test your boundaries and"—he turns to me and smiles—"that's a good thing, Nadja." I look away and squeeze my hands in my lap. I hear him flap down the lid of the water reservoir and press the "ON" button. There is an extended hiss from the coffee machine, followed by bubbling noises.

He sits down.

"I'm totally serious when I say that you can be proud of

yourself. Look at all the things you've managed up till now." The fake expression of enthusiasm on his face and sham euphoria in his voice make me burp up the plum schnapps from the petrol station. "You drove the car, Nadja. Just that on its own. You got into an unfamiliar car and drove it all the way here without a GPS or anyone beside you to help. Be honest, would you have ever thought that possible?"

I say nothing.

"I wouldn't," he says. "You really surprised me there. I mean, seeing as you can't even take the subway without practically having a nervous breakdown."

I look up. How does he know that?

"You overcame your fears to help Laura. Of course, we have to ignore the fact that this meant you'd committed a criminal offense, quite apart from the ethical dimension. But"—another smile—"now you know you can do more than you think, if you really want to. And I'm sure you're going to be a good lawyer for Laura if you make an effort. You can save her." The grin on his lips is broader as he whispers, "Save her, Nadja."

I shake my head in disbelief and immediately regret it when the pain inside flares up again.

"Herr van Hoven, I think I have to see a doctor. I might have a concussion from my fall in the petrol station this morning."

"Oh, Nadja."

"I really don't feel well."

"You can go and see a doctor when we're finished here."

I want to shake my head again, but decide against it, and instead channel all my disbelief into my voice.

"What the hell is wrong with you?"

For a few seconds he holds my gaze, then slaps the table and gets up.

"I'm just doing my duty here. And you're doing yours." He takes the bunch of keys from his jeans pocket and puts them in the middle of the table. I stare at them.

"Oh yes, the coffee," he says, before leaving the kitchen. "You can look for the cups. We need three of them, as we've got a guest, you see."

You can't go in there, darling. She's got a guest.

What's he doing in our bathroom?

He needs to take a shower before he goes home and she's helping him.

Huh? Why does he need a shower?

You don't say "huh," you say "pardon" . . . Because he'll smell of her otherwise.

But she always smells good, of roses.

Some people don't like roses. They think they stink. Others are even allergic to them. Roses make them really sick. Now please move away from the door.

But I really need a wee.

I'll take you down to Aunt Evelyn's, okay? You can go to the loo there.

That's our bathroom!

I know, darling. Come on, let's go before you have an accident.

I don't like it when we have guests.

.   .   .

Me neither . . .

I feel cold, I feel queasy, I can't move. All I can do is put my head back and look up at the ceiling when I hear the clattering on the floor above me. I know. I know what's about to happen. I think of the mobile phone in my handbag on the front seat of the Land Rover and of the bunch of keys just an arm's length away, in the middle of the table. I wouldn't be able to pick it up, unlock the door, run to the car, retrieve my mobile and call the police.

Footsteps on the stairs, the stifled sounds of a woman.

I start to tremble. Wonder when it was he saw through our plan. And especially how. I mean, I was there when he was picked up this morning. I'd been awake for ages, but I didn't dare come out of the van Hovens' spare room. The thought of bumping into him and having to look him in the eye was just too much. In truth I didn't even want to have to look at Laura after having heard her last night, but just for now I wasn't going to be spared that. So I simply sat on the bed and waited. Shortly after eight o'clock the doorbell rang. I heard two muffled men's voices, and when I peered out of the window a moment later I saw Herr van Hoven and Fred Mertens get into the public prosecutor's car and drive off. Almost simultaneously Laura knocked at my door and asked if I was ready.

There was only one possible answer: he must have eavesdropped on us. Maybe yesterday evening when we thought he was having a shower. That would have given him all night to think this through in his mind.

"Nadja?"

I recoil.

"I thought I told you to find the cups."

I don't want to look and I also ignore the sound, a broken, stifled whimpering.

"Nadja?" he says again in a nasty singsong. I play deaf.

"How impolite of you. Please say hello to our guest."

I begin swaying.

"You're wasting valuable time, Nadja."

I move my head sluggishly.

They're standing in the doorway, him pressing up against her from behind. His right hand is around her waist, his left around her neck, which is stretched back and leaning on his shoulder. I can't make out anything of her face, all I can see is the gag. She's wearing a thin white nightie. It's smeared with blood. My heart cries. *She's injured*, I think at first, but then I realize that she wouldn't be able to stand up if she was injured as badly as the stains suggest. It must be Aron Bruckstätt's blood. That's the nightie she wore when she stabbed him, the nightie from the plastic bag.

"Laura," I whisper, at which she makes another stifled sound.

"She's fine," Herr van Hoven says with satisfaction, pushing her into the kitchen. Laura is barefoot, tiptoeing in front of him, unable to see where she's going as he still has her by the throat. He guides her to the chair at the head of the table and pushes her down onto it. Her eyes stare at me; her neckline is glistening with sweat and her breasts rise and fall at alarmingly short intervals. I even fancy I can see her heartbeat. He steps behind her and unfastens the gag.

"Nadja," she pants as her hand shoots across the table. I grab and squeeze it tightly. Individual hairs that have slipped out from the Alice band are sticking to her brow. I really want to touch her face, stroke her pallid, tearstained cheeks and assure her that it's all going to be fine. But I suspect I'd be lying.

"How touching," Herr van Hoven sneers, before taking the bunch of keys from the table and slipping it into the back pocket of his jeans. "Now that Nadja is sufficiently motivated, I hope, we can finally begin."

AUGUST 2014

The night lay before them, as if it had been poured over the forest. The moon drew fine gray streaks across the sky, which could only be seen when their eyes had got used to the darkness. Nothing broke, nothing cracked beneath their heavy boots. They were silent, like ghosts. Two men in the face of whom even capricious nature capitulated, yielding to their footsteps and their determination. The first of the two men was Gero van Hoven; the second, his senior partner, Ludwig Abramczyk. They didn't have to speak. A look was enough, even in the dark. This was the right place to wait for the night to lift and give way to daybreak. Ludwig took a hip flask from his coat, had a sip and passed it to Gero, who took a sip too. At once a warm feeling washed down his throat and spread throughout his entire body. Single malt. Gero imagined his father in a wheelchair with a bottle of beer. He was about the same age as Ludwig, the only similarity. *Thank God.* Gero gave the hip flask back to Ludwig, who returned it to his coat. They waited. This was the real trick: to be able to wait without becoming impatient. Just as Gero had waited years for the right match and found it in Laura. They were made for each other; together they were whole, a serious this-is-forever. He was certain the feeling was mutual. *My parents got divorced when I was three*, she'd told him at the beginning of their relationship, with an expression in her eyes that was so damaged, so wistful that she looked like a little girl. Gero took her hand and immediately fell in love with her a little more.

He grinned silently into the darkness of the woods. This was clearly another trick worth mastering: waiting without becoming distracted. So he composed himself. Focused. Reminded himself that he was here because of *him*.

One hour later. First there was merely a rustling. Then he came. Trotting unwittingly to his demise. Gero and Ludwig exchanged glances again. Both looked satisfied. Ludwig pushed an annoying twig aside. They watched him for another moment, allowed him a few final seconds in which he could feel secure and invincible. Then Gero readied his rifle. Aimed. Shot. And triumphed. As if in slow motion, the legs doubled up before the rump of the beast fell onto the forest floor with a thud.

"Good shot, my boy," Ludwig said, clapping his hand on Gero's shoulder. Words and a gesture he'd have loved from his own father, but had never received.

They dragged the stag to Ludwig's holiday house, which stood at the edge of the woods. Here, in his old homeland between Poland and Germany, other laws applied. No one was bothered by game hunting. They attached the stag by his antlers to the thickest branch of the old oak in the garden. This made gutting the animal easier than if they'd hung it upside down. In the grass lay tools such as a hatchet and boning knife. Ludwig made the incision. The innards spilled out of the slit torso and blood came spurting out. They had to be quick; with every degree it got warmer the risk of the meat spoiling increased. And they were quick, because they worked as a good team. By breakfast time they'd cleaned the animal.

"We should do this more often," Gero said as they sat on the steps of the veranda, looking at the red-stained grass beneath the oak tree, and drank their coffee. He'd needed a weekend like this. Switch off his head, reduce himself to something archaic, pure. For although things were great with Laura at the moment, on the work front things were really tough.

"I remember when I took you hunting for the first time," Ludwig said, interrupting Gero's brief melancholy with a laugh. "Your arms were so weedy you could hardly hold the rifle. And then all the fuss." He raised the pitch of his voice to a girly whine. *"I can't do it, the poor thing."*

"And yet you didn't send me home."

"Because I sensed there was more to you than that." Ludwig brought his cup to his lips and took a sip of coffee through his teeth. "A will. And that's exactly what you need in this world: a will. And tenacity. It's like with hunting. If you hesitate and your shot merely grazes the beast, you cause it more suffering and make more work for yourself." He put the coffee cup to one side and instead fished out his hip flask again. "All or nothing, that's the only rule."

Gero nodded.

"But who is that tenacious?"

"Barely anyone," Ludwig replied between a couple of sips of whiskey. "They're all cowards. Talking of which, how's the Heger case going?"

"No change, at best," Gero said wearily.

It had all panned out as he'd predicted. The press had fallen in love with the victim and given her a face. They'd already published his—Gero's—too, under the headline: "HE is defending the monster." Gero thought he looked cold in the photograph, which showed him in a suit and sunglasses, getting into his Porsche outside the firm's offices. Some hack must have lain in wait for him once *woman (22)* became "beautiful Nelly," *husband and father (41)* "the A24 monster" and *discovery of a corpse* "treacherous murder." Gero gave a sigh of resignation.

"Heger is still refusing to confess," he continued. "So we'll go to court and feed him to the public prosecutor."

"Which you don't want."

Gero laughed out loud. *Caught.*

"As you know, I haven't lost a case in years. Heger is going to blot my record. The evidence stacked against him is really overwhelming."

"Perhaps," Ludwig deliberated, "you ought to go back to him with a different approach. The victim is dead and the fact that she has a family who are suffering because of this might be too abstract for him. Instead you should make it clear to Heger what a guilty sentence will mean for his own family, for his daughter. She'll grow up as the child of a cold-blooded murderer."

"She'll be that anyway."

Ludwig shook his head.

"She could also be the daughter of a man who made a mistake in a moment of madness. Perhaps he'd taken leave of his senses when he put his hands around the girl's throat. Maybe he was even trying to help her by ensuring a quicker, painless death after she'd broken her neck falling down the slope. An act of mercy." He shrugged. "Perhaps he'll confess if he feels that you're honestly trying to understand him and what he did rather than maintaining your success rate."

"Tell me, do you really believe all that or are you merely tossing me a defense strategy because in truth you're just as worried about our firm's reputation?"

"Oh, my boy," Ludwig said, placing a hand on his back. "Losing a case isn't nice, but ultimately it doesn't harm us as a business. We'll still be number one in Berlin, no need to panic."

"What is it then? The mellowness of age?" Gero smirked. "Weren't you just talking to me about tenacity?"

Ludwig smirked too, but wearily in contrast to Gero. Swimming in his eyes was something that Gero took to be melancholy. "It's probably just the day making me slightly soft. Today's the birthday of a woman I once knew." He looked into the distance, at the bloodstained grass. "Her name was Marta."

Gero was shocked. None of Ludwig's acquaintances had ever had a name before, and in any case it wouldn't have been worth remembering them because his women changed like the weather.

"Your great love?" he asked.

Ludwig shook his head.

"Only an idiot could love a woman like that."

That day, that day over and over again. She was ill. Jesus! She'd
fainted in the bath. I took her to bed and lay down beside her. The
next thing I remember is the doorbell ringing. I got out of bed and
opened the door. Aunt Evelyn in her colorful flowery housecoat stood
there, her huge hand holding that of a little blond boy with round
blue eyes. The boy was you.

"For goodness' sake," she panted. "Why aren't you opening the
door? Janek had to be picked up early from kindergarten because
he'd been fighting with another boy again. The teacher tried to call
you, but . . ."

"We haven't paid the telephone bill yet," I replied.

Aunt Evelyn rolled her eyes and sighed.

"What's new? Anyway, then she called me and I went to pick him
up." She made to come into the flat, but I held her back. I told her I
couldn't let her in because Marta was ill. Maybe a bad case of the flu.
I didn't want her to catch it too. As if at the flick of a switch, Aunt
Evelyn now looked worried.

"It's all right, Aunt Evelyn." I smiled, patting her arm. "I'll look after her, I've got it all under control, I really have. I've made her some tea and a hot water bottle."

"Come on, let me in for just a minute," Aunt Evelyn insisted, shaking you from her hand and telling you to wait for her outside the door. Before I could stop her again, she'd already pushed her way past me.

"Please, Aunt Evelyn. She needs peace and quiet!"

I hastened after her and grabbed her shoulder just as she was about to enter the bedroom. Marta hated being woken up. She didn't get enough sleep as it was because her guests were inconsiderate, calling for her at the most impossible times of day and night.

"She's . . . deathly pale," Aunt Evelyn stammered, now looking at me with a quite different expression. I just gave a curt nod, took her by the arm and pulled her down the corridor back to the front door. On the way she caught a glimpse into the bathroom, the chaos inside it. People had always gossiped a lot about us. About how slovenly Marta was at keeping our flat in order and that she couldn't even butter rolls for school. That she worked at night and slept during the day, or—like this morning—had a bubble bath, as if it were some cast-iron law that you were only allowed to take a bath in the evenings. It got to the stage where people had said so much that their words fizzled out and instead they sent the woman from the child welfare office.

"Child," I heard Aunt Evelyn say, but I'd already pushed her out of the flat. "Child," I heard her say a second time, now through the closed door. I went back into the bedroom and lay down again. Beside Marta, who was sleeping.

NADJA

The grandmother's house may once have been full of sun and warmth, a place where Laura used to spend her holidays, where it smelled of freshly baked cakes, where people hugged each other, were close, told stories. In my mind I see a small girl sitting here at the kitchen table. She's just been outside, bounding through the undergrowth in her sweet summer dress or sitting on the wooden bridge, her toes dangling in the cold water, before being called inside by her grandmother to help make supper.

"You be careful with that knife, now," I hear the grandmother warn the girl before the scenery in my head is cruelly torn apart. The image that appears behind looks as if the color has been washed away: it's cold, menacing. It's real life. The three of us—Herr van Hoven, Laura and I—are sitting at this kitchen table, each of us with a cup of coffee, surrounded by an oppressive silence that seems to have lasted an eternity. Laura, slumped on her chair at the head of the table, is staring torpidly at the ceiling; Herr van Hoven's lips are curled into a one-sided smile—a perverse pleasure he seems unable to conceal. I silently count the breaths I take, feel my nervousness in the throbbing of my neck. This waiting is driving me nuts; I'm dying for something to happen, but also apprehensive, for I suspect that sitting around here, however grueling, is going to be the most pleasant part of all of this. The least dangerous.

"Right, then." Two little words that rip through the silence like a thunderbolt. "The trial has begun. Let us begin with the particulars." Herr van Hoven clears his throat. "Laura van Hoven, née Brehme. Date of birth: April 29, 1985 in Oranienburg. Nationality: German. Family status: married. Current occupation: housewife and mother . . ." He glances to his right, at Laura, who has sat up in horror. In the thin nightie, smeared with Aron Bruckstätt's blood, she has started trembling and crying again. Laura, who is afraid because she doesn't know what's going on here. I'm trembling too. ". . . as well as all those things she gets up to the moment her husband turns his back."

"Herr van Hoven—" I begin, but fall silent the moment his hand shoots up in the air.

"No, Nadja, it's not your turn yet," he says, sounding as he sometimes does on the phone when Laura makes Vivi call him to ask whether he's going to be home in time to read her a goodnight story. "Are the details correct so far?"

Laura babbles beneath her tears.

"I asked you a question, Laura."

She nods with apparent difficulty.

"Please, Herr van Hoven," I try again. "All of this is—"

Now his fist crashes into the table. The coffee judders in the cups; I flinch and Laura gives a yelp.

"I said, it's not yet your turn, Nadja!" He turns back to his wife. "Is the information correct?"

"Yes," she whispers hoarsely.

"Good. Would you now tell us how you met the victim, Aron Bruckstätt, a photographer?"

"You know that."

With a sigh, Herr van Hoven leans back in his chair and his eyes dart between Laura and me.

"The two of you still haven't understood," he says, crossing his arms. He fixes his gaze on Laura, who swallows quietly. "Do you doubt me? Do you really doubt I'm being serious? Without this trial, the verdict is a foregone conclusion, my darling."

She puts a hand in front of her mouth to smother a sound.

"Poor Vivi!" he continues in a tone of fake sympathy. "How am I going to tell her that her mummy won't be coming home anymore?"

Please come back home. I cry all day long without you.

I'm afraid I can't, darling.

Why not?

Because people think I've done something really, really terrible.

But that's not true!

You're too young to understand. If people think you've done something terrible, you can't go back home. That's life.

Rubbing my forehead, I irritate my wound and the burning sensation makes me suck air through my teeth. All I keep thinking is, *I want to wake up*. At home, in my small, bare flat that smells so comfortingly of Ajax. I want to make my bed and do thirty knee-bends. I want to go to work, see the friendly man who's my boss and look at photos of Vivi.

His gaze is harsh. When he looks at Laura he doesn't blink; he stares right into her.

"So, where did you meet?"

"At the tennis club Christmas party," she replies falteringly.

Herr van Hoven rocks his head from side to side.

"More details, please."

I can see her struggling to retain her composure. Gasping for air, opening her mouth and closing it again. I know what it feels like to be desperate to give an explanation, but sense that with every word you're going to lose.

"Just try," I say, giving her a look that's supposed to be encouraging. So long as Herr van Hoven wants to listen nothing worse is going to happen, I tell myself. Perhaps Laura has realized this too. She takes another deep breath and then begins. "The Christmas party was on December 18. You took me along. For days I'd been looking forward to us spending a child-free evening together again, as we hadn't been out in so long. You're always working so much and you're tired when you get home. But when we got to the club, you abandoned me. I was standing there all on my own while you chatted to Herr Mertens, the public prosecutor, and a few others. Aron came over to me by the bar and we talked."

"About what?"

She shakes her head.

"Nothing in particular. When he found out that I was your wife, he told me you often played tennis together. He said you had a remarkable backhand. He also told me that he worked as a photographer and a book of his pictures had just been published. I thought it was interesting."

"Go on."

"That was it."

"For that evening."

"For that evening, yes."

"Did you find Aron Bruckstätt interesting?"

Laura begins to shift around in her chair.

"Gero—"

"That means yes, I suppose?"

"This is irrelevant," I interrupt.

"Ah!" Herr van Hoven smiles. "An objection! Good try, Nadja, but I'm afraid I'm going to have to disappoint you. It is, of course, relevant because, as we all know, the two of them proceeded to have an affair. I want to know how it happened and if my wife was up for something like that from the outset."

At a stroke Laura's face turns pale, even paler.

"No, I wasn't! I swear!"

"So why did you meet Aron Bruckstätt again?"

She lowers her gaze and says softly, "His book."

"His book," Herr van Hoven echoes faintly.

She nods. And goes on talking. It was late afternoon, two days after the Christmas party. The doorbell rang. Aron Bruckstätt, what a surprise. When they hugged she inhaled the smell of his leather jacket and the scent of his aftershave. I'm squirming inside; I don't know whether I want to hear this. Herr van Hoven, on the other hand, leans forward with interest, encouraging her.

"Did you find his scent attractive?"

I hold my breath and hear Laura say, "I . . . I think so."

Herr van Hoven bares his teeth like an animal.

"Go on."

Aron gave her a book, she says. The book of photographs they'd talked about at the tennis club Christmas party. *Places That Time Forgot*, she says, quoting the title, and smiles—inadvertently, I suspect. Having thanked Aron, she offered him a cup of tea out of politeness. Took his coat and showed him into the living room. She felt slightly uncomfortable, but also . . .

"Well," she says, then smiles. "I mean, I also thought it was quite nice that he'd come. Do you know what I mean?"

Herr van Hoven just keeps snarling. A predator watching its unsuspecting prey.

So she made some tea, she continues. Poured a cup for Aron, sat down with him and asked about his book and the journeys he'd documented in it. Which of the forgotten places had impressed him the most? He talked, talked about his work and the trips he'd made. It sounded exciting, Laura said.

Herr van Hoven laughs.

"My God, how pathetic."

"Yes," Laura says, then sniffs. "That was it. I don't know . . . but in Aron's presence the most ridiculous things started going around my head. I asked myself if I'd imagined my life would be like this—as just a housewife and mother. Making breakfast. Buttering rolls for kindergarten. Doing the cleaning, washing, cooking, ironing shirts, waiting for you—endlessly waiting for you! The moment he sat on our sofa, I realized how long it was since I'd last been to the hairdresser to get a cut or my roots dyed. How sloppy I must look in my leggings and baggy tops that were otherwise so comfortable and practical. When had I stopped wearing dresses, skirts and jewelry?" She looks down at herself, at the thin, bloodstained nightie.

"I'm all ears," Herr van Hoven says.

Do you know how beautiful you are? Aron Bruckstätt then asked. That was probably it. He just said it like that, out of the blue, as he was telling her about his next photographic project. *How beautiful she was* . . . She'd forgotten. Nobody had said this to her for a very long time.

She smiles, lost in thought. Herr van Hoven is still baring his teeth. A bad feeling tightens inside my stomach. She's doing exactly what he wants. She's talking in detail and hard-heartedly, given that every phrase, every word she says about Aron Bruckstätt is one against her husband. By whom she clearly felt neglected. But who doesn't stop grinning nonetheless.

"I think we've got a good idea now," I bring myself to say. "These things can and do happen. A marriage that—"

"Be quiet," Herr van Hoven hisses.

I can't. I don't know what's going on here, but I do know that I've got to prevent it.

"Millions of couples across the world go through this."

"Quiet!"

His pupils are gleaming.

"It's all right, Nadja," Laura says, forcing a smile. "I owe him the truth."

So, Aron Bruckstätt told her how beautiful she was. *Sure, sure,* was her response as she coyly swept a hair behind her ear and noticed that her fingers still smelled of onions, she added. They'd had osso buco the night before.

"Your favorite dish," she says to Herr van Hoven, his bestial grin only growing wider.

"Go on."

I'd love to cover my ears right now, just as I used to as a little girl when the walls of our flat were too thin and the noises coming from the bedroom too loud. Like Janek would do a few years later.

Laura obeys and continues her confession.

Aron Bruckstätt offered to take her on one of his research trips. She agreed.

"Are you telling me you were planning on accompanying a complete stranger on his," he says, making air quotes, "*research* trip?"

"No, I wasn't, actually," she replies hesitantly. "But I found the thought that I could somehow . . ."

"A turn-on?"

I shudder.

"No, Gero!" She shakes her head in panic. "It was more the . . . the idea of getting out, for once not having to be myself, that . . ."

". . . turned you on," Herr van Hoven says, finishing her sentence.

"And even if it did, there's absolutely nothing reprehensible in that," I chime in. "All of us feel like that sometimes, don't we?" I laugh stupidly and think of my mother, how she loved to melt away to the music of Johnny Hallyday. I think of how on Saturday evenings I used to sit by the open kitchen window of my flat and gaze down as I listened to the laughter from next door. Five stories: I could fly and disintegrate. How simple that would be. How much simpler sometimes.

"Well, then he gave me his telephone number."

"Which you rang."

"Shortly after Christmas," she confirms, her head bowed. "We'd had an argument, do you remember? I'd promised your parents that we'd go and see them with Vivi on Christmas Day, but you didn't want to."

"Because I'd been working like a dog," Herr van Hoven states. "I just wanted some peace and quiet. Was that too much to ask for?"

"No," Laura says. "Of course not. I understood where you were coming from. But your mother had bought a goose specially and you know what an effort it is for her to spend hours cooking after her hip operation."

"And we did go, as you'll recall. You got your way."

"But you didn't say a word throughout the entire meal."

"I let you talk me into coming. There was no mention of having to be in a good mood." He clears his throat. "Go on. So, you called Aron Bruckstätt and told him just what a dreadful husband you had and how awful your marriage was."

Laura nods and says softly, "Yes, that was about the gist of it."

"What then?"

I hear her swallow.

"We arranged to meet up for a drink."

"When and where?"

Laura doesn't reply. Now she looks at me.

"Don't you think that's enough, Herr van Hoven?" I ask circumspectly. "You now know how it all began with Aron Bruckstätt. Surely you can imagine the rest."

"No, Nadja, it's not enough."

Of course not. I feel my hands tense, ball into fists. Laura swallows again.

"Could we take a break?"

"Yes, please, let's have a break," I say, even though I harbor little hope that Herr van Hoven will agree.

And yet he does. With a smile and a friendly voice.

"Yes, of course." Bringing the cup to his lips, he says, "Let's drink our coffee." Above the rim of his cup I can see the predator lurking. Laura and I don't touch our cups; we merely exchange glances.

"I said," he growls, "we're going to drink our coffee now."

My head feels as if it's about to burst. I don't know if the tension I'm feeling is the aftereffect of my fall or my trying to understand Herr van Hoven. Laura cheated on him and he's furious—I'm with him so far. But, the way I see it, fury is like an avalanche: once it gets going it's unstoppable. *Who the hell are you?* I ask him in my head. A man who's clearly capable of standing up to an avalanche, of suspending it on a whim for a coffee break. I almost wish he'd scream, go into a rage, threaten us. I'd find it more natural, more human. Maybe even more computable. Instead it's as if he's a different person. Friendly. Calm. He asks whether we'd like milk with our coffee. "No, thanks," Laura says, her voice trembling. "It's perfect as it is." I take a sip too even though I can barely swallow. But I don't dare refuse to drink my coffee. I don't trust this peace.

"I owe you an apology," he says, so unexpectedly that coffee sloshes out of my cup as I put it down. "You're absolutely right, breaks are important. I simply forget sometimes. Laura says I'm a workaholic, isn't that right, darling?" She doesn't answer; she just looks at me. He laughs. "My, my, the two of you really are careworn souls. Hasn't either of you got a funny little story to tell? Nadja!" I give a start. "Tell us something about yourself! How long have you been living in Berlin?" I say nothing. "Okay, then. We can, of course, continue with the trial."

"Five and a half years."

Satisfied, he leans back in his chair.

"And do you like it here?"

I nod.

"Yes," he says. "Berlin's a lovely city, *my* city. Remind me where you come from originally."

"Zabrew, Poland."

"That's right. What about your family? Am I right in thinking you've got a brother?"

I feel a slight tweak in my heart.

"We're not in contact."

"Oh," Herr van Hoven says, sounding nauseatingly sad. "I'm sorry, I don't mean to open up any old wounds."

I want to scream, but instead I drink my coffee.

"Gero," Laura says. The tone of her voice tells me that she wants to embark on a new attempt. "Couldn't we sort all of this out differently? I can understand how angry you are, but first, Nadja hasn't got anything to do with this, and second—"

"Would you like to go, Nadja?" He cocks his head. Smiles again. I bite my lower lip. Think of John Haigh, the English serial killer with the perfect plan, with crimes and victims he simply sluiced away with the waste water. Who was caught nonetheless, but only because his lengthy criminal record put him on the police's radar. When they searched his flat they found the container with the sulfuric acid, a foot that hadn't quite dissolved, three gallstones and a set of teeth. My whole body tenses at the thought that Herr van Hoven has no criminal record to give him away. That he might be even more adept at covering up crimes than John Haigh. That he knows all the legal ruses and the work of investigation teams by heart. That the public prosecutor is one of his best friends. That Berlin, as he just emphasized, is *his* city, and he has it totally under his control.

"Nadja?"

"If I go, you're going to kill Laura."

"Possibly."

I consider my options and realize I have only one. I'd never be quick enough to fetch help. "Let's continue with the trial."

JULY 2015

FOUR YEARS EARLIER

It was a Tuesday when the boy turned up at Gero van Hoven's office. As Laura had also come in that day to introduce newly born Vivi to her former colleagues, the visitor was able to walk unhindered into the office through the empty anteroom. Gero had just got out of his chair to go to the staff canteen, where the employees were gathering to toast the baby, when the boy came through the door and said, "Are you Gero van Hoven?" His voice was quivering as badly as his hands, one of which was holding a newspaper, the other an envelope.

"Would you be so kind as to introduce yourself too?" Gero asked the boy as he sized him up. He might be about twenty, and his mother had probably never fed him enough—at any rate there was something rather woeful about his weedy stature in the washed-out black Metallica T-shirt and the shorts that ended just above his bony knees, even though he seemed to be a good head taller than Gero. His pale face was dotted with pimples and nervous red blotches, which his light-blond hair only accentuated.

"You *are* Gero van Hoven," the boy said, nodding furiously as if to confirm to himself that he was in the right place. "I saw you in the newspaper." By way of evidence he unfolded the tabloid and held it up. On one half of the front page was a photograph of a tearstained Paul Heger leaving the court the day before with Gero; on the other a picture of Nelly Schütt. The headline above read: "Eight Years for Motorway Monster."

Manslaughter was the judge's verdict—finally, as Nelly had already been dead for over a year now, and the case had been in the media spotlight all that time. It had been a difficult trial, not just for Gero, but also for his new friend, the public prosecutor Fred Mertens, who'd gathered plenty of pieces of evidence against Heger, but no definitive proof. As Gero anticipated, however, unanimous public opinion had been an advantage for Mertens. Paul Heger was a well-off family man, whose life was simply too good. Although he had it all, he seemed incapable of appreciating everything he did have. He'd danced on thin ice, made a hole and dragged an innocent country girl into the cold, dark depths. For the sake of the firm's reputation and his own, Gero was relieved about the result of the trial; Heger's sentence could have been much harsher, and had he been the judge rather than the defense lawyer that would certainly have been the case. He loathed Heger, even more after the latter had cried and screamed upon hearing the verdict rather than thanking Gero for the lenient sentence. On the contrary, he'd insisted on his innocence till the bitter end and called Gero a "bastard in league with the public prosecutor." He'd been transferred from custody in Moabit to Tegel prison, where he would serve his sentence.

"Okay," Gero said to the boy. "I don't have the time or the

inclination for guessing games, so let's keep this brief. Who are you and what do you want?"

"In the paper it says he'll spend eight years in prison."

One of the sensitive ones, Gero thought. One of those who couldn't get over the fact that someone could extinguish another person's life at the trifling cost of eight years of their freedom, and that the system had proved itself to be as it sometimes was: dreadfully unjust.

"Listen," he began, raising his hands sympathetically.

"I thought he'd get off."

Gero faltered.

"What?"

"I thought they didn't have enough evidence and he'd definitely get off."

"Who are you?" Gero asked again, more calmly this time. He could see the Adam's apple in the long, slim neck bob up and down as the boy swallowed hard several times. It seemed as if he had to summon his courage before approaching Gero and handing him the envelope.

"Here is my confession."

Gero was so surprised that to begin with he was unaware of the commotion in the corridor outside. But then Laura came running into his office, waving her arms and screaming.

Like in pass the parcel, Vivi had gone from arm to arm, from colleague to colleague. One hand after the other had stroked the fine, soft hair, felt the delicate curve of the tiny back of the head; one nose after another had taken in the unique, sweet fragrance that only a newborn baby could emit. This went on until the short-lived need for purity and innocence had been sated and they wanted their hands free again for the glass of Sekt they were drinking to toast the child. But there must have been a break in the chain, someone who hadn't passed the baby on, for now she was missing and everyone was in uproar. Nobody could remember whose arm she'd last been seen on. Vivi had disappeared and Laura was in a total state. After an attack of hysteria, she slumped like a sack of flour onto Gero's chair and sat there apathetically while a few colleagues attended to her with tissues and hugs. Gero couldn't bear seeing his wife like this; it was as if an unbridgeable gulf had opened up between them. Of course he was the stronger of the two—he always had been and gladly so—but when it came to Vivi he expected Laura to behave like a lioness, not a cowardly meerkat who stood at a safe distance, just gawping idiotically. This character trait of his mother's had troubled him greatly; it had been too painful. But he'd have to sort that out later, because now everything was about finding his daughter. He organized search teams to cover the lower three floors and the reception area, while he took charge of the top floor, the fourth one. Those who accompanied him soon fell behind. Unlike them, Gero merely needed one glance inside a room to know that Vivi wasn't there. He didn't have to check under desks or behind doors; he would have sensed her presence immediately, even if she'd been shut in a filing cabinet. From the open stairwell in the former boiler works he heard panicked shouting, which shot around the thick old walls like out-of-control bouncy balls. He really wanted to shout, "Be quiet!" He was nervous enough without the screaming that only emphasized the seriousness of the situation. He mustn't become infected by the hysteria; he had to keep a clear head. But the more rooms he passed by, the more profusely he began to sweat. It was seething anger aimed at Laura, who clearly hadn't been keeping a close enough eye on Vivi, who like a child had allowed herself to be distracted by the attention, who'd cheerfully stood around chatting with her glass of Sekt, while someone had dared make off with their daughter. *I'll find you*, Gero growled silently, although he was unsure whether he meant Vivi or her abductor. Thousands of possibilities shot through his head. An unhappy client or the relative of a victim. He even thought of Paul Heger and Laura. Heger hated him because Gero hadn't prevented him from going to prison, and Laura had burst into tears when she found out she was pregnant because, as she said, she didn't feel ready to have a child. At the same time Gero knew that both were nonsense. Heger sat locked up in his cell in Tegel, while Laura had quickly got used to her role as a mother and loved her little daughter more than anything else. *When she wasn't allowing Vivi to be abducted.* Gero pushed open the last door before the end of the corridor—no Vivi. He rubbed his brow. His skull felt as if it had been locked in an invisible vise. He realized he had to notify the police. This was serious, this was real: someone had snatched Vivi away from him and every second counted. With child abductions the first forty-eight hours were crucial. Gero felt his insides wrench. He didn't want to think of his daughter as a victim; she couldn't be one. As he took his hand from his brow, his gaze fell on another door: the metal one that led to the roof terrace. He went over to it as if on automatic pilot, pressed the handle and climbed the first few steps of the metal staircase. And then he suddenly sensed it: Vivi's presence. He sensed it even before he saw her in the arms of the woman who was standing perilously close to the edge of the roof. Only the panel railing—a thin sheet of perforated metal—lay between her and the ground below, between Vivi and a good fifteen meters of free fall.

"Nadja," he said, stretching out a hand. "Please don't do anything silly."

From: Letter #31

The world seems so strange; I slink through it like a ghost. I am merely the wisp of an existence, translucent somehow. Easy to see through. And yet nobody knows the entire truth, not even my therapist. Some days I talk and spit out undigested lumps at her feet, on others I just sit there and answer with a terse yes or no, or give a vague shrug because I think it's not going to get me anywhere. How's she going to help me? Can she turn back time and undo things that have happened? No.

Even you only know part of the truth and what people have told you are the "facts." But you don't know what it was really like that day, June 17. You've no idea what it felt like—why should you? I mean, I can't write this letter. I can't find words that you'd be able to understand. Perhaps I'll never manage to write this damned letter, and yet I try to over and over again. I take a new, blank sheet of paper and write for you. June 17, 1999. That day, that day, that god-awful day.

NADJA

In the kitchen of the Spreewald house Laura pulls her legs up onto the seat of her chair. She wraps her arms around her knees and rocks, either in discomfort or back into the past. Her first date with Aron Bruckstätt. She had to arrange a babysitter. And something she refers to as an "alibi," without thinking too hard about it. She trembles as she talks.

First she called her husband in the office and said she was meeting a friend. As these words had passed her lips, she hunched her shoulders and screwed up her eyes as if expecting him to see through her immediately. *Which friend?* he should have asked, well aware that since their marriage she'd hardly ever gone out without him, and not at all since Vivi was born. A friend—which friend? Which friend could be left? Just like Gero, all her former friends and acquaintances worked during the day, leaving just the evenings to meet up, but she preferred spending the evenings with Gero—otherwise they'd barely see each other. In the early days, right after Laura had given up her job as an assistant, how she loved to lie in without any time pressure in Gero's smart flat. Later, when they moved into a house, she relished sitting outside with a cappuccino from the expensive, gleaming coffee machine, pitying those who at that hour were hastening to work and living their lives at a rush. Laura, meanwhile, was seeing to the wedding preparations, going for massages, to the hairdresser, shopping. But later . . .

"I loved our evenings," she slips in as if to justify herself. "Do you remember? We'd sit by the fire, drinking wine, planning trips we were going to make when you'd taken over the firm from Ludwig and so could be freer with your time. We fantasized about what it would be like to live in the country. You would only work a few days a week and would commute. We always agreed and sometimes even came out with the same word. Then we'd laugh and do silly high fives. All of that was much nicer than the prospect of meeting up in a bar with a friend and indulging in trivial small talk. I turned down lots of things around this time until people stopped asking me if I'd like to go out. The answer was probably obvious to them anyway. *I can't, evening in, winking smiley.*" A rapt smile fades from her lips. "So it should have been obvious I was lying when I told you I was meeting a friend. Secretly I might have even been wishing you'd see through my plan and thwart it. Then I'd have known that I was still important to you."

But nothing. No questions, no word of doubt, just a muttering from which she concluded her husband must be otherwise occupied. While on the line to her he was probably looking through a case file or putting his signature to various letters. At the end of the call he wished her a nice evening, which sounded like he was just being polite, and he hung up before she could reply with an equally polite, "Thanks, darling."

"Go on," Herr van Hoven growls.

Laura nods.

She took Vivi to his parents, who were delighted to be able to look after their granddaughter for the evening. *Such a shame that you had to leave straight after Christmas Day*, his mother had said with a sad smile on her face. Gero was very stressed at work, she'd replied, comforting Irma with a stroke of her arm. *He always is, Laura*, the mother said with a sigh.

And then—she did it. She got into her car and programmed the GPS. She and Aron had agreed not to meet in town, as there were too many people and in the worst-case scenario they'd bump into someone they knew and have to come up with an explanation. Who would believe they'd met only to have a chat? So she drove thirty kilometers just for him. To a truckers' pub on the highway. They wouldn't meet anyone they knew here, who might gossip and give them away. All the same, what a dreadful, filthy place it was! Someone had gone to the trouble to build a metaphor out of wood, stone and neon signs for the dreadful, filthy things she was about to do. Oak-paneled walls, dim light, the air stuffy from cigarette smoke and the clientele from another world. Washed-out individuals, long-distance truck drivers, prostitutes. And *him*, of course. Aron Bruckstätt leaning against an old jukebox when she came in, feeling idiotic in the tight red dress she had on beneath her overcoat. He embraced her for rather longer than he had two weeks earlier by her front door. Gave her such a long, close look, as if she were a potential subject for a new photo series, and said: *Who'd have thought you could be even more beautiful? I love your new haircut.*

Why did you choose to meet here? she asked as he helped her out of her coat.

I'm studying the place for my next project. He grinned, laid her coat over a barstool, went back to the jukebox and pressed a button. Frank Sinatra and his daughter sang "Somethin' Stupid." Aron put out his arm, helped her up and they danced. The only ones in this dive, under the gaze of the strange customers. *Embarrassing*, she thought. *Unpleasant.* And yet she laid her head on his shoulder and let him show her the way. She felt his heartbeat, the warmth of his body, his firm grip around her waist. She knew full well she wasn't here just for a bit of a chat. She'd organized a babysitter and an alibi. She'd shaved her legs and ironed the red dress she'd last worn on New Year's Eve two years earlier. She'd put on lipstick and entered the address he'd texted her into her GPS. She also knew full well that she could have turned around. She could have driven straight out of the car park and back home, to the man she'd promised to be faithful to forever.

"Yes," Herr van Hoven said thoughtfully. "That's exactly what you ought to have done. But instead you did what?"

She just looks at the floor.

Herr van Hoven turns to me.

"I think she cheated on me that night. Is that what happened, Laura? Did you have sex with Aron Bruckstätt that night? Did you immediately find a hotel?"

She shakes her head and goes on talking.

She and Aron Bruckstätt in the ladies' lavatories. She stood there, bent over, her hands clutching the rim of the sink. The soft feeling in her knees made its way up to her thighs. She felt ashamed. What on earth did she think she was doing? In the grimy loos of this run-down pub, standing up, uncomfortable and painful in every respect. *A study for his next project*, she thought. Maybe she was merely a study for him too. Maybe he'd just wanted to test how far she would go with him. Whether he could really have her that easily. A little bit of attention, a dance to a kitsch love song, half a beer and he'd already reached his goal. From the corner of her eye she saw him standing at the other sink, washing his face and hands, washing her off him. She imagined her dignity seeping away down the plughole, down the filthy old pipes and into the sewer, to the rats. Scraps of an AC/DC song drifted into the lavatory through the closed door. One of the truckers must have chosen the track on the jukebox, irritated by the schmaltz and misery he'd just been subjected to. She was already dreading leaving the loos and exposing herself to the gaze of the characters in the bar, but she'd have to do it as her overcoat was still on the stool.

Everything okay?

She hadn't noticed that he'd turned off the tap and stepped behind her. Without thinking, she looked up when he grabbed hold of her hips and caught sight of the smeary mirror that was fixed above the sink. So that was them: a pathetic woman with red cheeks, smudged mascara and strands of hair stuck to her sweaty brow; and behind her a man who looked fresh and satisfied. Laying his chin on her shoulder he whispered, *My little whore.* It was beyond her how her smeary reflection could smile at this.

Laura's crying. Her body quivers as she sobs. She apologizes and begs for clemency. She was stupid. She was ungrateful. In the meantime, I'm now leafing through the criminal code. Somewhere there has to be something about a reduced sentence in exceptional situations. The letters blur; I blink furiously.

"That very first evening," Herr van Hoven remarks, shaking his head. He sighs.

"She was looking for appreciation after years of neglect from her husband," I say, flapping the book shut. The tiny letters are driving my eyes crazy. "She was lonely."

"Lonely," Herr van Hoven says. "I see." He gets up, feels in his pocket and takes out his mobile. Laura and I exchange glances as his fingers dart across the screen and a second later guitar chords echo throughout the kitchen. "Somethin' Stupid." Satisfied, he places the mobile on the table, walks around and puts out his hand. To me.

"May I?"

I freeze. He actually means *me*.

"Come on, up you get." His hand wiggles beside my face.

"What's going on, Gero?" Laura asks softly.

"Don't you like the song, Nadja?"

I don't reply.

"That's not possible. Everyone loves good old Frank."

I'm still silent and completely stiff, even when he grabs my hand and hauls me up from the bench.

"Gero, please," Laura says.

His hands. The right hand tightens around my wrist; the left is on the small of my back, pulling me toward him. I struggle but he leads me ruthlessly. All I can do is stumble along as he moves to the music, as if this dance and the unbearable physical proximity were completely natural. He hums along to the melody, keeping his eyes shut. I peer over his shoulder at Laura, who has shifted to the edge of her chair and is now sitting so upright it's as if her body were in a steel corset. I can see the look of disbelief in her pale face and how she's agonizing over whether to do something that might turn out to be a mistake. Mustering my courage, I pull against the firm grip on my wrist. Herr van Hoven opens his eyes and smiles.

"Are you feeling something already, Nadja? Are you feeling what Laura must have felt that evening?"

"Let her go, Gero!" Laura says, leaping up from the chair.

"That's how they danced, Nadja." He twirls me around and the movement makes me feel sick. My head is buzzing, bright lights flash before my eyes and my legs are on the verge of buckling like two burned matches. Herr von Hoven's unyielding grip keeps me upright and he twists me so he can look at Laura. "This is how you danced, isn't it? Where was his hand, Laura? Here?" I feel a movement on my back—his left hand sliding further down, pushing me tighter against him. "Or like this?" I pant. I wriggle. But I can't get free.

"Please let her go, Gero! I'll tell you everything you want to know!"

"Oh, Nadja, this is getting exciting," I hear him say right beside my ear, too close, his breath damp and hot. "Perhaps you have a few more details for us from your first evening together, Laura."

No response.

Instead there's a sudden shove. The abrupt movement makes me reel backward against the moving boxes by the window. They wobble and clatter, and I collapse on top of them like a puppet whose strings have been cut. A brief moment of confusing silence and everything's dark before my eyes. I feel my lids fluttering their way to unconsciousness; I want to abandon myself to it. But then: shouting.

"Give it to me, Laura!"

I blink desperately to recover my sight. I can make out Laura, but she's blurred. She's standing in the kitchen, not moving. She doesn't even recoil when he stands in front of her, a tall and broad man. In her hand is his mobile, which she must have grabbed from the table. Only now do I realize that the music stopped playing precisely a second before he pushed me away. Laura says in a surprisingly firm voice, "I'm going to put an end to this crap. I'm calling the police."

That was it, the mistake.

I must have been five, maybe six years of age. Janek hadn't been born yet. The men were called "guests" and as such they paid their visits, usually after their shift at the steelworks. My mother said you had to be friendly to guests so I smiled when I opened the door to them and allowed them to pat my head by way of a greeting. I said she'd be here in a minute and invited the men into the kitchen, where I gave them a beer from the fridge. The men were friendly too. In the beginning I was just as unsettled by the sounds that came through the closed bedroom door as Janek would be later, but each time my mother came back out of the bedroom—exhausted but unharmed—I realized that there wasn't anything bad going on in there. Besides, the men paid for our rent and food, which we had to be grateful for. Admittedly, she would cry sometimes. Her beautiful body could have danced on a large stage in Paris, beneath glittering spotlights and to rapturous applause. Sometimes she gave a throaty laugh—*Oh, screw it! Such is life, eh?* I'd learned to apologize when she cried and to laugh whenever she did.

But then there was that time when I was five or six. The man who came to visit that evening was friendly, almost the friendliest of them all. He said, "Hello, Nadja. I'm Uncle Fedor," and brought me a bar of chocolate. Nothing about him was strange; he merely seemed to be in a bit of a hurry to get her into the bedroom. But we'd seen this often enough in the past. There wasn't much time between the end of work and family supper. I sat at our kitchen table and unwrapped the chocolate, very carefully so as to avoid tearing the beautiful shiny silver paper. When I heard screaming I didn't think anything of it. I smoothed out the silver foil; I was going to put it away and keep it like some treasure. Her screams and the first piece of chocolate dissolving on my tongue—so soft, so sweet, so wonderful. Her screams suddenly perturbing me. Because they sounded different from normal. Louder, yes. More real. And then there was something else. A strange thundering and crashing. It wasn't the bedframe knocking against the wall, no. I slid off my chair, some chocolate still sticking to the inside of my cheek. My mouth was dry, so was my throat. I crept out of the kitchen, through the hall and to her room. Pressed the handle. The door swung open and I held my breath. The man, Uncle Fedor, standing over her. Like a giant. His fist pounding her as she lay on the floor. Him kicking, her screaming.

It's happening all over again here, except this time Herr van Hoven is the giant and Laura is the one lying on the floor, screaming and writhing. And me, I'm five or six again, I'm no longer breathing and I want to be blind, don't want to see anything. As I did back then, I screw up my eyes. I want him to stop. *Please, please, dear God, make him stop. Do something. No*, God says—or at least that's what I imagine. *No, Nadja*, he says with painful determination, *you're the one who's got to do something. Get on your feet, help her, save her. Can't you see he's beating her to death? Here, right before your eyes, he's beating her, beating the very life out of her, and you, you're doing nothing, you're just letting it happen.*

"Marta," I whimpered back then.

"Laura," I whimper now.

Laura, who he threw to the floor after she'd grabbed his mobile and threatened to call the police. I try to move, to free myself from the firm grip of the shock. I can't get to my feet, I can only make it to my knees, but that doesn't matter, the main thing is that I'm moving. I crawl over to them, put out my hand, grab his trouser leg, tug at it and beg him to stop, but I sound so pitiful.

Leave my mama alone, you bastard!

He turns around and looks me in the eye. Grabs my arm, pulls me to my feet.

"Just look at her," he says, pointing to Laura, who is rolling on her side. She has her hands in front of her face, so I can't see if she's bleeding. I want to help her, but he won't let me. I wave my arms about, balling my fists to hit him, but they just find thin air. He pushes me out of the kitchen and up the stairs. I stumble and think I'm screaming. For God, for Laura, for help. Now one of his hands is over my mouth. I stagger and keep screaming. He shoves me into the room and I land hard on the floor by the bed. From the bedside cabinet he takes the roll of packing tape, ties my hands behind my back again and sticks another strip over my screaming mouth.

"I gave you both the opportunity of a fair trial."

I growl into the packing tape.

"But now . . . what's that nice phrase? 'The right to appeal has been exhausted.'"

I shake my head, grunt and try to stand up, to stop him from leaving the room. I'm too slow, too weak. By the time I get to the door he's already locked it from the outside. I ram my shoulder against the wood, but it remains firm. I keep trying nonetheless, first with my left shoulder, then my right, until dots start dancing on my retina again. I sink to the floor. In my mind I see him going back down and wish there were a thousand stairs. But there are only seventeen of them—I counted. I don't want to think that Laura will only be alive for another seventeen steps. I want to think that he's changed his mind. Time passes and I listen intently. My head, the concussion, the strain makes me giddy. I could fall asleep on the spot. A peculiar twilight inserts itself between me and the world. I've just got used to it when a sound blows everything apart in the space of a single second. The silence, my thoughts, my beliefs.

It was a shot.

From: Letter #32

What do I remember? . . . Noises. A sort of stamping or drumming
of fists. A dream. I woke with a start. Beside me lay Marta, asleep.
I felt her head. To begin with I was sure the hot water bottle had
increased her body temperature by a few degrees—thanks, dear God.
But then I remembered the smell again and, more important, I real-
ized something. Although I was awake, I could still hear the noises,
the stamping and drumming. My heart followed suit, stamping and
drumming in the same way and hurting my chest. I carefully pulled
back the duvet and got out of bed. I crept out of the bedroom, wan-
dered along the corridor, all the while following the noises that were
getting louder and louder, their rhythm drawing me closer, and now
I heard shouting too.

"Police! Open up!"

I stopped as if rooted to the spot, put a hand in front of my mouth
and gasped into it. The police. Not Aunt Evelyn or the annoying
woman from the child welfare office, but the police. I swallowed hard
before dragging myself the last few meters to the door, turning the
key and opening up.

At first I could only see him: *Uncle Fedor, the local police inspector.*

I don't know if you remember him. He was a tall, round man, forever trying—and failing—to conceal his bald patch by combing the few strands that remained from right to left across his shiny pink head. And he was one of Marta's guests, who always came on Mondays and Wednesdays after his shift. At once my entire body went stiff and cold. Peeping out from behind his right shoulder was Aunt Evelyn, whose face looked red and swollen. I was going to ask her if she'd been crying, but thought better of it. Of course she had. I mean, she was still sniveling. Beside and behind her stood uniformed police officers—more and more police the longer I looked. Numbed, I took a step backward. Uncle Fedor took a step forward, into the flat, very slowly as if he were approaching a dangerous animal. In the same vein he put out his hands, then gently moved them up and down in the air. "Stay perfectly calm," he said. "I'm going to come in now, okay? I just want to take a quick look around. Okay, Nadja?" I took another step backward and bumped into the wall beside the kitchen door. "I just want to make sure that everything's okay here, do you understand?"

"Marta is ill," I said robotically.

That smell . . . Once again I recalled how she smelled before I fell asleep next to her. I threw up my hands and pressed them to my throbbing temples. Marta was a beautiful woman with her long dark-blond hair, slim figure and delicate features—and beautiful women didn't have a smell. Beautiful women had a fragrance. Marta's fragrance was lavender and roses, always. No matter what she did, no matter how much she exerted herself and sweated. Not even the smoke from all those cigarettes seemed to linger on her. Marta's fragrance was lavender bath foam and rose shampoo. I hiccuped.

Uncle Fedor crossed the hallway. When he passed the bathroom he said, "Bloody hell!" As if this was their code word, Aunt Evelyn and the other police officers came pouring in through the door to our flat. Aunt Evelyn grabbed me in her arms, while the uniformed officers swarmed to the various rooms in the flat, most of them to the bathroom. Someone started retching loudly. "Here!" Uncle Fedor yelled from the bedroom, and then I suddenly knew it again for sure. If Marta no longer had a fragrance, that meant something strongly metallic had overpowered the lavender and roses. I knew this smell from Aunt Evelyn's kitchen when she'd slaughtered a chicken in the yard and put it in the sink, waiting to be processed. The smell of blood.

In Aunt Evelyn's embrace my legs went weak and a black curtain drew across my eyes. The last thing I heard was Uncle Fedor's voice coming closer and saying, "Battered skull. You ought to get her a lawyer, Evelyn."

JULY 2015

Gero van Hoven had found her holding Vivi on the roof of the law practice.

"Nadja," he'd said. "Please don't do anything silly."

She let him take the baby without objection. Looked at him like someone who'd just woken up. Shook her head as if she couldn't believe it herself. And Gero, who finally had his daughter at his chest, started to bawl her out. What the hell did she think she was doing? She'd pay for this. With his chin he motioned for her to move away from the edge of the roof. She gave a feeble nod, trotted sniveling and head bowed to one of the pub benches, slumped onto it and buried her face in her hands. Gero couldn't believe it. Nadja, his assistant. That inconspicuous woman in her mouse-gray suit with neatly ironed white blouses and a tight bun, a woman who was always quiet and cautious, unobtrusive, had never complained once when made to work overtime during the entire eighteen months she'd been with the firm, who was nice and acquiescent, a perfect assistant—this woman was a *lunatic*.

"I demand an explanation!" he spouted at her. "What was that all about? Were you going to jump? With my child on your arm?"

As if on cue Vivi made a noise of discontentment and wriggled. He stroked her back, lowered his voice and hissed, "I want an explanation."

Shaking, Nadja took her hands from her face, stuttered apologies and hiccuped. Gero lost patience.

"I'm going to call the police."

"No!" she cried, leaping to her feet. "Please don't, Herr van Hoven! I wasn't going to hurt her! I'd never do anything to hurt her."

"So what were you going to do?" He was almost expecting to hear something about maternal love, from a woman who years earlier had lost a child herself—and because she was unable to get over the pain, one day decided on the spot to get a replacement. That was very possible—he didn't know much about her apart from the fact that she originally came from Poland, just like Ludwig, who'd been the one to employ her. Gero recalled that he'd once asked her if she was married and she'd said no. Just "no," not *I've got a boyfriend* or *I don't have a boyfriend* or *I've got a girlfriend* or *I don't have a girlfriend* or *I'm a widow* or *I'm a confirmed single woman*. Reluctant to continue with such small talk, he'd sent her off to get a coffee.

"I couldn't help but think of my brother," she said now, falling back onto the bench. "Vivi reminded me of him when he was small. His big blue eyes, his tiny little head . . ." Lost in thought, she gave a fleeting smile, then shook her head briskly, as if to return the mixed-up thoughts inside it to their rightful places. "A few of the people in the canteen started smoking when the Sekt was handed around. My brother had asthma. I know it sounds stupid, but I thought it would be good for Vivi to have some fresh air."

"Don't you dare call her Vivi," Gero growled, turning to go. "I don't want to ever hear you say her name again."

"Please, Herr van Hoven, no police," he heard her say pitifully behind his back. "I'm not dangerous, I really wasn't going to hurt her."

"You're sick."

She bawled.

"Pack up your belongings and get out of here," he said as he left. "I will notify Ludwig of your dismissal."

Ludwig Abramczyk was fascinated by this view. First the pain, and with it, the horror and the fear. Then defiance, the expression of a determination to resist. The realization that it wouldn't help. That he would wear himself out for nothing. That he might as well relax instead and just let it wash over him. And finally, peace. Peace in his view, peace flushing through his naked, withered body.

From behind the gag he smiled at his reflection. It showed a sixty-year-old man with gray tousled hair and outstretched limbs, his hands tied to the head of the bed, his ankles to the posts at the bottom. Some of the women he'd taken to his bedroom in the past just giggled bashfully when they noticed the huge mirror on the ceiling, others were plain angry, and almost all of them insisted on having the light turned off, or at least the curtains drawn in front of the floor-to-ceiling windows of the villa in Grunewald. The Madame was different. Whenever she came, all the lights stayed on and if his eyes occasionally strayed to her, she would murmur, "Don't look at me, you pathetic dog. Look in the mirror." And he obeyed. Allowed himself to be fascinated by the sight of himself, his twitching body and the expression in his eyes.

"Everything all right?" The Madame lifted her long, black dress to sit on the edge of the bed. She cautiously removed the gag from his mouth and placed her warm hand with its long, delicate fingers and red nails on his pumping chest. Once she'd performed her services and put the tools aside she was a gentle woman, almost caring. Ludwig could imagine that she might have been a nurse in an earlier life.

Instead of answering, he just gave a sigh of pleasure. The Madame came to relieve him twice a week, every Tuesday and Friday. He needed the pain, he inhaled it like others did oxygen. There were impecunious people of his persuasion who had to shut their fingers in doors or put a hot iron to their inner thigh to experience this ecstatic emotional cycle of repentance and redemption. Ludwig pitied them. He could afford professional pain, someone who could inflict it upon him without lasting damage, which represented the additional charm of being at the mercy of another. The Madame was expensive and discreet; their business relationship went back years. Nobody apart from her knew that the great Ludwig Abramczyk enjoyed being the prey rather than the hunter twice a week. Nobody must find out.

"Would you care to stay for dinner?" he asked the Madame, and as ever she replied, "Next time, my dear."

She got up from the bed, undid the shackles from his wrists and ankles and handed him his dressing gown. Then she gathered up all her tools and packed them into her large black wheelie case, which made her look like a traveler. Sometimes Ludwig wondered who she might be visiting next or whether she was simply going home, back to a husband and a family.

"See you on Friday, my dear," the Madame said, but Ludwig

insisted on accompanying her to the door, from where he watched her, now with a plain coat over her lace dress, wander down the drive with her wheelie case. No sooner had she turned the corner than from the other side Gero van Hoven's Porsche announced its arrival with a dramatic sputter. Ludwig stayed in the doorway while Gero parked, tied his dressing gown a little tighter and smoothed down his gray hair.

"My boy!" he said to his guest, with as much surprise as affability in his voice, but Gero just pushed past him into the house. He waited for Ludwig to close the front door from inside before letting rip.

"What kind of madwoman did you hire for me?" he thundered, his nostrils flaring like a wild bull's. When Ludwig didn't react, he added furiously, "I'm talking about Nadja!"

Ludwig hadn't been at the office that day as he'd had a trial in court, and so had no idea of what had happened. After Gero filled him in, all he said was "Oh" and invited his younger partner into the library where he gave him a glass of whiskey. They sat facing each other in the thick, brown leather armchairs, between them the globe whose northern hemisphere gaped open, presenting an array of bottles within arm's reach.

"You were the one who took her on," Gero said, emptying his glass in one. "You said you'd stake your life on her when I asked about her lack of references. You said you knew her and she needed a chance."

Ludwig rubbed his forehead.

"I'd never have expected something like this to happen," he said quietly.

"But it did," Gero retorted.

"But she's undergoing therapy and she's on medication."

"She's . . . *what?*"

Gero put down his glass and shifted to the edge of his seat. A furrow buried itself deep into his brow and his eyes burned with a combination of anger and disbelief. Ludwig felt the latter too.

"But she's in good shape," he said, although this sounded more like a question than a statement. "She's in the best hands. I hired her therapist personally and she reports back to me after every session."

Gero's hands unexpectedly shot forward, grabbed Ludwig by the lapels of his dressing gown and pulled on them.

"You're not seriously telling me that you knowingly put a mentally ill woman in my office? Are you out of your mind?"

"She's not mentally ill," Ludwig croaked as he shakily tried to pry Gero's fingers from his collar. "She's just a girl who's had a lot of bad luck in her life. Please, my boy." The agitation was now tugging at his heart, a sharp, menacing pain—not the good sort this time. "Let me explain."

Gero abruptly let go of him, picked up his glass and reached for the bottle of whiskey in the globe for a refill.

"I'm all ears."

Ludwig closed his eyes. Another secret he'd never wanted to see the light of day.

"It was Thursday, June 17, 1999," he began. "The day when Marta . . ."

NADJA

My angel,

I've written you dozens of letters and, now more than ever, regret never having sent a single one of them. I ought to have done. Definitely. You've every right to find out what really happened back then. To find out from me, in my own words, words I always believed to be inadequate. I don't know what you remember, or if hidden somewhere at the back of your mind there's still a fragment of our last meeting. I promised to catch the evil man. I tempted you with the sea, and you must have thought you could rely on me. That everything would turn out fine and that I would be the one to make sure it did.

All words are irrelevant now and I can only write this, perhaps my final letter, in my thoughts.

It's over, my angel.

Today I'm going to die.

Just like her. Laura. He's shot her. When he's fully aware of what he's done, when the penny drops, he'll panic and realize that he'll have to get rid of me too. He no longer needs me as Laura's defense in his sick game, and he certainly doesn't need me as a witness. Now I'm convinced we never had a chance. A fair trial? How ridiculous. As far as he's concerned, it was never about Aron Bruckstätt's murder, only that Laura cheated on him. He'd already decided that she would die. The only reason for his mock trial, his game, was to torture her. Other psychopaths enjoy slitting throats with a knife, slowly and slightly away from the major veins and arteries, to ensure the victims experience as much as possible of their own death. Because they want to see them suffer, take delight in their eyes—the fear, horror and disbelief raging inside them, but also the absurd hope they briefly cling on to. The hope that the monster will realize their mistake and stop in time. But in the end, it's in vain.

He's won.

He slit Laura open with his humiliating interrogation. And me too. Everything surfaced again, the entire story with Marta. June 17, 1999, the day when she didn't faint after a bath that was too hot, or lie in bed because of the flu, but because her skull had been smashed in. The day when Uncle Fedor arrested me as her killer and wrenched us apart.

I remember standing in our flat that was overflowing with police officers—really there were so many that we needed bigger rooms—and feeling as if the top of my skull had been opened and someone was stirring inside vigorously with one of Aunt Evelyn's wooden spoons. They were right when they said that the chaotic state of our bathroom that afternoon was considerably different from the usual chaos that the woman from the child welfare office had identified in her report. I was standing in the bathroom doorway—I couldn't go inside because of the forensics officers—and thought: yes, of course they're right.

The blood. So much blood, everywhere. On the floor. On the bathmat. On the wall. It had even spurted all the way up to the ceiling. Then the water in the bathtub that I must have forgotten to drain away after I'd heaved Marta out. At once the calendar picture of Aigues-Mortes flashed in my mind. At the same time, what my eyes were seeing in the real world looked totally new. I could have sworn that the blood simply hadn't been there before.

"You're going to tell me now exactly what happened," Uncle Fedor said strictly. Unlike me, he was allowed into the bathroom, having put on blue plastic overshoes and latex gloves. I opened my mouth, but nothing came out. I mean, I had no idea how my mind had clearly blanked out all the blood, let alone . . .

"Marta's dead," Uncle Fedor said.

Dead, not ill.

I'd taken her corpse from the bath, dragged it across the hallway, put a nightie on her and evidently I even tried to brush her hair. I'd put her into bed and lain down beside her; I'd shown her the patterns on the ceiling and snuggled up to her.

Sleep well, Marta.

I panted, but nothing else. Uncle Fedor shook his head in resignation. I felt Aunt Evelyn's hand on my shoulder. She was standing behind me, still sobbing. Of course she'd seen the blood in the bathroom earlier, and she'd seen Marta too, who wasn't pale because of the flu. And of course she'd notified the police. I reached up for her hand on my shoulder and squeezed it hard. The thought of her heart tore me up. That poor old heart which must have missed several beats when she was in our flat earlier. "I'm really sorry, Aunt Evelyn," I whispered. Her response was only to sob slightly louder.

I noticed a movement behind me. A policeman came down the hallway from the bedroom. He was holding a plastic bag containing a hairbrush. I could make out tufts of hair that were dark blond only at the tips and otherwise sticky red. Clamped under his arm was a pillow, also in see-through plastic. Marta's pillow that had once been white and now had an ugly red stain in the spot where her wounded head had lain. The policeman passed us and straight after that I heard the front door. I imagined this was only the beginning. All these people would now carry piles of things from our flat, pack them into boxes and drive them with their blue lights on to some laboratory in the nearest major town. I imagined that next they'd carry Marta out of the flat and I'd have to explain to you that our mother was dead. I felt utterly rotten.

"Aha," Uncle Fedor said, bending down to a bloodstained object on the toweling bathmat. "We've probably got the murder weapon now too." He waved one of his men over, who squeezed past me into our narrow bathroom.

I picked up scraps of words, mere noise, as I stared at the object that Fedor was now turning over in his hands and weighing up. Murder weapon—that was crazy. A knife was a murder weapon, like you always saw in films. A knife with a long, sharp blade. Or a pistol. But surely not . . . I wanted to leap forward and snatch it out of Uncle Fedor's hands: the bronze ballerina with Marta's blood dried in the folds of her dress. Her right arm pointing upward, her left pointing to the side at chest height. Her legs were mounted on a black marble plinth that looked like a small, flat brick. "TRZECIE MIEJSCE" was engraved on a plaque: Polish for "third place." Marta had won it when she was sixteen at a ballet competition in

Gdansk as the third-best dying swan. That wasn't a murder weapon, was it? The bronze ballerina was Marta's most treasured item.

"You always liked it," Uncle Fedor said, holding the figure out toward me. "You enjoyed playing with it when you were a little girl." What he omitted to say was that I'd sat on the cold tiles in the kitchen and played with it while he was in the bedroom with Marta getting what he could from her for twenty marks or fifty zloty. He narrowed his eyes and allowed his gaze to linger on me for a moment, before asking, "What the hell have you done, my girl?"

I faltered. My churned-up brain could only think of one right answer: "It wasn't me."

But of course he didn't believe me. I was at the mercy of him and his men, just as I'm now at the mercy of Herr van Hoven.

Right now there's nothing I can do apart from tug at my bound hands. If I managed to free them I could try to block the door with the chest of drawers. Then I'd open the window, jump and run for my life. I can't just give up and actually that surprises me. I'd always thought I wouldn't mind dying. That it might even feel right, fair. But now that death is so close, I'm seized by this peculiar determination and I know it's got to do with you. You give my life meaning, sense. I will make it, Janek, for you. It was only ever about you. At every moment of my life . . .

JULY 2015

Ludwig Abramczyk took a deep breath.

"You came hunting with me a few times to my old home, Gero. What you know is the wild nature, the empty forests, the peace—idyllic. What you don't know is the town itself. Zabrew—dirty, poor, drunken. More of a situation than a place. A hopeless situation, much worse back then than today. Most of the population, one generation after another, used to trudge off to work in the steel factory. You didn't think about it; it was just how things were. The factory determined day-to-day life and was part of your family, like a mother who gave you a home and fed you. But who was also strict and demanding. You'd get worked up about it over a beer with friends and then you'd vent your feelings on prostitutes. Not a good life, not for anybody. That's where they grew up, Nadja and her little brother Janek, pretty much having to fend for themselves. Their mother Marta was . . ." Ludwig broke off, shaking his head. Even uttering her name was painful, the sort of pain that was only bearable because the Madame came twice a week and diverted his mind from internal to external matters.

"My cousin Evelyn lived in the same building," Ludwig continued, now in a different, less painful place. "She looked after the children as best she could, but she didn't have an easy time of it. Nadja was particularly tricky. No sooner had she learned to walk than she started climbing the banisters and falling down all ten flights of stairs. She made Evelyn's life a misery. My cousin often said to me on the phone: *One day that little brat is going to break her neck and I'll have to mop up the blood.* Then, as soon as she was big enough, Nadja would creep around the building and steal from the ground-floor windowsills jars of preserves or even entire pots and pans that the housewives had put out to cool. Later they caught her and her brother trying to leave town on foot or by bus; she always blamed the little one, claiming that he urgently had to go to the sea to cure his asthma. When she was twelve she was found blind drunk in the rear yard. She'd taken beer from her mother's fridge because she was so dreadfully thirsty, as she said. Those sorts of things."

Gero looked unimpressed.

"She delivered her baby brother with a pair of kitchen scissors," Ludwig went on, to emphasize how difficult her life had been, and indeed there was a flicker of a reaction in Gero's face. Ludwig nodded. "Apparently Marta was ill, a bad case of the flu she'd been suffering from for months, and which simply wouldn't get any better. But this illness turned out to be a concealed pregnancy."

He pulled the lapels of his dressing gown across his chest. He was still chilled to the bone by the idea of a ten-year-old girl snipping away at her own mother and a newborn.

"And even so, after all these incidents, nobody could have predicted something like that would happen. A tragedy, that June 17 in Zabrew . . . Evelyn had to pick up Janek from kindergarten because they couldn't get hold of Marta. She took him home, but when she rang the Kulkas' doorbell it was Nadja rather than Marta who answered. Nadja said her mother was ill and didn't want Evelyn to come into the flat. But when she did, she saw Marta lying in her bed. She also saw blood in the bathroom and notified the police. When they entered the flat they found Nadja, who'd clearly just woken up, and was totally bewildered. She kept insisting that Marta was ill. But she wasn't ill, Gero, she was dead."

Ludwig instinctively made a grab for his heart, where Marta had settled many years before the tragedy and which still lamented her absence by tugging and cramping when he focused too closely on her. He took another sip of his whiskey, his medicine.

"Fedor Botzki, the local police inspector, advised my cousin to get some legal help for Nadja right away, so she rang me. Uncle Adwo, they called me," he said and smiled briefly. "'Adwo,' from 'adwocat,' the Polish word for lawyer." Now he turned serious again. "To begin with I couldn't believe what I was hearing on the phone. Marta was dead and they believed little Nadjeschka had killed her in their flat. From the traces of blood, they were able to conclude that she'd been battered to death while she was in the bath. I went there later myself. So much blood, Gero. It had even got on the ceiling."

Gero shook his head, but said nothing.

"The presumed murder weapon was also found in the bathroom," Ludwig continued. "A trophy that Marta had won as a young woman in a ballet competition. Nadja admitted to taking the body from the bathroom to the bedroom, where she dressed her in a nightie and put her into bed. But she continued to insist she hadn't realized Marta was dead. She said she thought she was ill and wanted to help her. She'd even made her tea."

"But that's ludicrous."

"No, it's perfectly possible. Nadja's therapist told me later that it might have been a protective function of her mind at work. Unable to comprehend the fact that Marta was dead, it offered her an alternative scenario."

"But she must have seen the blood."

"Blocked it out," Ludwig said curtly. "She just blocked it out."

"Maybe it was, in fact, a lie to cover her actions."

Ludwig sighed.

"Of course that's possible too. Anyway, after Evelyn called me I went straight to Zabrew and met Nadja in a consultation room at the local police station. She sat facing me, misery personified, just saying again and again: 'I swear it wasn't me.' But she also claimed that a man had been in their flat. One of Marta's guests."

NADJA

For years I've been trying to find the right words. For years I've been trying to put down on paper what happened on June 17, 1999, because you've never heard it from me, only ever from those for whom the story is merely a succession of appalling facts. Two children having to fend for themselves, and an ignorant mother who won't even allow them to call her "Mama" because it makes her feel old and it might scare away her "guests." A home that is anything but—the filth, the screaming, the sleepless nights, physical violence. And then, all of a sudden, this woman is lying in her bed with her skull bashed in. They find a bath full of blood and beside it the presumed murder weapon. Everything appears quite clear: the daughter, seemingly the only other person in the flat at the time the crime was committed, and troubled for years by the conditions at home, must have killed her in the heat of the moment. But is it always so simple?

Marta was dead. Dead, not ill, as my crazed mind tried to delude me at first. I begged to be able to see her, but they wouldn't let me. They said you were staying with Aunt Evelyn for the time being and took me to the police station. I thought only of you. Someone had to explain to you what had happened to Marta and I would be the best person for the job. There was just one little problem—what would I have said? I didn't even know myself.

Aunt Evelyn rang Uncle Adwo to get him to act as my lawyer, and he actually did come all the way from Berlin. Now we sat opposite each other in a police consultation room.

"I'll do everything in my power to help you," he said. With this promise and the caring expression on his face that accompanied it, a thought came to me that briefly made me forget everything else. I remembered how as a child I'd always fantasized about what would happen after Marta died. The women from the neighborhood would bring cakes—which of course didn't happen given the circumstances—but most important he turned up, my father, with a promise. Do you remember? We'd often wondered who our fathers were. It seemed pretty obvious that we didn't have the same one. Yes, we did look similar: both of us had inherited Marta's eyes and her mouth. But there were other features which were totally different and which couldn't be put down to Marta. The recognition literally burst out of me: "You're my father!"

I could barely believe how long that had escaped my attention. Uncle Adwo, who I'd known all my life, who didn't live in Zabrew, but was here time and again, like a shadow formed by the cycle of the sun. Uncle Adwo, who sometimes brought Marta flowers when he came to visit. And who had dark hair. Like me. I shuddered with excitement, as if I'd just been injected with pure adrenaline.

But Uncle Adwo shook his head.

"You're mistaken, Nadjeschka. If you were my daughter, we wouldn't be sitting here." He lowered his gaze; it was an embarrassing situation for both him and me. I crumpled, no longer any trace of adrenaline, just shame. Had I really believed that the worst day of my life would turn out in the end to be a blessing? Had I seriously doubted even for a moment Marta's answer to the question *about our fathers, which I'd asked her so often?* You were brought by the stork. *Or some guest. It could have been any man in town, anyone or no one.* "I'm sorry," Uncle Adwo added.

I just nodded. *Crossed my arms on the table and laid my stupid, heavy head on them. All of a sudden I felt tired, so unbelievably tired from everything. I thought of the flat cola in the bottle beside our bed, which I'd washed my mouth out with at some point that morning because I hadn't brushed my teeth. I thought too of the little white bits that had settled on the bottom of the bottle. I ran my tongue over my teeth and felt a slimy film.*

"Hey!" Uncle Adwo clicked his fingers right in front of my face, as *if he were an impatient diner summoning a dawdling waiter.* "Wake up, Nadjeschka! Look at me."

I raised my head sluggishly and asked, "Could I have a cola? I'm really tired."

"Okay," Uncle Adwo said with a sigh. "I'll get you one."

His chair scraped across the floor when he got up and then he left the room. I put my head back in the nest of my crossed arms and closed my eyes.

You weren't the first one in our family to have sleeping problems, you know. *Marta always had terrible trouble trying to get me to bed when I was small. She told me good-night stories and sang me* chansons. *The time came when I knew her entire repertoire.*

Go to sleep now, for God's sake!

There was nothing I'd rather do right now. I drifted into a kind of doze, a sphere where I was able to consciously direct my dreams. I saw Marta. Not as she'd have loved to see herself: a beautiful, sylphlike ballerina with a tight bun and perfectly extended limbs and movements, which for all their grace always had something mechanical about them. No, I saw her as she was when she forgot she'd have loved to have been a ballerina. Her dancing and singing "Retiens la nuit." Do you remember what she was like then? So wonderful, so happy.

The door opened and Uncle Adwo came back with the cola. As tired as I was, I immediately sensed that something had changed. He'd probably been having another chat with Uncle Fedor in the corridor. I sat up.

"Okay, it's like this. Fedor seems determined to clear this up fast. Which means he and his people are now going to get their machine going at full tilt. They'll question people who know you and Marta. They'll analyze the traces they found in your flat and on Marta's body. They'll definitely identify and analyze the murder weapon. Do you know what DNA is?"

I shook my head feebly.

"There's a particular method of analysis that the police have been using for over ten years and it's being refined all the time," he continued. "They can analyze any foreign matter that they find on a body. Flakes of skin, hair, sperm, vaginal fluid, cell material beneath fingernails from scratching, fibers from clothing."

I said nothing.

"Listen, Nadjeschka, I don't want to frighten you. All I want from you is the truth. Only when I know exactly what happened in your flat this morning can I help you. Do you understand?"

"Yes."

"Good. Okay, what do you remember?"

I thought about this. Something had to occur to me. There must be something left in my churned-up brain. I mean, I could remember that I hadn't brushed my teeth. That I'd drunk the rest of some flat cola. There had to be more. That morning . . .

There was more.

"We overslept," I began hesitantly. "I sent Janek to Aunt Evelyn so she could take him to kindergarten and then I went back to our bedroom because I was so tired. I planned to skip school and lie down instead."

"Okay, that's good. Go on."

"I don't know exactly."

"Think hard."

I tried, but in vain.

"I don't know. It's just gone."

Uncle Adwo breathed out loudly. "Marta was a difficult woman, everyone knew that. Did she provoke you? Did you have an argument and then it just happened? You left the bathroom and went to fetch the bronze figure. You swung your arm back and hit her. Those things happen, Nadjeschka. There are some moments when people do things they never intended to."

I tried to imagine that this was what had happened, but that didn't work. The picture in my head seemed completely wrong. And you know it too, don't you, Janek? You know how much—in spite of everything—I loved her. Oh God, I hope you do.

"No, that's not what happened. Not at all."

"How can you be so sure when you can't remember anything?"

I didn't reply.

"Manslaughter: ten years," Uncle Adwo said. "Seven, if the judge is having a good day and feeling sympathetic to you for some reason."

"What? No!" I leaped up.

"She's dead, Nadja."

"I didn't touch her!"

"Then tell me what happened!"

I slumped back down in my chair. I had to think. Get a grip on it. I had to bloody, bloody, bloody well get a grip on it. Think, think, think. That morning . . . Marta in the bathtub, alive. The scent of lavender bubble bath and rose shampoo. Is that why I left our room and crept down the corridor to the bathroom? Did I hear sloshing sounds, Marta's body moving in the bathwater? Marta happily humming to herself?

No.

No, it was different.

First the sloshing sounds, yes, I did hear them. But then . . . I slapped my palm on the table—four times. Thud-thud-thud-thud. I heard the muffled sound four times in succession. The blows on Marta's head.

A spark. A shadow coming away from the white noise of my memory. The outline of a person standing there, arm raised. Holding something: the bronze ballerina. It was as if the image in my head was printed on blotting paper, something red dripping on it and immediately creating a huge stain. Until that was all I could see: red, everything red. Blood.

I flinched.

"Someone was there. A man."

"A man?"

I nodded eagerly. Suddenly everything made sense. A man. A man in our bathroom. The man who'd struck Marta, killed her.

"Did you recognize him?"

"I only saw him very briefly and from behind." Again I hit the table four times. Thud-thud-thud-thud. "Maybe a guest."

"Who?"

"I don't know. I was so shocked and I hid behind the chest of drawers in the hallway."

Uncle Adwo cocked his head.

"Are you sure?"

"Yes."

"That's what happened?"

"Yes!"

Uncle Adwo's jaws moved and for a moment it looked as if he were chewing on something.

"I'll do what I can," he said, before getting up and leaving the room.

JULY 2015

"I knew she was lying," Ludwig Abramczyk continued, "and that I had to dissuade her as quickly as possible from sticking to the story of the punter who'd supposedly killed Marta. Her strange behavior in the flat, the fact that she'd claimed not to have seen the blood—that could be explained by shock. Everything else, however, could give my defense case huge amounts of trouble. All of a sudden a man was there, she said. How had he entered the flat? Who had let him in if Marta was in the bath? And why did Nadja only remember him after I'd asked her several times about the events of that morning? No." He shook his head resolutely. "I had a different theory. Nadja overslept, which led to an argument with Marta. Perhaps Marta called her a lazy bitch, a parasite. Maybe she painted her a future which was no different from her life at that moment: in a shabby flat, in a run-down block, with endless money worries and men who treated her like dirt. In which she was like her mother. That made her furious, she told Marta to stop. And then—"

"She blew a fuse," Gero said. "Nadja went for her mother and in the heat of the moment killed her."

"Exactly." Ludwig pointed a finger at Gero to show that he'd grasped the circumstances of the case. "However, Nadja was stubborn. The police interrogated her for hours, but she kept insisting it had been one of Marta's punters. At some point I got them to break off—it was late, already nighttime. I wanted her to have some sleep. Maybe she'd come to her senses overnight. It was one thing building a defense case on the basis that she'd acted in the heat of the moment. But the longer she stuck to her lies, the more negatively that would affect the verdict. Of course, forensic science was less sophisticated than it is now . . ." Pausing briefly to refill his glass, Ludwig recalled a recent conversation with his good old friend Ansgar, a professor at the forensic institute of the Charité. He'd learned that nowadays scientists needed only six skin cells to draw up a meaningful DNA profile of a criminal. Six paltry skin cells which, as Ansgar had explained, roughly corresponded to what was left behind when you touched a light switch. "But," Ludwig continued, brandishing his freshly filled glass, "the methods were sufficiently advanced to easily solve a murder with that amount of evidence left behind. The truth would come to light, I was certain of that."

NADJA

I remember sitting in my cell, knees up to my chin, staring into space. From the wall opposite, a patch of bare concrete stared back. I estimated it must be at least half a square meter. On the floor, flakes of paint lay on a thin bed of gray cement dust. Paint and cement dust sat beneath my fingernails too.

The cell I'd been shut up in was drastically different from the cells I'd seen on TV. In Zabrew there weren't any beds, just a saggy, bare mattress on a floor of cracked tiles. A mattress on which a number of people had slept off their drunkenness and—judging by the smell and stains—relieved themselves in every way. There was no shiny aluminum toilet, just a bucket with a lid that was supposed to prevent the worst odors from escaping—and failing miserably. No window either, not even a narrow gap with bars, to allow me to glimpse the sky and estimate the time of day. There was a sink fixed to the wall, though, and when my thirst became unbearable I would take a gulp of rusty water from its tap. It had been a long night, cold and sleepless. Merciless on me and my thoughts. My fists had pounded the hard metal door dozens of times. I wanted them to let me see you. I'd shouted your name till I was hoarse.

At some point I heard a key in the lock and I turned my head to the door. Uncle Adwo came in. I wiped my nose with the back of my hand and got up.

"Where's Janek?"

"Evelyn's looking after him," he replied. In his left hand he held a plate with a jam roll on it, while a thick yellow cardigan and a pair of tracksuit bottoms hung over his right arm. I immediately understood what this meant.

"I've got to stay here."

"I'm sorry," Uncle Adwo said, holding out his arm with the clothes like a gentleman inviting a lady for a walk. "Evelyn gave me these for you."

I knew that they were Aunt Evelyn's things, from which I assumed that our flat had already been sealed off by the forensics team. I took the clothes from him and put them on. I had to roll up the waist of the bottoms several times so that they didn't slide down my bony hips. The cardigan was several sizes too big as well; the shoulder seams almost came down to my elbows. When I was done I grabbed the plate, sat on the mattress and started scoffing the roll.

"Zabrew is a difficult town," Uncle Adwo said, getting down beside me with his creaky knees. "I know what it's like to grow up here. And I also know what it's like to feel different. Like you don't belong anywhere."

I put the half-eaten roll down on the plate and changed my seating position so I could look him in the eye.

"Please, you've got to believe me when I say it wasn't me. The man . . ."

"Marta's last guest?"

"Yes."

"What did he look like?"

I shook my head.

"Do you know what, Nadja? Fedor Botzki and his people went to your school right at the beginning of lessons this morning and took witness statements. Including from the boy whose cheekbone you almost broke last week. Milosz Nowak. It wasn't the first time you'd been involved in a fight."

"And it wasn't the first time he'd insulted Marta either. He provoked me."

"Did Marta provoke you too?"

I shook my head again.

"Right now she's lying on a mortuary slab in the forensics department, Nadja."

I saw it in my mind. They'd shave her bald to investigate the hole in her head. Her beautiful long hair would sail to the floor; it would sound like a breath, one last exhalation. They'd cover her body with special sticky strips in the hope that these would pick up useful evidence when they were torn off again. They'd thrust a scalpel into her chest and make an incision across her entire torso. Her organs would be cut out. She'd be gutted like a slaughtered cow. I burped, but the taste in my mouth wasn't jam roll, it was something else, something far sweeter. I began to tremble, I heard sounds in my head. Blows—thud-thud-thud-thud—blows and the rustling of silver paper. A memory.

"Nadja?"

Hello, Nadja. I'm Uncle Fedor.

Uncle Adwo clicked his tongue.

"I don't think you understand the seriousness of the situation, Nadjeschka. Fedor and his people also talked to your friend Aniela

at school." He got to his feet and looked down at me. "She is your friend, isn't she?" I nodded eagerly and got up too. "So, can you guess what Aniela told him?"

I expect I smiled. I expect I thanked God and all the higher powers I could think of for making Uncle Fedor and his people talk to Aniela. She would have told them how much fun we had together, how much we laughed when we spent afternoons in each other's company. How we lay on the grass behind the disused railway line and identified pictures in the clouds while listening to Marta's old cassettes on Aniela's Walkman—Aniela with the left earphone, me with the right, and the lead connecting us like a thin, black umbilical cord. Aniela would have told them that since the second year I'd hugged and thanked her every day for bringing me a roll at break time, even though by now I could have taken it for granted. She would have confirmed that I only hit people because I was hurt when they said bad things about Marta. Yes, I expect I was smiling and my smile must have been the most stupid and least appropriate answer I could have given Uncle Adwo at that moment.

"You regularly forced your friend Aniela to steal money from her mother's purse. She said she was scared of you, scared that you might turn aggressive toward her too—"

He broke off abruptly. He'd caught sight of the patch on the wall where the paint had flaked off. It was extraordinary that he only just noticed it now.

"What on earth have you done to the wall?" At first he ran his hand along the bare concrete in disbelief, then he squatted down, grabbed a handful of cement dust and let it trickle to the floor, looking utterly perplexed. I closed my eyes for a couple of seconds and thought of the sand on the beach. And then of you, Janek.

"The lady from the child welfare office is coming at eleven to give a statement," I heard Uncle Adwo say, who sounded distant. The thing with the wall seemed to have completely thrown him. "You've met her a few times, I think."

That was the moment I gave in. I suspected I didn't have a chance. My future was determined. But you, Janek, you at least might be able to see the sea one day. For that to happen, however, I had to let you go now.

JULY 2015

"She said I should tell Fedor to stop. She'd tell them everything they needed to know. On one condition: she wanted to see her brother again so she could say goodbye to him." Ludwig Abramczyk was now on his fourth glass and even he noticed himself slurring slightly while Gero took his first sip of his whiskey in a long time. But the alcohol didn't seem to extract anything from him apart from a shake of the head and a quiet "Unbelievable."

"She never commented on the circumstances of the crime," Ludwig went on. "She just agreed to the record of the facts reconstructed from the evidence. But she didn't have to do much more than that anyway, as it was perfectly clear. A rebellious teenager known to be a troublemaker had killed her mother, a prostitute who neglected the girl and her little brother, with a ballet trophy."

"And she was sentenced," Gero inferred. Ludwig nodded.

"Seven years' youth custody. In mitigation, the judge accepted that the two children had indeed spent a long time living in unacceptable conditions. The flat was filthy and the children were left to their own devices. If it hadn't been for my cousin Evelyn . . ." He broke off and swallowed audibly. "I expect Marta hit them quite often too."

Gero looked bewildered.

"She wasn't altogether bad," Ludwig's pained heart urged him to point out. "At least not in the early days." A dreamy smile swept across his lined face.

"So you *were* in love with her."

"Yes, I was the idiot who really did love this woman. She was the sweetest, most beautiful girl in the entire town."

"Who later became a monster."

"Many of us did," Ludwig said seriously. "Me too."

"What do you mean?"

"We were together when I was young. I would have married her on the spot. But I also wanted to go to Berlin and become a lawyer. Marta, meanwhile, wanted to go to Paris to dance. Because we couldn't agree, we split up over the issue after lots of arguments. It was almost another three years before I came back to Zabrew, because I was anxious that everything there would remind me of her. I even ignored my cousin's telephone calls for fear that she might mention Marta. But when I did come to visit one day, I realized that Marta had never left. Now she had a little daughter and worked as a . . ." He gazed into his glass. "Well, you know."

"You think everything would have been different if you hadn't left her back then."

"I don't only think that, I know it. And that knowledge tortures me every day."

"Regardless of what Marta did," Gero said after a moment of pensive silence, "do you really think that a fifteen-year-old girl would be capable of killing her own mother?" He moved forward on his seat. "Did you never consider that Nadja might actually have been telling the truth? That it might have been one of Marta's punters after all?"

Ludwig felt his face hardening.

"No."

"No?"

"It *was* her," was all he said, failing to mention that doubts over Nadja's guilt had occasionally nagged at him down the years. For then he'd have had to admit that he'd been wrong and made the worst mistake of his life. "Anyway," he continued, changing tack, "thanks to my contacts I was able to have her transferred to a youth detention center in Frankfurt an der Oder. Legally she should have been locked up in Poland, and you don't want to know what conditions were like there back then. They allowed me to bring her to Frankfurt personally, in my car. I remember her begging me to find her brother somewhere nice to live. Before we got out I handed her my hip flask, allowed her to take a large gulp of whiskey and said, *See it through, my child. Take your punishment with dignity and consider your incarceration as an opportunity.*" He cocked his head. "Really, Gero, I swear she's harmless now. Those years in prison changed her. She can't even get on the subway without coming close to a nervous breakdown. She's suffered enough."

Gero rubbed his forehead. Ludwig fancied he could read the thoughts churning away behind it.

"I said she's harmless," he repeated emphatically. "Take that as a given. And another thing: I want you to take her back and treat her well, as if this incident with Vivi never occurred."

"But it—"

"Enough!" Ludwig said harshly. "You know I love you like a son,

Gero. But I'm not kidding about this. It's still my firm and I'm the senior partner. Understood? Life's been hard enough on that girl."

Gero van Hoven sat in his Porsche, where a feeling was unfurling that he'd unwittingly picked up in Ludwig's villa. He himself had been a misunderstood child, with a father he could never do anything right by, and a mother who, instead of intervening, had withdrawn to the kitchen to cook, or the laundry room to iron. If he concentrated, he could still hear the sound his father's belt made when he pulled it out of the straps of his trousers, and how the leather cut sharply through the air before lashing his bare back after he'd got a bad mark at school. He heard his mother promise him a thousand times that she'd leave his father and begin a new life with her son somewhere else. A promise never kept, which hurt almost more than his father's beatings. Then he heard himself, years later and despite everything, sitting on the edge of a hospital bed, holding his father's hand and telling him he'd decided to study law. One day he'd become a judge, so he could mete out just punishment to those individuals like the driver who'd failed to notice his father and sealed his fate as a cripple. Children loved their parents, unconditionally and hopelessly—that's how nature arranged it. So what sort of a person would you have to be to repeal a law of nature and kill your own mother? On the other hand, people did make mistakes . . .

Mistakes, he thought, sneering at himself. A murder wasn't a mistake; a murder was a murder. Or was it? Again he thought of his first love, Lilly Kössling, and that night when he'd been angry enough to make more than just one mistake. He'd trusted Lilly, trusted that her "forever" had been meant seriously. But she'd let him down, just like his mother with her useless promises, and he'd suffered terribly for weeks after that. Determined that Lilly ought to be the one to suffer for her actions, he made his way to her hall of residence in the middle of the night. When he saw the special light on in her room, his blood began to boil. Seething with rage, he marched to the car park behind the hall, where he found Lilly's little blue Polo. She'd had to scrimp and save to buy it and do even more hours of overtime in the café where she worked part-time as a waitress. The little blue Polo, her most precious possession. He took a final swig of the beer he'd brought along, then hurled it at the right-hand mudguard. He ran the sharp, jagged neck of the bottle along the paint of the doors and the hood, again and again and again. And he relished the grating noise, oh yes, how he enjoyed it, every single piercing, high-pitched sound. He imagined Lilly's despair the following day when she saw what had happened to her car. Gero only stopped when one of the windows in the building opened and a man's voice shouted, "Hey!" down at him. Then he ran. Things like this were mistakes, especially as Lilly reported him to the police afterward.

But what other choice did he have than to do what Ludwig had told him? None, he concluded, and activated the speech function of his onboard computer. He said her name and waited. The first time it just kept ringing, the second time she answered.

"Van Hoven," he replied to her quivering "Hello?" Nadja Kulka, who'd been locked away from the world until she was twenty-two for having killed her mother. Then she returned to her home-town of Zabrew, where she'd looked after Ludwig's cousin Evelyn, who was suffering from a heart condition. After Evelyn's death,

Ludwig brought her back to Berlin, and set up for her the basic elements of a normal life: a therapist she could consult regularly and who prescribed her medicines, her own flat and a job to earn a livelihood. Ludwig ultimately left Nadja to take care of herself because, as he'd said, he couldn't spend that much time with her. She reminded him too much of her mother, who he'd loved, hated and lost.

"I'm taking back my decision to dismiss you," Gero said, though he didn't mention his meeting with Ludwig. "I think that today was just a silly misunderstanding and I overreacted." She answered hesitantly with "Oh" and "Thank you, Herr van Hoven."

"See you tomorrow, then, Nadja," he said.

Gero resolved to keep an eye on her. To test her. Maybe show her the odd photograph of Vivi from time to time, to check her reaction. The moment he noticed anything unusual he'd go back to Ludwig and confront him, he decided as he drove home.

It was chilly in the living room—Laura, who was sitting on the sofa, held Vivi wrapped in the cuddly toweling blanket she'd bought in anticipation of the autumn—and yet a certain warmth filled the room, which immediately penetrated Gero's chest and found his heart. The smell of dinner simmering away on the stove wafted over from the open kitchen and mingled with the delicate floral notes of the scented candles that stood on the set table. For a moment he stood in the doorway to the living room, marveling at all the wonders that surrounded him. A beautiful home, a proper family—just as he'd wanted when he was a child. Laura looked up and smiled as he went over to her.

"What a day, eh?" She pulled down Vivi's blanket so he could see the little face. Every single day of his life he would be the father to her that he would have loved to have himself. It was what he'd promised her at her birth. "And all of this just because of a crazed woman who was reminded of her asthmatic brother," Laura said, shaking her head.

Gero nodded, sat beside her on the sofa and gave her a summary of what Ludwig had told him. Not only because it seriously bothered him, but also to make Laura think. She hadn't kept a close enough eye on Vivi today. In his eyes she'd failed slightly as a mother and he thought it was salutary to point out the dangers lurking in the wider world. Dangers you often failed to see coming, beginning with people you regarded as harmless. Only if they stuck together and continued to function as an indissoluble unit would they be able to defy these dangers.

In the end Laura looked just as perplexed as he'd been.

"I always thought there was something not quite right with her. But I . . ." Although she didn't manage to complete what she was saying, Gero understood well enough. No, nobody could have expected that Nadja Kulka was a convicted killer.

NADJA

Do you remember the last time we saw each other? You cried. Both of us cried when Uncle Fedor honored his side of the bargain and brought you to me so we could say goodbye.

"You said we'd be going to the seaside soon!"

You were wheezing with anxiety; I was worried you might have another attack. Aunt Evelyn, who had you on her lap as we sat facing each other in the consultation room at the police station, took your inhaler from her bag. You kicked and thrashed about when she held it up to your face. And you shouted, "You lied, Nadja! You lied!"

"No, no, no!" I opened my arms and asked you to come over to me, but you turned away and pressed your tearstained face into Aunt Evelyn's chest. She'd already warned you that I wouldn't be coming home. I wasn't sure whether I ought to hate her for that or feel grateful. You started coughing, just as I'd feared. Your whole body twitched so violently that Aunt Evelyn had difficulty holding on to you. I leaped up from my chair. Uncle Fedor stood by the door like a guard dog and cleared his throat. I immediately had the taste of chocolate in my mouth again, but I tried to suppress the feeling of nausea this produced. Only you were important now. He wouldn't be able to keep me away from you and in the end he didn't even try to. I squatted in front of your chair and put out my hand to stroke your back. Aunt Evelyn waved the inhaler. I nodded.

"Listen, my angel," I began. "It's true that I won't be able to come home for a while and that some things are going to change." You panted and Aunt Evelyn waved the inhaler more frantically. "But you will see the sea—that was no lie. I swear."

You tentatively turned your head toward me.

"What about Marta?"

"Marta can't go, she's asleep. She has to rest. Her last guest really tired her out." Ignoring Aunt Evelyn's look, I continued in the way I felt was right. "You'll see the sea on your own soon and when I come back, we'll go again together and you'll show me everything, okay? Shall we do it like that?" I took the inhaler from Aunt Evelyn and held it up to you. "It's got sea air in it, Janek," I said, smiling. "So you can get used to it."

You looked doubtful.

"Please come back home. I cry all day long without you."

I explained again that you'd have to get along without me for a while.

"What does 'a while' mean, Nadja?" you asked after taking two big puffs on the inhaler. "When will you come home again?"

"Just as soon as the people who think I did something bad realize that they're mistaken and they catch the evil man."

"What if they don't catch him?"

"Then I'll get him, my sweetheart. I'll come home, I promise."

"And then we'll go to the seaside."

"Yes. Then we'll go to the seaside."

.   .   .

You've seen it in the meantime, the sea. You really have been there, I know. Last summer, for example, you went to the Baltic with your wife. This year you're planning to go to the Adriatic—the first time all three of you. Now you know if gulls squawk or crow and what it's like to be in the salty air.

I really wished you could have told me about it. I really wished I'd had more than just my thoughts of you. That I'd had the courage to send my letters. But I was cowardly, Janek, cowardly and selfish. I was afraid you'd rebuff me. I only thought of myself. Me, who'd sworn I'd always do everything for you and that you were the most important thing in my life. That's why I've got to get out of this alive. I have to do it.

So I tug at my bound hands like crazy and yell my struggle, my sorrow and my pain into the packing tape over my mouth. I want to tug harder, struggle harder, but the very opposite happens. I become weaker. And tired, unbelievably tired. The groggy feeling inside my head spreads to my entire body. For a moment it's not unpleasant: I want to give in; I like it when everything fades away. But then it all goes terrifyingly quickly. When I try to order my thoughts, I realize it's getting more difficult. I remember the letters blurring when I tried to read the criminal code in the kitchen earlier. Wanting to stop Herr van Hoven from beating Laura, but not being able to stand up, only crawl. Only having enough strength to tug on his trouser leg. I see Aunt Evelyn before me, hands on her broad hips and saying in the voice of Annelies, the woman from the petrol station, I told you it was a concussion and that you should go see a doctor. If you'd listened to me, you wouldn't be here now. It's your own fault. *Your fault, always your fault . . .*

I can't go on anymore, I'm surrendering to nightfall, I'm drifting off. I don't know what's going to happen when I wake up again. Apart from one thing: if it should happen, if I really am to die soon, all I hope is that you can forgive me one day. Please forgive me, Janek.

I love you.

JULY 2015

The boy was there again. He'd been waiting for him in the underground garage. It couldn't have been difficult to find Gero van Hoven's car. In its report on the Heger case the paper had said how he was wearing a suit and sunglasses when he got into his Porsche outside the law firm. Recognizing the boy from a distance, Gero slackened his pace. It was already gone ten in the evening and the garage was dark. The caretaker still hadn't solved the problem with the lighting; the fluorescent tubes on the concrete ceiling flickered dismally.

"Hello, Herr van Hoven," the boy said.

Gero had soon forgotten his sudden appearance in the midst of the chaos surrounding Vivi's disappearance a couple of days earlier. Especially as the boy had left as abruptly as he'd arrived and was gone when Gero came back from the roof with Vivi.

"Okay," Gero said, defeated, as he neared the boy. "Let me ask you again: what do you want from me?"

The boy reached into the inside pocket of his baggy denim jacket, which he wore over the same band T-shirt he'd had on a couple of days earlier, and pulled out the envelope once more.

"You have to help me make everything right again, Herr van Hoven."

Gero remembered. *My confession*, the boy had said when he tried to hand him the envelope for the first time two days earlier.

"So you knew Nelly Schütt, Herr . . . ?"

"Hannes Liewert," the boy said, offering Gero a trembling hand. Gero took it; the hand was clammy and the boy's grip was weak. "Yes, I knew Nelly. We went to school together. Sometimes she let me carry her satchel, but otherwise she didn't want to know me at all." In response to the abortive smile that dashed across his pockmarked, spotty face, Gero raised his eyebrows, a gesture designed to express his desire for the boy to come to the point. It was late, after all, and he wanted to go home to his loved ones, little Vivi and Laura, who after the shock of the "abduction" was like a different person, like she used to be. Before the incident she was always complaining, bored by her day-to-day life, but also unable to cope with it: the crying baby, the household, no time for herself, no Gero when she needed him. Some evenings she hadn't even cooked and he had to order some takeout, while she showed zero interest when he talked about his work over dinner. But now she was smiling again. Cooking, embracing him for no particular reason and saying things like "We're so lucky to have each other."

Hannes, however, seemed to take Gero's expression as a judgment on Nelly and he came blustering to her defense. "She didn't have anything going with anyone else, she was a decent girl," only to add quietly, "until Heger came along."

Gero was no longer surprised by what the boy said after that. Hannes had thought that after Nelly split up with Paul Heger he'd finally have a chance with her, but he was forced to face the fact that she was only using him for comfort until Heger was back on the scene.

"I visited her that morning and brought her flowers. But she sent me packing," the boy said, wiping the tears from his face. Because he'd immediately suspected that Nelly's change of heart must be to do with Heger, he followed her in the afternoon to the hotel on the A24, where he confronted her in the car park. "She started off denying that she was meeting him, claiming that a friend of hers worked at the hotel." He shook his head energetically. "I know all her friends. Everyone knows everyone else in our village." Finally Nelly realized that Hannes wasn't going to be fobbed off, not this time. At Nelly's request they drove in her car to the nearby woods to talk it through. "I expect she didn't want her stallion to turn up at the hotel and see the two of us together." He looked at the ground. "I was an embarrassment to her." Gero opened his mouth to say something nice, but he couldn't think of anything. *Yes, that's probably what happened,* he thought, giving a dismissive look to the scrawny, spotty boy, compared with whom even an idiot like Heger looked classy, especially to a village dolly like Nelly Schütt. "And in the woods," the boy said, his eyes fixed on his grubby, worn trainers, "it happened." He'd only wanted to make her realize how much he loved her and that Heger wasn't good for her. She laughed.

"I shoved her. Not to push her down the slope. I just wanted her to stop laughing. But there it was, the slope. I tried to grab and hold on to her, but I missed and she fell. And when she was lying there, so strangely contorted, staring up at me . . ." He dramatically raised the hands that had lain around Nelly's neck.

Gero nodded thoughtfully and didn't probe further. He'd be able to read the rest of the details in Hannes's written confession. The question that was uppermost in his mind was what to do with this new information. He could go straight to his friend Fred Mertens, the public prosecutor, and have Hannes arrested. He could be a hero—for Heger, for the media—Berlin's top lawyer who at the end of an odyssey for a wrongly convicted client ultimately ensured a happy ending after all. Or he could simply send Hannes home and instruct him to burn the letter containing his confession and live his life. Nelly Schütt's death was undoubtedly a tragedy, but she was partly responsible for it. She shouldn't have got involved with Heger, and certainly not a second time. For what did they say? *The first time it's a mistake, the second time it's a choice.* Nelly Schütt had made her choice and now she was dead.

Gero sensed the corners of his mouth twitching. It didn't feel good to be the judge for once.

NADJA

Time has passed; I fell into it as if it were a black hole. I'm lying on the bare, slightly moldy mattress in Laura's grandmother's bedroom. The packing tape over my mouth has slipped, loosened by spit, snot and tears. My wrists are still bound; the tape has twisted and is cutting into my skin. The black night seeps through the window and somewhere in the room a weak light is flickering—candles. I can make out a strip of dazzling white in the dark sky: a shooting star. I'm too tired to make a wish. My head is porridge.

Laura . . . Grief is a creature with sharp claws. It makes a cruel cut down my torso like in an autopsy. It pushes my ribs apart and reaches right into my open chest to squash my heart like an old sponge. I know it hurts, that in different circumstances it would be unbearable, this pain, which is so much more than just grief, of course. It's the awareness of my failure. Laura is dead and the belief that I couldn't have done anything about it has gone. I ought to have played along with his mock trial. I ought to have made more effort. I didn't fulfill my role as lawyer in the way he'd expected.

He would have killed her anyway.

I could have bought us more time at least.

Now it's too late. I fail in my attempt to maneuver my body into an upright position; the packing tape binding my wrists behind my back gives me too little leeway. I keep wriggling nonetheless, like a fish pulled from the water, until my body lies quite still from exhaustion. But the mattress continues to move. I heave myself around and groan. Beside me sits Herr van Hoven. He's looking at me intently. He nods as if I'd just asked him a question. There are many I would like to put to him and most of them begin "Why?"

"You're awake," he says. "That's good."

The mattress undulates beneath me again when he leans over and manhandles my enfeebled body to sit it up. Now I'm leaning with my back against the headboard. My heavy head rolls uncontrollably on my neck; it's as if I'm drunk and maybe I'm even slobbering. My vision is blurred; I have to concentrate to work out what he's got in his hands now as he sits beside me in the exact same position, his back against the headboard.

It's a glass. I can see a colorless liquid: water. I bet he's mixed something with it. Maybe the pills from my handbag. Maybe too many, an overdose. I shake my head in panic, everything about me is shaking, and the mattress swells even more. The water sloshes over the side of the glass.

"Shhh," Herr van Hoven says, switching the glass to his other hand. "Calm down."

But I don't, I continue thrashing about as far as my weak body will allow, with the result that he puts the glass down on the bedside table and grabs my upper arms.

"I told you to calm down." His eyes are in the shadows, but

I can still make out his pupils. I'm frightened by the way he's looking at me and it paralyzes my fidgeting body. "Yes," he says, "that's better."

"What happened?" I ask circumspectly, glad that the tape has now fully gone from my mouth, at least.

"You passed out," comes his reply. "But now you're awake again. Which is good, because we've got a lot to do."

"What have we got to do?"

"First you need to come to your senses fully. Here." He lets go of my arms and picks up the glass on the bedside table. I press my lips firmly when he moves it close to my mouth.

"It's only water, for God's sake, Nadja."

My lips are tightly closed. His left hand reaches for my face, squeezes my cheek as if it were soft clay and painfully forces my jaws apart. I cough when he pours the contents of the glass into my mouth with his right hand.

"That's good," he says. "Drink up to make you fit again."

"Are you going to kill me too?"

"Of course not."

"I'd like to go home. Please."

"Home," he repeats thoughtfully. "Laura told me how she took you home once when you worked together. She said there was barely any furniture in your flat, no carpet, no pictures, just white walls. As sterile as a hospital, was how she described it. Is that how you live, Nadja?"

I nod mechanically. That's how I live.

"So why do you want to go back there? It's not a real home. There's not even anyone waiting for you."

"Yes, there is." I'm nodding as if my life depended on it and maybe that's the case. "Someone is waiting. My brother has been waiting for me for twenty years. I have to go to him, today has made that clearer than ever."

"Twenty years. Then you would have had plenty of time already." The softness of his tone shocks me. He's right. I feel a warm tear run down my cheek. Wiping it away, he says, "Everything's going to be all right," and tells me he's never broken a promise. Then he gets up from the bed and goes over to the chest of drawers, where the candles have burned down to stubs. I hear rustling: a plastic bag. I crane my neck, but can't see anything as his back is blocking the view. When he turns around again, one hand is holding the wig I wore on the way here, the other a tube. I don't understand. At least not straightaway.

OCTOBER 2017

TWO YEARS EARLIER

All the employees had gathered in the staff canteen that Friday to raise a toast to Ludwig Abramczyk, who over the course of the past thirty years had turned the old boiler works in Kreuzberg into the largest and most successful law firm in Berlin—and to him: Gero van Hoven, the most worthy successor. He started as a lanky young law graduate who carried Ludwig's briefcase and made him coffee. Over time he not only became an important cog in Ludwig's machine, but a bearing axle. Eight years ago they'd toasted the fact that Gero could now call himself a partner, and today, today he was taking the final step. The prince was taking over from the old king and ascending his throne.

"I'm proud of you, my boy," Ludwig said, raising his glass to Gero who, as he returned the toast, thought of his father once more.

"Do you really want to go back to your old homeland?" he asked to distract himself. His father wasn't here to share this moment with him—of course not.

Ludwig shrugged.

"My little house in Poland, the wild forest, hunting whenever I want—I think life could be worse."

"But won't you miss anything here?"

"Oh, I will!" Ludwig laughed. "Work, of course! And so much so that I'll pop in every few days and claim it's purely coincidence. I'll tell you, Gero, and all the rest of you, too, how to do your jobs." He shook his head. "You have to know when a chapter of your life has come to an end."

"I'll come to visit you," Gero said softly. A few strange feelings had knotted in his throat, making swallowing difficult. Feelings nourished by all those years spent together and moments when Gero recognized that Ludwig was the father he'd never had.

"You certainly will," Ludwig replied with a smile, putting a hand on his shoulder. "As often as you like, my boy."

"I'm proud of you," Laura had told him earlier too, although only via WhatsApp. Vivi was ill with measles, and in any case Laura felt uncomfortable about bumping into Nadja at Ludwig's farewell. The incident two years ago had affected her permanently, which to Gero's mind wasn't all bad. Laura had understood how precious life was and how sometimes everything could turn from one moment to the next. She was the most caring mother and best wife. Now he realized he really did have it all. He'd taken over from Ludwig Abramczyk. He had a wonderful wife and a healthy two-year-old daughter. He had a beautiful home. Money. His life was perfect. Gero touched his face, felt the corner of his right eye and indeed there was a tear.

"Surely you're not going to cry." Ludwig laughed again.

"Never." Gero laughed back and swore silently to himself that he'd protect this life forever.

NADJA

I resist. Not at once, because it had to sink in first. Because my head is still porridge and far too slow. In one hand the wig, in the other the tube. Herr van Hoven put them both on the bed and sat cross-legged beside me. Then his hands came close to my head. Smoothed my hair down. It wasn't until I saw him unscrew the tube and rub the inside of the wig with a milky-white fluid that comprehension shot through my body. Now it's wriggling, thrashing and kicking, and if the wrists weren't bound it would drive its claws into Herr van Hoven's forearm and sink its teeth into his flesh. If only it had a chance, this body, just the hint of a chance.

But Herr van Hoven is stronger. Invincible. He fends me off as he attaches the wig firmly to my head. I think I can feel the sticky fluid trickling onto my scalp. Wig glue. I scream until I'm out of breath. He lets me. Watches me in silence, still smiling. When I'm finished screaming, he says, "Suits you much better."

I howl. He's mad.

"Calm, calm, Nadja," he implores.

Clearly he is mad, he's going to kill me. He's got a gun. Maybe it's still downstairs in the kitchen, or maybe it's at the back of his waistband, hidden by his shirt, like you sometimes see in films.

At any rate he's got one and he's used it once already today. He killed Laura with a single shot.

"I ought to have realized that something was up," he says, holding on tight to my body, which is still writhing. "In the past, you know, Vivi was everything to Laura. Recently she'd been taking her to my parents' more often, supposedly because she was meeting friends or going to the gym. And like an idiot I believed her. She bought new clothes and got a new haircut. She even started using perfume again. You know, you read about this sort of thing everywhere, it's in all the silly magazines. The first sign your partner's cheating on you: they take more care over their appearance and take up new hobbies. Even so, I failed to notice. I was still working like a dog, as ever, because I wanted to provide for my family. It was never about me. No one ever asked about me. About how it feels to step into the shoes of the great Ludwig Abramczyk. The pressure his successor is under. What it's like to know that more than one hundred people are my responsibility. Besides, the loan on our house is 1.3 million euros and that has to be paid off. And what does my wife do?" Full of scorn he spits out the title of Aron Bruckstätt's book of photographs: "*Places That Time Forgot . . .*"

My body goes limp in his arms. I have no strength left. I whimper.

"Why the game, Herr van Hoven? Why the trial? Your verdict was already decided. Why did I have to defend Laura?"

"Life itself is a game, Nadja, a game in which there are winners and losers. Come now, we're not finished yet." He removes the tape from my wrists and pulls me off the bed.

"What do you mean? What do you mean 'we're not finished yet'? What's going to happen now?"

All he says is, "I've found a nice place."

The "nice place" is right behind the house with a view of the over-grown stream, which looks even more mysterious in the dark of night. Where there's nobody and nothing to disturb you. Where you can listen to the whoosh of the wind and water, feel at one with nature and the cycle of life. Now, in the middle of the night, the air is clear and cool, a blessing for my sleepiness, whereas the daytime temperatures have been climbing above eighty-six degrees for weeks now. In the heat a few trees have dropped their leaves prematurely, which now cover the ground like a dark blanket. They will cover everything with a final rustle before they crumble or rot in the next long-awaited rain.

The ground is hard, the spade heavy, and my hands hurt from the rough wood of the handle. Sweat is tingling on the back of my neck and my forehead, my scalp itches beneath the fake hair, and each time I blink an image of Laura flashes behind my lids. Laura, and on top of the older brown bloodstains on her nightie, another bud in a brighter red color blossoms rapidly until the thin satin can hold no more and her blood forms a pool on the kitchen tiles. A pool that grows larger and larger, a puddle, a pond, a sea, Laura drifting on red water. Gasping, I ram the spade into the ground. Somehow my body is functioning, everything freewheeling; my head is stuffed with thoughts, too many of them, none able to stand out clearly from the others. With the last of my strength, I keep thrusting like someone obsessed with the idea of making it to the center of the earth. Or to the core of the story. Something lies buried, an image or a thought—I can't put my finger on it. I pause my shoveling and rub the back of my neck. A few paces behind me stands Herr van Hoven, brandishing the flashlight.

"Keep going."

I obey. He's mad and he's got a gun. As I thrust the spade into the earth, I can't help but wonder whose grave I'm actually digging here. Aron Bruckstätt's? Laura's? *No*, I say, giving myself the answer. If Herr van Hoven has his way, all three of us will lie buried here in the end. I dig deeper, farther down and into this strange feeling that there's something there. It's inside my head. I can practically sense myself unearthing it layer by layer, but I haven't got to it fully yet.

The hole before me is ankle-deep.

"I can't go on anymore."

"Keep digging."

Keep digging and then you're going to die, just like the others. Aron Bruckstätt, who probably just wanted to have a bit of fun. Laura, who was seeking attention and found it in the arms of another man. And finally me, Nadja Kulka, an unwanted child without a father, foster mother to my little brother, imprisoned for seven years for Marta's murder. As I play back my life I find dirt, shouting, blood and wasted chances. A flat that's not a home. A job that's nothing more than a façade to preserve the semblance of normality. I realize that I did nothing to live my life. I've only ever existed. Hidden myself. Run away from people, but most of all from myself.

"Please." I turn around and hold out one of my sore palms to Herr van Hoven. "Just five minutes' break."

He says nothing. I imagine what would happen if the gun were in his waistband. If he now reached behind and pulled it out. If it were suddenly over here and now. If this here really had been my life and I had to go to my death with the knowledge that I'd always been a coward.

Herr van Hoven moves. Bends down. Puts the flashlight on the ground. He comes up to me and reaches for the spade. Finally he says something: "Okay, give it to me. I'll have a go for a bit."

Enough. That's all I think. I've done enough suffering, enough whining. *Enough, for God's sake.* I let out a scream, I scream out the pain of the last few hours, all the pain of the last few years, and my scream tears through the silence of the night. Simultaneously the head of the spade crashes hard into Herr van Hoven's left temple. He collapses like a felled tree, like Milosz Nowak did that time in the playground. For a moment I stand there motionless. I can't do anything but stand where I am and look at him, lying there among the dried leaves and small islands of earth I heaped onto the grass while digging the grave. Blood, which in the pale torchlight looks black, runs from his temple onto the leaves, the grass. His rib cage is still. I shake myself from my paralysis. Grab the torch. Run and tug at the wig—it's stuck fast. I run around the house, ignore the fact that my head is humming again, ignore the nausea and the flashes on my retina. Across the bridge. I have to get to the car. If I'm lucky my bag will still be on the passenger seat. If I'm lucky my mobile will still be in it and I can ring the police. I'll tell them what he did. That he shot Laura and was going to kill me too. Then I'll drive into the village, look for refuge and wait for the police. I run; I can already see the Land Rover, I'm only a few meters away now, almost in safety.

I'm coming home, Janek.

A moment later the engine roars into life and the car speeds away. Behind me I hear shouting. Herr van Hoven, yelling after the car like an animal turned feral.

JULY 2019

TWO NIGHTS AGO

He drove too quickly. In the pitch-black night he had a bleary view of the road. Gero van Hoven was blinking wildly. He couldn't believe it. It couldn't be true. The phone call.

His mobile had rung shortly after midnight, waking him in his Magdeburg hotel room. After the last conference presentation, he'd wandered into the city center with a few other lawyers. Over dinner they'd drunk to their respective health.

"Hello?" he'd mumbled. Nothing initially, just a soft crackle on the line. Then a woman's voice he didn't recognize to begin with. Maybe because he wasn't fully awake, maybe because she was hysterical. It was probably a bit of both.

"Laura?" he said in his confusion, and briefly took the mobile away from his ear to check the number. It didn't ring a bell. "Laura, is that you?"

"Yes," she sobbed. And told him he had to come at once. Something dreadful had happened. She needed his help. Gero was familiar with these sorts of calls from clients and mostly they were exaggerated. This one wasn't. "I think I've killed him," she said.

"What? Who?"

"Aron . . . I'm really sorry, Gero."

Somehow he immediately knew that her apology was less for the crime she'd claimed to have committed, and more aimed at him, her husband. Perhaps the tone of voice reminded him of Lilly and how she'd sounded when admitting all those years ago that there was someone else.

"What's happened?" he growled, his teeth clenched. Something about an argument and blood, so much blood. He didn't understand any more than that at first; she was speaking so indistinctly. As if she had the hiccups, that's what it sounded like. All the same she kept trying, starting over and over again until something in him snapped and he hissed, "Shut up, now!" She yelped as if he'd kicked her. He took a deep breath and talked more softly.

"Just tell me where you are. I'll come."

Not some cheap motel. Not some shabby room with a worn, stained carpet, furniture with the varnish peeling off and bedclothes washed so many times they were thin and full of holes. Not an obvious place of disrepute. When she told him where she actually was, every bone and muscle in his body contracted until he had the momentary feeling he'd completely disintegrated.

"What should I do now?" she said, hiccuping.

"Nothing," he said. "Do absolutely nothing till I'm there, agreed?" He listened but couldn't hear anything meaningful. "Do you understand, Laura?" he asked again.

"But he—"

"I said, do you understand?" The severity in his voice really was a kick. After all, she'd been the one to kick first. She'd almost kicked him to death with her confession, leaving him lying on the ground, bleeding emotionally.

"Yes," he heard her say softly, but clearly—*that was something at least.*

"Good," he snorted. "I'm leaving now."

"Darling, I—"

After he'd hung up, the screen briefly showed the length of the call: two minutes forty-seven. It had taken two minutes forty-seven seconds to set his world on fire. Two minutes forty-seven and the promise they'd made to each other five years ago had burst as insignificantly as a gum bubble. *Two minutes forty-seven . . .* Gero shook his head in disbelief. He got dressed and stormed out of the room.

Then he drove off. Now he was sitting stiff-backed in his Porsche, digging his fingers so hard into the leather of the steering wheel that it hurt. As the car careened on a bend, he heard good old Ludwig in his head, saying, *What use is the best lawyer if he's dead?*

No use at all, Gero thought and cut his speed. Then he decided to stop altogether. He vomited right by the side of the road.

Laura and Aron.

He'd had another call from her between a couple of lectures that day. She'd decided to go out in the evening, she said, and she'd probably be late if he wanted to get hold of her. She might even stay the night with a friend. He'd only been half-listening. More important as far as he was concerned was what was happening with Vivi.

"Don't you worry; she's spending the weekend with your parents."

Gero wasn't particularly pleased by this. Vivi had been spending a lot of time with his parents recently. The only consolation was the fact that he had to admit his old man was doing a better job as a grandfather than he ever had as a father. So he'd muttered "Whatever" into the phone and politely told his wife he hoped she had a nice evening.

He was feeling better now; his stomach had settled. Gero took a handkerchief from his jacket and wiped his mouth. Then he leaned against the hood, took a deep breath as if to revive himself, and gazed up at the sky. The moon looked like a nipped-off thumbnail. Around it sat stars, millions of speckles. Gero tried to think when he'd last paid attention to the stars. Had he ever been someone who'd found beauty and significance in them? Probably not. He'd overlooked things. He'd overlooked his wife slipping from his grasp. They'd been happy, hadn't they? Didn't they have it all? . . . *Pull yourself together*, he urged himself, before getting back into the car and driving off. Ahead lay the cold, black horizon. Gero tried unsuccessfully to follow its example. Instead another thought had taken root.

What if . . . ?

His head was buzzing. A vague feeling that something wasn't quite right had lodged in the back of his neck. He tried to picture Laura, sweet, gentle Laura, attacking a fully grown man. One moment she was holding a kitchen knife, the next a hunting rifle. He saw a vase breaking on a skull, he saw the skull gape open. But whichever scenario he let play out in his mind, the man who died didn't have Aron Bruckstätt's face. Each time it was his, Gero's.

And now he knew. All of a sudden it was no longer a vague,

twisted feeling. He'd seen through it all. A trap. A plan. There was no dead lover. Laura's call was merely a dramatic excuse to lure him home. He was the one who was to die tonight. She wanted to get rid of him because he was standing in the way of her happiness. She'd decided he had to die.

NADJA

I knocked him down with the spade. He was lying there on the ground, beside the half-dug grave, not moving. I ran around the house, across the bridge; I could already see the car. I stopped abruptly. First it was just the taillights of the Land Rover that suddenly lit up. The next moment the engine roared to life and the car raced off. Without me.

Suddenly there was shouting in the distance. Herr van Hoven running and yelling after the car. He ran past me, waving his arms about, cursing, shouting.

"Laura!" he screamed.

"Laura!" he now screams once more, and up ahead the car comes to a stop.

I'm dreaming.

It's just my addled mind, which has had too much to cope with over the past twenty-four hours. The crazy girl who twenty years ago failed to see copious amounts of her mother's blood is now seeing a ghost. Laura getting out of the Land Rover. Laura who's nothing more than a vision, like Marta drifting on the red water in my dreams. Laura who can't be anything *but* a vision.

"For Christ's sake, Laura!" Herr van Hoven, bearing down on her, grabbing her by the arm, shaking her.

Laura, who is real.

The realization whacks hard into the back of my knees; I drop the torch and collapse to the ground. Stare with wide eyes. I can just make out Herr van Hoven's voice; it sounds gruff. "Have you gone mad? Where do you think you're going?"

I can't hear what she says in reply as it's about fifty meters between me and the car. All I see is her knock his hand from her arm and gesture to him. He then nods toward the house. In my direction. I try to get to my feet, but the full force of the realization has broken my legs. I can't move.

Laura.

Laura, who's no longer wearing the bloodstained nightie, but trousers and a light-colored shirt. Laura, who's alive. For a second I feel the relief of the most stupid idiot on the planet. The shot I heard was probably just a warning. Herr van Hoven trying to intimidate her. Afterward he locked her in a room like me and kept up the delusion that he'd killed her because he was trying to intimidate me too. Finally, as he stood by the grave with me, she made a miraculous escape.

A second later, even the most stupid idiot on the planet realizes that Laura wouldn't have stopped the car if she were actually trying to escape. She would have let her husband run, wave his arms and yell all he liked, but would have driven off as quickly as possible and as far away as possible. What's more, once she'd spotted me in the rearview mirror she would have opened the car door and helped me escape too. I become aware that my mouth is opening as if to scream, but instead starts to retch. Everything is spinning and all reason is falling apart.

Life itself is a game, Nadja, he said earlier up in the bedroom.

I sense that I've lost, only I don't understand. I don't understand any of it.

Herr van Hoven points at me and their footsteps speed up in my direction.

Stand up, I bark silently at myself. *Run!*

Run! Janek's voice barks inside my head too.

I can't. I'm paralyzed. I topple over the white cliffs, but I don't scream, nor do I ever hit the bottom. I just fall, I fall forever. Time doesn't exist anymore. Nothing exists anymore, it's over.

They come, they're here. They stand on either side behind me, pull me to my feet and drag me back into the house, into the kitchen. Herr van Hoven maneuvers me back onto my regular place on the bench.

"Why am I really here?"

Without giving me an answer, they sit down too, Herr van Hoven opposite and Laura on the chair to my left. The same arrangement as during our mock trial earlier.

"This is about Aron Bruckstätt, isn't it?"

Still they say nothing. Laura, head bowed, removes the hairband from her plait and then takes off the Alice band. Now she's got a blond bob that comes down to her chin and a fringe. Instinctively I feel for the wig stuck on my head.

And finally I understand.

JULY 2019

TWO NIGHTS AGO

Not wanting to risk the noise of the engine announcing his arrival, he parked the Porsche a good two hundred meters away, on the next corner. He thought of the wooden box he kept on the top shelf of his wardrobe, behind some old sweatshirts he claimed he was keeping for gardening. The wooden box lacquered with a dark varnish and faded golden letters that read *Mémoires*. It was the sort of box you kept things in you no longer needed, but couldn't throw away. Photographs, shells from the last beach holiday, postcards, old tickets to important events you'd felt proud to have been invited to. Or even the .22 that Ludwig had given him after he'd once been attacked by a male boar on one of their hunting trips, the shot from his rifle having only grazed the beast. An old, but fully functioning gun that Gero would have liked to have in his waistband right now. Only he had to go inside the house to lay his hands on it. *His home.* He couldn't seriously believe that Laura had the audacity to desecrate this place with her grubby fling. *His home.* In the drive was her Mini Cabrio with Vivi's chair fixed in the passenger seat as ever. Gero felt the artery in his neck throbbing. But he couldn't see Aron's old Land Rover. Like Gero, he must have parked it away from the house to avoid being seen by nosy neighbors. *By witnesses.*

Gero took the path to the Grunewald. He would approach his house from the rear and not, as they'd no doubt planned, straight through the front door and into their trap. At this time of night the lights in the park had already been switched off, but as a hunter he didn't find it difficult to move around in the dark so long as he focused on precisely that: hunting. He mustn't be tempted to ask himself whether he was capable of killing Laura if his suspicions proved correct. He would imagine he was shooting a beast, and if all this were true, if it were really as he feared, then Aron and Laura were nothing more than that: beasts. Crazy, sick, rabid animals the world had to be rid of. Sometimes three were two too many. *No*, he thought, *no doubts.* Just act, show resolve. Once you had doubts, you were doomed.

Like that boy, Hannes Liewert, the pitiful, unlucky fellow who'd unintentionally become Nelly Schütt's killer. Gero had sent him home, given him a second chance. And how had Hannes made use of this chance? He hadn't. Instead of simply turning down Gero's generous offer and continuing to insist on Heger's innocence, the boy had plodded back to his village like a meek sheep and just vegetated there. Until this May, five years to the day that Nelly Schütt died, he was found in his parents' garden hanging from the branch of a tree. He'd always been a sensitive soul and had never got over the death of his first love, his mother was quoted in the newspaper as having said. Apparently in his heartache he'd even dreamed up morbid fantasies and started hearing Nelly's voice. *Idiot.* At least he hadn't left behind a suicide note stating that Gero had prevented him from handing himself in after Heger's conviction.

No doubts, Gero thought once more. Behind the beech hedge separating their property from the park he stopped for a moment, like a long-distance runner needing to catch his breath. Or someone sensing this might be the last chance to change their mind before events snowballed. He allowed himself a glance at the black sky, across which gray strands of cloud, illuminated by the moonlight, passed in quick succession. A storm was brewing. In the ripples of cloud a good-night story was being acted out, images from different, happy times. Laura, him and their first kiss. Laura, him and their first Christmas together, stomping hand in hand through the white cotton-wool landscape, her wearing his hat that was much too big and continually falling over her eyes. Laura sitting on the edge of the bath holding the little plastic stick with two blue lines in the panel, first crying in despair, then for joy after he kneeled before her, pushed up her sweater and kissed her belly. He shook his head. Let these images be torn away by the storm; as far as he was concerned, it couldn't be violent enough.

No doubts, Gero told himself for the third time.

He carefully opened the garden gate and crept up on the house. Light. He saw it coming from behind the drawn curtains in the living room. Movement behind them. As in shadow puppetry, a dark silhouette scurried across the pale curtain material, first from right to left, then from left to right. *They're expecting me.* He tiptoed over to the back door and pressed the handle; his luck was in. As ever, Laura had forgotten to lock it. Before him lay the darkness of the hallway that led to the bedroom. He listened out, but heard nothing, so went into the bedroom, took the .22 from its box and left the room. He was ready. Gripping the pistol tightly, he moved silently down the corridor, past the kitchen and into the yellow shaft of light that slanted through the entrance to the living room and landed at his feet.

There she was, her back turned to him. She was wearing a nightie. And he saw him too, Aron Bruckstätt. His rival, who didn't have a hope.

Laura van Hoven was inexperienced when it came to death. The few people she'd lost in her life had either been old or not close enough for their passing to have seriously upset her.

Her first vague memory was of a great-aunt's funeral. She remembered holding her mother's hand as a coffin decorated with lilies was lowered into the ground. Laura's mother had sobbed so much that her entire body seemed to vibrate. Laura had sobbed too, not because of the great-aunt, whose name she didn't even know, but because it felt bad when Mama cried. She remembered people dressed in black and an unfamiliar living room into which the funeral procession shuffled after the cemetery. There was coffee, cake and apple juice, and a photo album was passed around. Laura sat in her dark-blue dress on a thick carpet, playing with a dachshund. Mama had refused to buy her a black dress too, as if she were determined to prevent the adults' grief from spilling over too much onto her little girl. Laura also remembered people telling her lots of things about heaven, even though she hadn't asked any questions about it. They assured her that people had a better time in heaven. In heaven, they said, there wasn't any pain, hunger or thirst—nothing to torment you anymore. Heaven was a kind of wonderful garden where the sun always shone. But no matter how much she loved fairy tales and stories, Laura thought this was totally absurd. How could flowers grow on clouds? And how were people supposed to sleep up there if the sun shone all the time and it was never night? Because nobody was able to give her a satisfactory explanation, she decided to keep playing with the dachshund. Later, when they were back home, her mother wanted to talk to her about death again. Probably in an attempt to allay a fear she didn't feel. But that's what good mums were like, wasn't it? They thought ahead, sometimes a bit too far ahead. She held Laura in her arms and Laura listened, because it felt nice in Mama's arms. Mama said that when you died your life played out again in front of your eyes, like a film rewinding. You saw again the faces of your favorite people. You saw all the lovely places you'd been and the great moments you'd experienced. Maybe the wasted opportunities too. Those things that could also have been lovely and great if you'd been more courageous. *Or more careful.*

And that's what it's really like, Laura thought now, thirty years later. *Yes, that's exactly what it's like.*

The first thing that came to her mind was her daughter's face. That pretty little face with the pudgy cheeks, cute snub nose, fine light eyebrows, blue button eyes and heart-shaped mouth. In the past Laura often used to slip into the nursery at night, sit on the edge of the bed and gaze in silent awe at this tiny, extraordinary miracle that she and Gero had created. *In the past . . .* when Laura still jumped in puddles with Vivi and crawled through the grass without caring whether she got dirty. When she fought space battles with Vivi as if her life really were at stake. When she sank, rasping, to the ground, her palms clutching her chest in the spot she'd been hit by the lightsaber, then lay there, eyes closed and tongue lolling out to one side because she knew it would make her daughter laugh. *In the past.* That couldn't be so long ago and yet it felt like an eternity. When had all of this become unimportant?

Now she realized she'd never sit on the edge of Vivi's bed again, hadn't spent nearly long enough gazing at her daughter, and far too seldom got dirty in muddy water or died in space battles. She thought of Gero too and suddenly, unexpectedly, she knew she hadn't looked at or loved him enough. No matter how alienated she'd felt recently, it was now that the feeling returned.

Yes, it was true. At the moment of death you saw your life again, and perhaps differently too. And this, even though it wasn't Laura herself who was dying. Laura was just watching. Laura was responsible.

She looked down at Aron Bruckstätt's body, which lay motionless on the white marble. She hadn't just destroyed his life; she'd brought misfortune on them all. She'd screamed when this dawned on her, not stopping until the yelling made her sick. Then, rummaging around in her bag for her mobile, she'd found the prepaid one which was meant only for communication between Aron and her, and rung Gero, who she was now waiting for. She'd briefly considered waiting outside the house so she'd hear him the moment his Porsche drew up. But she was cowed by the thought of the darkness outside, the black, accusing night. So she suffered being in the same room with the man who was no longer Aron, but just a lump of dead flesh.

Suddenly, Laura heard a clearing of the throat and she whipped around. Gero was standing in the entrance to the kitchen. "Oh God," she sighed, hurrying over and pressing herself to his body, urging him to hug her and for this hug to make everything all right again, somehow.

Gero stiffened. Looked down at her. Her white nightie was soaked in Aron's blood. Mortified, she threw her arms around his torso, to hide not just the blood, but her nakedness too. The expression on his face remained severe; her husband was made of stone. Panting, she staggered backward. Her husband was made of stone and he was holding a pistol.

"Surely you're not . . ." she begged, throwing her hands up to pacify him.

"Give me one good reason why I shouldn't." He lunged forward and grabbed her. "Why not?"

Without waiting for an answer he slapped her face. The force of it knocked her to the floor and she let out a cry. Again he made to hit her, but stopped in midmovement. Simultaneously their eyes darted to the opposite corner of the living room. To Aron Bruckstätt, who was lying on the floor and had just let out a quiet, but clearly audible "Help!"

NADJA

I was stupid to scream. A stupid, stupid, useless brat. It's what Marta said, what many people in Zabrew said about me. Now I know they were right, all of them were right.

It's here. What I'd sensed was buried. The moment Laura shook her hair was evidently the last invisible thrust of the spade it needed inside my head. It's here, only too late—it always comes too late for the stupid, the losers.

Time no longer exists.

I'm somewhere that time forgot.

"He lived here, didn't he?"

I remember. My fleeting glance into the living room when Herr van Hoven led me down the stairs this afternoon to the kitchen for Laura's trial. What I saw was the back of a leather sofa, a standard lamp with a semicircular metal shade and curved arm that looked like an oversized flower stem, and a bookcase that was empty apart from one compartment. And this compartment housed multiple copies of the same book. A thick book, a book of photographs, and on its spine the title in bold letters: *Places That Time Forgot.*

"No," Laura says softly, without looking me in the eye. "He

lived in Berlin, in a flat on Potsdamer Platz. But he inherited this place. After his grandmother's death Gero helped him clear it and rip out half of the kitchen. Aron was planning to move in; he loved this house. When I asked him which place in his book had impressed him the most, he said: *The Spreewald. Where my grandmother's house is.* He asked me if I'd like to come here with him one day." She smiles sadly.

"They were here a few times," Herr van Hoven says, and Laura's smile becomes distorted.

I nod, then pull pointedly on a strand of my fake blonde hair.

"And going by appearances, he could have met me too, couldn't he?"

Herr van Hoven nods as well.

"All the witnesses who might have seen Laura and him together will remember a woman with blond hair and a fringe. The drinkers in the truckers' pub, Aron's neighbors, one or other of the people here."

"Just like the guy at the petrol station this morning," I add listlessly. "So, I was on my way to our supposed love nest. Only thing is, his wife wrote down the registration number of *your* car."

I look at Laura, a brief moment of triumph until she points out that the car I drove here from Berlin was Aron Bruckstätt's Land Rover. Aron Bruckstätt's car with my fingerprints all over it.

"The police will question us too, of course," Herr van Hoven says. "And we'll tell them that you'd always been a bit obsessed with Laura. A few years ago you almost abducted her child. So nobody will be surprised that you bought a wig resembling her hairstyle. Nor, more important, that you went for a man she knew. I mean, you always wanted to be like her, didn't you?" I grab my throat as I feel an invisible noose tightening with every word. "Besides, in your flat they'll find a red dress and a few of Aron's personal effects." He gets up. "Now I'm going to fetch the body from the trunk."

"Because I killed him here, I assume."

"Correct."

I shake my head. Think of the bucket and sponge I used to scrub the van Hovens' living room floor. I think too of the knife block in Laura's kitchen, another detail buried. I'd presumed the one empty slot in the block was where the murder weapon had been, but I failed to notice that Laura was cutting up the tomatoes with a knife from the block. I thought of how she'd asked me to cut up the meat and told me exactly which knife to use. Like hell she'd hidden the knife under a compost bag in the shed.

"I was holding the murder weapon, wasn't I?"

"Correct."

"And I assume you brought it here?" Just as they'd brought the bucket and sponge, and would place them here in the house. "But they won't find any traces of blood here."

Herr van Hoven, who's now standing by the kitchen door, says, "Of course you gave the place a thorough clean to cover your traces. We've brought along a few detergents from your flat. You're a cleaning obsessive, which is very handy—you know how to be thorough. You'll even put Aron Bruckstätt's body in the bath and give it a good shower to remove all traces of you. Which is a bit of a shame, but a necessary evil in view of the fact that Laura and I had contact with the body too. So we'd rather do without traces of you than run the risk of them finding traces of us too." He looks up at the ceiling. "Although the bathroom's on the first floor, you're strong enough to haul him upstairs. After all, when you were fifteen you managed to drag your mother's body—how much did she weigh?—the length of your flat, so no doubt you'll manage this too. What a nice coincidence that she lay dead in the bath as well, eh?"

I pant.

"How . . . ?"

"How do I know the stuff about your mother? From Ludwig, of course."

"He'd never have—"

"Oh, he did. Otherwise I wouldn't have known."

I feel myself open and close my mouth a few times before the next words come out.

"But they'll also find traces of you and Laura here in the house. Here in the kitchen, upstairs in the bedroom—"

"Of course," he interrupts me and laughs. "Don't forget we helped Aron clear the house and rip out the kitchen." He leaves the room.

"I'm sorry, Nadja." Laura's voice sounds gentle, whereas mine is croaky from the invisible noose choking my neck when I say, "Spare me your sympathy."

"You should have left when I showed you Aron's body. Or called the police."

"Of course. How stupid of me to want to help you."

"Nobody forced you to. On the contrary. You really insisted."

I look at her incredulously.

"You were my friend, Laura!"

Her head twitches.

"There's no other way. You yourself put it in a nutshell: I can't go to prison because I've got a daughter to look after."

I can't believe that now my own words are tightening the invisible noose around my neck. I can barely breathe.

"Why did you have to get me mixed up in this in the first place? Why didn't you just get rid of the body?"

Laura looks at me sympathetically.

"Because ninety-five percent of all dead bodies eventually turn up again somewhere."

"You didn't want to run any unnecessary risks." I wipe my eyes and sniff. "Let me guess what the final stage of your plan looks like: the crazed killer is found dead too." How could it work any other way? They can't allow me to survive and make a statement which will send them precisely where they don't wish to go: prison. "How am I to die, Laura? Do I kill myself overdosing on my own pills?"

She shakes her head and looks seriously surprised.

"Of course not. When you've killed him, you ring Gero and ask desperately for help."

I have to laugh.

"And what is that help supposed to look like?"

"Nadja," is all Laura says, and along with my name my death sentence hangs unspoken in the air.

JULY 2019

TWO NIGHTS AGO

"He's still alive!" Laura van Hoven began to tremble as if in a flash her entire body had been covered in a thin layer of ice. "He's alive, Gero!" She got to Aron Bruckstätt first; Gero followed a moment later. Both of them were now standing over him. He'd opened his eyes and one hand was moving feebly in the air.

"Help!" he said again as he looked at his hand. When he saw it was full of blood his eyeballs rolled.

Laura looked at Gero. She was expecting him to kneel beside Aron, but he remained on his feet so she did the same. She whispered, "We need to call an—"

"How did it happen?" he interrupted, his eyes not moving from the bloodied man lying on the floor, who started writhing in pain.

"What?"

"Tell me how this happened."

"We . . . we had an argument," she said hesitantly, unsure of how to go on.

"Help me," Aron gasped, undertaking fruitless attempts to sit up. But Gero made no move to help him.

"I told him I was going to finish our affair. Because of you. I told him I loved you and no one else. He got furious and came rushing at me. I fled to the kitchen and the first thing I saw was the knife block." She tried to ignore Aron's eyes growing bigger with every sentence she uttered; now they almost seemed to be bursting from their sockets.

"Is that what you want, Laura?" It didn't sound like a question, nor did Gero's voice seem to contain the slightest emotion. He didn't even look at her; his gaze was still fixed on Aron. Who was in urgent need of help. Who was silently imploring them to do something, call an ambulance. "Do you want to be with me? Love me and nobody else? Just as we promised each other on our wedding day?"

"Yes," Laura said, nodding energetically. "That's right. I don't want anything else until death do us part."

Only now did Gero take his eyes off Aron and look at her.

"You'll forgive me if right at this moment I have serious doubts about your love."

"I know."

Without another word Gero slid the pistol, which was still in his hand, into his waistband. He left the living room and a moment later Laura heard him turn on the tap in the kitchen. From the sounds that followed she concluded he was making coffee. Laura looked down at Aron, who was shaking his head as best he could given the severity of his injuries. "Laura," he begged in a whisper. "Laura," when she bent down to pick up the knife that lay on the floor a few meters away. "Laura," when she raised it aloft. "Laura," when she kneeled over him, and again "Laura"—one very last time.

NADJA

"Did your husband tell you?"

"What?"

"What happened to my mother."

Laura doesn't answer.

"Of course he did. That's why you chose me to be your scape-goat, isn't it?"

She still says nothing.

"But did he also tell you that there was no conclusive proof at the time? Clues, yes, but no proof. I was put under pressure to confess and in the end that's exactly what I did, I confessed to killing my own mother. I was fifteen years old and terrified. Not just because Uncle Fedor, the officer investigating the case, was known to be a very violent man. All I wanted was to spare my brother the sight of our family being dragged further through the dirt. I wanted him at least to have the possibility of a normal life."
I recall the moment in my cell when Uncle Adwo let the cement dust trickle through his fingers and I thought of sand on the beach. The moment when I decided to give up my fight. Against the people who'd never seen anything good in me anyway. And especially against Uncle Fedor, who had the upper hand and was

determined to see me convicted as Marta's killer at any price. If necessary, I expect he would have fabricated more evidence to reach his goal. I would have lost one way or another. I'd only have protracted the inevitable, painfully so, and Janek would have suffered. There's much I regret, but not the decision I took at that moment in the cell. "I did it for my brother," I conclude firmly. And something happens. Laura's shoulders start twitching, barely noticeably: she's trembling. I sense her uncertainty; it's like a revelation, a tiny hole in the van Hovens' net and Laura is a loose thread. She's afraid. She's a coward. I think of how she tried to escape earlier in Aron's Land Rover after she must have seen me knock Herr van Hoven down with the spade. She would have simply left her husband lying there. She didn't even check to see if he was really dead or still alive.

"Oh, so that part of my story is new to you," I assert. "You didn't know I spent seven years locked up for a crime I might not have committed. And now I'm to die for another murder I had nothing to do with."

Laura is shaking more visibly now and her face is pale.

"What was that shot I heard this afternoon?" I ask. "Were you just trying to scare me, or were you fighting over the gun because you weren't in agreement?"

She just shakes.

"Maybe you really did intend calling the police when you picked up his mobile as he was dancing with me." I lean a little further across the table. "What's happening here is wrong. You know that."

Finally she opens her mouth.

"Everything you did, everything that brought you here, happened of your own free will."

"But I won't die willingly, you can be sure of that. Always bear that in mind, especially all those times you're feeling particularly happy. When you're sitting in your beautiful, expensive house watching your little girl play. When you go on holiday, visiting all those places I'll never see. At every delicious meal and every glass of wine—"

"Quiet!"

"That's how guilt works, Laura."

"I told you to be quiet!"

"You'll carry it within you like an incurable disease, like a tumor growing inside you until one day it's eaten you up completely."

For a moment she looks as if she's going to pounce on me, but the moment passes and Laura stays where she is, limp-shouldered and slumped on her chair as if she'd been beaten up.

The front door. Herr van Hoven is back; I hear him panting.

"You'll never forget me," I whisper to Laura.

"Gero!" she cries, leaping up so abruptly that her chair almost topples over. She manages to catch it just in time. I can hear a thud in the hallway; it must be Aron Bruckstätt's dead body that Herr van Hoven has rudely dropped on the floor.

"You'll think about me for the rest of your life."

"What's wrong?" Herr van Hoven says, standing in the kitchen door.

"Laura's no longer sure that your plan's such a good idea," I translate before she can say anything herself. Herr van Hoven looks confused. When I see the wound on the side of his head I have to smile. I did that. I can see that my smile unsettles him even more. His eyes twitch and his hand unconsciously moves to the spot. He grimaces briefly when the pain flares up as he touches the wound.

"Don't make things more difficult for us all, Nadja," he says finally. "It'll be over soon," he says, making to leave the kitchen.

"Gero!" Laura says, her eyes wide. I presume she wants to ask him not to leave her alone with me again, only she doesn't want to spell it out in my presence.

"Sit back down, Laura." He sounds annoyed. "I need to take him up to the bathroom now and get everything ready. We don't have much time left," he says as he goes.

Until I die, I add in my thoughts.

JULY 2019

YESTERDAY MORNING

Laura van Hoven was tired. Her head was buzzing and every artery throbbing. It was six o'clock in the morning. She stood at the kitchen sink, showered and in her tracksuit, holding the knife beneath the jet of water and trying not to look at the streaks of red dancing in the plughole. Gero had just left to drive back to Magdeburg, a necessary move if they wanted to preserve the semblance of normality.

Last night.

"Until death do us part," she'd said, repeating her wedding vow before dropping the knife in the entrance to the kitchen and collapsing. Flinging the spoon he'd just used for the coffee onto the work surface, Gero rushed over to her. He grabbed her beneath the armpits, pulled her weak body into his arms and covered her head with kisses. Thus they sat, on the floor, clasping each other and weeping. As horrific and final as this moment seemed to Laura, she didn't want it to pass. It was Gero who brought it to an end by saying, "Now we have to think."

Like a caged tiger he proceeded to prowl around the house, a sight that in a different way bothered her as much as the lump of dead flesh on the living room floor, the dead flesh who had once been her lover. She was desperate to know what he was thinking, but she realized there was no point in asking. He had to come up with the solution. He was the one who would take the decisions and make everything right again, as ever. *As in the past.* After all, that was why she'd first fallen in love with him. She'd been the daughter of a single mother; her parents had divorced when she was young. Whereas her father with his second wife and her new half siblings only played a walk-on role in her life, and without much enthusiasm, everything else was on her mother's shoulders. To pay the rent she worked overtime as a nurse; she helped Laura with her homework, read to her and did her plaits. A good, self-sacrificing mother, who she often heard crying at night because it was all simply too much to cope with alone. Laura realized early on that she didn't want a life like that. She wanted a husband she could rely on, who would relieve the burden when she didn't have the strength to do something herself, and who would look after her. A man like Gero. How could she have forgotten all of this and risked everything so frivolously? Laura tortured herself as she watched him pace around the living room, lost in thought. She heard him speak. Say that the risk of calling the police and insisting it had been a tragic accident was too big. Even if he defended her—and of course he would—it would still come down to manslaughter and thus five years in prison, in the best-case scenario.

"You couldn't defend me on the grounds of bias," Laura said.

"Yes, I could," he said, nodding. "It would be permissible. It might not be advisable in every case, because personal feelings often cloud objectivity. On the other hand, I am a lawyer and so I automatically take my client's side whether I'm related to them or not. There would only be a problem if I were the presiding judge and had to give a verdict on my own wife. Then I'd be excluded from the trial on the grounds of bias." He sighed. "But that's not our problem, Laura. Our problem is the five years. Five years at least."

"No," was all she said. Vivi couldn't do without her for five years, and then there was prison. Laura in prison, Laura locked away in one of those miserable hunks of concrete. She'd wither like a neglected plant. She wasn't particularly tough—not like a dandelion that pushes its way unperturbed through any soil and can be ripped out again and again, but still takes advantage of the tiniest crack to force its way back up to the light. Laura was an orchid. Elegant, sensitive, demanding and high-maintenance.

"I can't go to prison."

"I know that," Gero said, rubbing his brow. "And you don't have to, either."

Then he contemplated getting rid of Aron's body, but only briefly because he knew the stats. "Ninety-five percent of all dead bodies eventually turn up again somewhere." And seeing how precise and accurate forensic analysis was these days, such a plan would in all likelihood end in the same place: prison, for both of them, for now he was an accessory. Vivi would no longer have any parents.

"No," Laura bawled. "No way. No prison."

"I told you, you're not going to prison." He sounded surly—she tried not to hold it against him as it was only because of her that he was in this position.

"I'm really sorry." She took her hands from her face. "I'm really, really sorry."

"Stop."

She couldn't. She cried and screamed. She couldn't go to prison; it was no place for her. She was a perfectly normal person, a mother, a wife. She'd never done anything wrong in her life, not even steal a sweet as a child or get a parking ticket as an adult. She wasn't like the real murderers, the mad people of this world, the deranged, the malicious, the psychopaths, the Nadjas, the—

"Wait a moment," Gero said, raising his hand for her to be quiet.

He thought out loud.

A murder had been committed and it couldn't be undone. Or could it? What if this murder were to happen again, but differently? Under different circumstances with a different killer. Someone who would certainly be thought capable of such a crime. Someone who'd already committed such a crime before. A madwoman, a deranged woman—a Nadja. What if it wasn't Laura who'd been Aron Bruckstätt's lover and killer, but Nadja?

"What if we simply give her your role?"

To begin with Laura thought he was joking. Not a good joke, either, of course. He was letting his imagination run riot, as often happened when people were put off their stride by sheer desperation. But it seemed as if Gero was dead serious.

"Aron's death is an incontrovertible fact," he said. "Everything else we can twist. Who do you think deserves prison more? You or Nadja?" Laura remembered how a few years back Gero had found Nadja on the roof with Vivi. The horror she'd felt at Vivi's disappearance. For which Nadja was to blame. Afterward she'd often wondered what might have happened if Gero hadn't gone up to the roof in time. And she'd hated Nadja.

"Nadja."

"I think so too," Gero said, getting the ball of his plan rolling. If they wanted to serve the police with a different set of events, then Aron Bruckstätt must not have died in the van Hovens' house. Aron's flat was out of the question too—trying to smuggle his corpse unnoticed into a multistory building with more than two hundred residents would be a futile undertaking.

"The house!" Laura remembered. "The house in the Spreewald!" Aron had taken her there a few times, the last occasion being two weeks ago when her husband had been off hunting for the weekend with Ludwig in Poland.

"Very good," Gero said, sounding like a teacher commending a pupil who's surprisingly come up with the right answer. In the version he was now fabricating, Laura had inherited the house rather than Aron.

"Nadja mustn't be able to make any connection between Aron and the house," he said. "She mustn't become at all suspicious . . ."

Five past six. Laura turned off the tap. She briskly rubbed the stainless-steel handle of the knife with some kitchen paper. She shook the blade dry rather than polish it, as it would be handy if forensics later found faint traces of Aron's blood still on it. Then she put the knife back in its slit in the wooden block. She'd have to ensure it was covered in Nadja's fingerprints, then plant it in the Spreewald house. Laura would dispose of the block with the other knives so the police investigation wouldn't be able to establish that the murder weapon had actually belonged to the van Hovens. She checked the time again. As soon as the shops opened she'd go into town and buy a wig. "With cash," as Gero had impressed on her.

They'd hit on the idea of the wig after realizing that no matter how hard Laura had tried to keep the affair a secret, she would definitely have been spotted with Aron at some point over the past few months. By the drinkers in a truckers' pub. By the waiting staff in a Potsdam café where they'd met once. By a ferryman in the Spreewald, with whom they'd taken a romantic barge trip only a couple of weeks ago—and probably by plenty of other people she couldn't immediately recall.

"They must believe they saw Nadja instead of you," Gero said. "So we have to ensure that Nadja looks like you." He poked his finger excitedly in the air. "You've got to buy a top—one with a really striking design!" Laura nodded knowingly. In psychology this was known as the "peacock effect," based on the finding that after seeing a peacock, the human brain remembers only the feathers. In precisely the same way, they had to give Nadja striking features so that nobody would pay attention to irrelevances such as the face or height. If this worked, it wouldn't matter that Laura was shorter, her nose slightly narrower or that she had higher cheekbones than Nadja. People, potential witnesses, would focus exclusively on the hair and the eye-catching top.

Then—"And now listen very carefully!"—Laura would put on the top and drive to Aron's flat on Potsdamer Platz. She'd got the key from his coat pocket. She would give the flat a thorough clean, getting rid of all traces of her left behind over the past few months, and pack a few of his personal effects.

"And don't worry if you bump into any of the other residents. On the contrary, just imagine they're seeing Nadja rather than you. The more witnesses the better."

The clock in the kitchen now said ten past six; its ticking was loud, too loud. Laura pressed her palms against her temples.

"Help," came the voice from the living room, Aron's voice which wasn't real, which was only in her head. "Laura, help me!"

No way, it was impossible. She couldn't handle this. She couldn't cope on her own in the house with his dead body.

"Couldn't we at least take him into the garage?" she'd asked last night in the middle of Gero's deliberations, when she realized she was finding it increasingly difficult to follow his complicated plan. He'd said a decisive no. Everything—the dead body, the blood—had to stay exactly as it was. This was exactly how Nadja had to find it later; only that way would it look real.

It was real, for Christ's sake! Laura slapped her head. She had to remain lucid and not lose sight of the plan, but most of all the goal: Vivi.

Vivivivivivivivi.

She took a deep breath. So, dressed in the new T-shirt, she would drive to Aron's flat, clean and pack some of his things. Then she'd get changed again and drive to the office to perform her little act to Nadja. They hadn't seen each other for years; Laura had avoided her since the incident with Vivi. She could only hope that she'd judged Nadja correctly, that she was still lonely and pitiful and would do everything she could to be Laura's friend again. Because however she ended up doing it, she had to lure Nadja to the house in the Spreewald.

"But is it really so important that she knows about Aron and his death? I could also revive our relationship by inviting her to a girls' weekend in the Spreewald and we could secretly get the body there."

"No," Gero insisted. "She might be a sad case, but she's not stupid. Why, after all this time, would you suddenly want to make up with her? You have to stay as close to the truth as possible, that's the only way it can work. You need a common cause—the body—and a common enemy—me. Make her feel that she's having a say and don't forget she has two weak points: death and her self-doubt. Try to mirror her own story. The more she's reminded of her own life, the more willing she'll be to help you out."

Laura had looked at Gero and started crying again. All these details, this imaginary script he'd drawn up in a very short time, would now determine how the rest of her life panned out. She ran to the loo and threw up. He followed, kneeled down beside her and held her hair away from her face.

"Hey. We're doing this for our family, okay? We're doing it for our daughter and our marriage. Until death do us part. Don't forget that."

She'd nodded and kept gagging, because of what she'd done, her fear, the plan and the question of what would happen if anything went wrong. Some overlooked detail that would break her neck. What if Nadja clocked off early and wasn't at the office anymore? What if someone else at the firm got wind of Laura's visit? What if at some important moment Laura fell out of her role and simply broke down?

"It's going to be fine," Gero said, sounding like a hypnotist, "just so long as you keep focused on why you're doing it."

Nadja, he then thought out loud, must spend tomorrow night at their place. This would allow them to keep a close eye on her and prevent her from backing out. Also it would give Gero the chance to pinch Nadja's keys from her handbag and drive to her flat in Marchlewskistrasse, where he'd plant the red dress as well as some of Aron's belongings.

"And in the morning you'll make her put on the wig and the top, then you head for the Spreewald."

"How will we play it when we're there?"

"You concentrate on the first part of the plan. I'll explain everything else later. And please don't worry, okay? I've got it all under control," he replied with a smile.

A quarter past six. Laura slid to the floor with her back to the sink. She was feeling cramps in her stomach again. The pain came in thrusts, a stabbing pain. *Knife stabs.* What had she done? She'd knifed Aron one last, decisive time, to prove her love to Gero. She imagined going over to the telephone, calling the police and making a confession. It still wasn't too late. It was up to her to end this nightmare before it completely outstretched its cold, black claws and dragged them all into the abyss.

It's going to be fine, just so long as you keep focused on why you're doing it.

Laura was going to nod into thin air, but she couldn't—her neck was stiff; her entire body felt paralyzed. Gero had said he had it all under control. For some reason she couldn't put her finger on, she found this anything but comforting.

NADJA

I think of Zabrew. A summer's day. A sky that appears yellow because of the dust from the steelworks. I think of children's laughter in the yard, small hands reaching for a preserving jar on a windowsill and nimble, bare feet that dart around the next corner. I think of giggling as pointy fingers dig out stewed mirabelles while an incensed grown-up's voice thunders in the yard, complaining about their disappearance and scolding the thief. I think that nothing can reach us there, where we are. No pain, no accusations, no shouting. We have our own little world and we have each other. I think of hugs, solidarity and how we'll make our way to the seaside, hand in hand, with a jar of mirabelles and bags of determination. We can already hear the gulls; we hold our noses in the air and smell the salt, and it doesn't matter that we've only got as far as the main street and that in a few minutes' time we'll be scooped up and taken back home, because we don't know that yet, not right at this moment. I think back further, back to the beginning. To the tiny, slippery bundle in my arms and the first sight of his eyes, which doesn't fill me with fear or shame, only confidence. I think of tiny hands that grip mine tightly, uncertain, shaky legs with their little rolls of fat and his first timid attempts at walking. I think of spidery, colorful tokens of love on A4 paper, a stick-figure Nadja and a stick-figure Janek, walking together on a beach. I even think of a woman dancing around the living room, oblivious to the world, and two children joining her, dancing along with her.

And when I now sort all my memories as Cinderella does her peas, and only look at those that have landed in the pot, I know that my life hasn't been altogether bad. That I have been happy and in fact know more than just what people are capable of.

I know what love is.

And I know that it's time to make my peace. I deserve to live.

So, taking another deep breath, I lean across the table and motion to Laura to come closer.

Do you two want to play? I'll play too.

"I've got to tell someone, Laura," my hushed voice says. "I've got to get it off my chest before I die. You should know who killed my mother."

And then—I play with my toy.

My arm, which shoots forward; my hand, which grabs Laura's head. Just one determined movement with strength and without hesitation. A brief moment, just like when I ignored the dosage instructions for my pills and my head smashed on the kitchen table.

Laura's head hits the table with a thud; I hear something crack. She doesn't scream, just makes a noise. The surprise, the shock, the blood—for a few seconds it's as if she's paralyzed. Taking advantage of the opportunity, I leap from my seat and dash behind her. I yank her head back up and put my arm around her neck so it's clamped tight between my stomach and elbow. She's wheezing. I hear the water being turned off in the bathroom, then footsteps coming down the stairs. The anxiety makes my breathing shallow. This is it. One more second.

Now. Herr van Hoven enters the kitchen and immediately recoils. I can literally see the shock pump through his body. His carotid artery is throbbing. His eyes are like saucers, darting between me and Laura. I open my mouth; the supposed sacrificial lamb has something to say.

"You think it doesn't matter with someone like me. You think my past history means my life is worth nothing. Nobody's going to be surprised, are they? I'm just a killer who's murdered someone else. And you're off the hook."

Herr van Hoven clearly hasn't regained his composure yet. The sight of his wife's bloodied face makes him teeter in the doorway.

"Please," he gasps. Warm blood drips from Laura's nose onto my bent arm.

"But you know, you might be right, Herr van Hoven. Some things must just be innate. Even at school I used to beat up the strongest boys if they dared insult my family. And just because I haven't done anything like that in the past twenty years, it doesn't mean that I'm not capable of it anymore. I can easily hold my own against your wife, at any rate."

"Please, Nadja, let her go." He moves into the room very slowly. "Laura, are you okay?" In my tight grip she attempts a miserable nod.

"Sit down." I make a jerky movement. The chair scrapes, Herr van Hoven sits. I carefully remove my arm from around Laura's neck, but to be on the safe side I remain standing right behind her. She puts a hand up to her nose and screeches when she takes it away again and catches sight of the blood. *No pity*, I tell myself silently. *No pity, just as they have no pity for me.*

"Where's your gun?"

"In the living room."

"Good."

Herr van Hoven makes to get up.

"Stay right where you are."

He begins to laugh; it unsettles me.

"You don't seriously believe you can keep me at a distance with your headlock routine, do you?" And he does it: he stands up. "The wicked girl from the playground. How terribly sweet."

"Sit down!" My voice cracks and I automatically wrap my arm around Laura's neck again. She grabs it, pulls, digs her fingernails into my skin, but I don't flinch. This time, however, Herr van Hoven looks unimpressed.

"Think about it, Nadja. Everything you're about to do to Laura will only make the murder of Aron Bruckstätt more believable."

I falter. He's right and yet I can't believe that he's going to calmly watch me hurt Laura, for whom all of this has been set up. She's panting and wheezing continually. Her neck is stretched back; I can see her wide-open, terrified eyes.

He moves closer.

"It's like in the courtroom, Nadja: you have to know when you've lost."

I yank Laura up from her chair, my arm still around her neck. She is my human shield.

"Keep away from me!"

Ignoring me, he lunges toward us. At that moment I shove Laura away and she falls straight into him. Without a moment's hesitation, I rush at them, give another shove, then race out of the kitchen into the hallway. The key is still in the front door; he must have forgotten it when he dragged Aron Bruckstätt's body into the house. I have to make a decision: get the gun which he says is in the living room, or get out.

I decide.

The bunch of keys jangles wildly; the door flies open. I run, I stumble—the dark night and the uneven ground beneath my feet, the cracking of twigs. They come after me, I can hear them. My first thought is to cross the bridge to the car, in the hope that Laura left the key in the ignition. But she seems to have had the same idea and shouts, "The car, Gero!" so I double back and head into the forest, into the pitch blackness.

JULY 2019

THIS AFTERNOON

"What the hell?"

Laura van Hoven thrashed her fists against her husband's chest. To begin with he let her, but when she kept going, just kept going and wouldn't stop, he grabbed her wrists and held her tight until she tired of flailing around in his grip. He'd tricked her. He'd been playing his own game and made her his pawn, just as he had Nadja. And she hadn't realized a thing.

Everything went according to plan at first. Fred Mertens, the public prosecutor, arrived at eight o'clock on the dot to pick up Gero for their game of tennis. Originally Gero was going to spend the whole day with Mertens as an alibi and wait for Laura to ring him on Nadja's phone. It was going to be the call that Nadja had allegedly made to ask him for help. In case the police checked the connection data later on, his mobile had to be logged to a phone mast in Berlin at the time of the call. In their story, he would then hurry to the Spreewald, find Nadja and the body, and notify the police. It was important, essential even, for him to be there when the police arrived.

He'd also spent time thinking about Laura's alibi. She'd gone to his parents' with Vivi. Ever since his father was confined to a wheelchair Gero had been giving his parents generous financial support, without which they'd have had to give up their house long ago. It would be enough to remind them of this fact when asking them to confirm to the police that Laura had spent the day with them.

In the meantime, Laura was to meet Nadja at the Spreewald house. In the trunk of the Porsche she had the murder weapon, the cleaning things from yesterday and some detergents that Gero had taken from Nadja's flat last night. She would make Nadja dig the grave, covering the spade with her fingerprints. She would ensure Nadja covered the entire house with her fingerprints.

But Gero hadn't stuck to the plan. As predicted, Laura had arrived at her supposed grandmother's house long before Nadja. And she was unsuspecting when she went in. Gero, however, had interrupted the tennis game with Mertens and also made his way to the Spreewald, in Laura's Mini, arriving before her. "Hello, Laura," he said when she found him sitting in the kitchen. He'd changed the plan without telling her, and she realized at once that this couldn't be a good sign. When she saw the smug look on his face and his teeth bared like a predator, she was sure of one thing only: she had to get away, away from here and fast. She tried to escape, but he overpowered her.

"We're going to play a game now," he said, his hand over her screaming mouth. He'd hustled her into the second bedroom, forced her to take off her clothes and put on the bloodstained nightie. Then he tied her up, gagged her, locked her in the room and didn't come back for her until it was time for the trial.

"Why did you do that?" she tried to shout now, but his hand was over her mouth again.

"Be quiet, for God's sake, or she'll hear us."

She: Nadja. Nadja, who'd collapsed in the kitchen of the Spreewald house after Gero pounced on Laura because of the mobile phone. Nadja, who he'd just taken upstairs and locked in the bedroom, for the second time that day.

Laura nodded as a sign that he could take his hand from her mouth. He did.

"What was all that trial crap?" she hissed. "You really scared me!"

He jerked his head and smiled.

"That was the price I set for my help, Laura. My lawyer's fee for sparing you prison. I wanted to find out the truth. I wanted to know how it all began between you and Aron Bruckstätt."

"You could have simply asked me, yesterday, today, tomorrow, whenever." She gesticulated wildly. "Now you don't have an alibi anymore!"

"I'll think of something. You'll see, I always come up with something."

Like changing the plan and really frightening her. Laura froze.

"It's your ego, isn't it? It can't cope with the fact that I cheated on you with Aron. You wanted to torment me."

"Everything in life has its consequences."

"Then there was the dance to 'Somethin' Stupid!' I actually thought you'd gone mad."

He grinned.

"Were you really going to call the police when you grabbed my mobile from the table?"

She started trembling and stammered, "Gero . . . perhaps we ought to abort this. The whole thing has clearly got out of hand."

"What do you mean? I thought it looked authentic the way I fell on you and wrested the mobile away. Nadja was terrified for you. Now she'll do everything I ask her to." *It didn't just look authentic*, Laura corrected him in her head. *It* was *real*. The way he stood over her, looking so unfamiliar and unpredictable. The way he grabbed the mobile, twisting her wrist and pulling her to the floor. Laura thought he was about to kick her, so she curled up into a ball and shielded her face with her hands. Her fear was unfounded in the end, but that made no difference right now. She put a trembling hand on her chest.

"And I was terrified of *you*."

Gero looked unmoved. "Perhaps that's not such a bad thing, my darling. It means next time you'll think twice before cheating on me."

"You know what I did to prove my love to you." She shook her head in disbelief. Aron. He could now be lying seriously injured in intensive care after an argument that escalated. Instead he was lying in the trunk of his car, dead. For Gero.

"And I'll prove my love to you by what I'm doing here."

"Please, Gero." She pressed herself against him, threw her arms around his waist. Felt something in his waistband at the back. She knew what it was before she took hold of it and pulled it out. "You brought the gun?" She recoiled. The .22 shook.

"Give it to me." Gero wanted to take it off her.

"Why did you bring the gun?"

"Just as a precaution. Now give it to me, please."

He moved toward her; she retreated farther.

"Are you going to shoot us both? Nadja and me? Is that your new plan?"

"Nonsense. Give me the gun before something happens."

His fingers fluttered in the air. Laura pointed the gun at him. She didn't want to contemplate what he might do if he had even the slightest suspicion as to why she and Aron had got into an argument. That it had been him rather than her who'd wanted to end it. Because for him she'd never been more than his *little whore*. Something to play with for a while.

"No. We're going to finish this now. We'll call the police and tell them what happened."

"Then you'll go to prison."

"So be it. Look at us, Gero. What happened to us? What are we doing here?"

"We're saving the life we have together," he said, then made a hand movement she hadn't seen coming. The shot was fired and the bullet entered the wood of the cupboard below the sink. Laura dropped the pistol, put her hands over her ears and sank to the kitchen floor. Gero grabbed the gun.

"I love you, Laura. And because of this, you'll do what I tell you. We've almost done it, we're almost there. So now pull yourself together, for God's sake."

She looked up at him and cried. Again.

"I can't."

He helped her up from the floor.

"Yes, you can. You'll go upstairs now, get changed and just

wait. I'll check on Nadja." He stroked her bare arms. "Everything's going to be fine."

"Promise me you won't use the gun." He nodded and reminded her that he'd never broken a promise. Then he reminded her of the most important promise of all, which he'd made five years ago: "For better or for worse." Until death did them part.

NADJA

In the forest the night is shapeless. I can't run anymore, I can only advance one step at a time and with my arms outstretched. It's as if I'd been blindfolded and spun around a few times. I feel my way between obstacles, from tree trunk to tree trunk. Beneath my feet twigs snap and leaves rustle; in my ears the blood roars like a waterfall. I suppress a cry when I miss my footing and slide down a bank that ends in a canal. The water is bitterly cold and within seconds soaks my jeans up to the knees. I reach out randomly into the blackness for something to hold on to and find a tree root, which I use to pull myself up out of the water.

"Behind you!" I hear Herr van Hoven say, then more loudly, "Nadja! You must realize you won't get out of this forest!" A white dot of light is dancing around—from a flashlight or mobile phone. I use the opportunity to orient myself; I make out the shapes of the surrounding trees and keep moving on all fours.

"I'm a hunter, Nadja!"

A hunter with a gun. Who easily finds his way around, even in the darkest forest. A hunter following the tracks of his prey. Following me. Somewhere a tawny owl shrieks, waking the green woodpecker who immediately gives an angry laugh by way of an answer.

"Nadja!" Laura shouts shrilly.

I stand up. The cracking beneath my hands and knees is too loud. I stand there, perfectly still, wondering whether to get into the water where nothing rustles or breaks.

"Nadja, please! We just want to talk."

Laura's voice and the dancing light move away. I breathe. I have to get out of the forest and make it to the nearest house. I picture myself hammering on a door with my fists, begging for help. I see flashing blue lights, Laura and Herr van Hoven being led away in handcuffs, and feel a fleeting, exhausted smile flicker across my lips. I just have to get out of the forest. All of a sudden there's another crack, right behind me. As I spin around, a light flashes, blinding me. I throw my hand up to my eyes, shielding them from the dazzling light. I squint and recognize the silhouette of the hunter before me.

"I've got her, Laura!" he calls out.

Staggering backward I knock into a tree.

"Come on, Nadja, it's all over. You know you're not going to get away from here."

The light from the torch brings tears to my eyes.

"And you're not going to get away with all of this," I croak. "Even if you've spread all the traces around the house and washed the body, the forensics team will establish that Aron Bruckstätt's time of death was considerably earlier and isn't consistent with your story."

"The hot weather simply accelerated the natural process of decay," he replies, unfazed.

Another twig snaps and the flashlight moves; he steps closer.

In defense I put out my hands. I know that this is the end. It's the moment when fate makes me hear voices. Uncle Adwo, saying, *You had a second chance, Nadja. You had a second life and you didn't use it.* Aunt Evelyn: *Everyone knows what you're really like, Nadja Kulka. You're misfortune personified.* And finally Marta, who doesn't say anything, but just laughs. It's the end, I know it is—the only thing I don't know for sure is how it's going to be.

"I took the body up to the bath and washed all traces of me off it, is that right? So, what was the next thing I did according to your story?"

Herr van Hoven sighs.

"You're really stubborn, do you know that? Well . . . after you've cleaned the body you begin digging a grave. But it's too exhausting and you realize you'll never manage it. Then you're struck by the enormity of what you've done: you've killed a person. Again. In despair you ring me and ask me to come."

"Why would I do that?"

"Because I'm a lawyer and one of the few people you trust." Who's always been good to me. Who's always treated me normally and shown me photographs of Vivi.

I bawl. Think it through. It is the end and it looks like this: "You come, find the body, shoot me and claim afterward it was self-defense because I attacked you. This way you ensure I'll never be able to tell my version of the story . . ." My legs give way; I fall to the ground.

I'm so sorry, Janek.

I have to tell you something, darling. I'm the girl who's slate-gray inside.

That's rubbish. I can see inside people too and I'm sure that you're a different color.

What one?

Mirabelle yellow.

Oh, Janek . . .

But it's true. I can see it perfectly clearly. You're really yellow.

I'm afraid you were mistaken, Janek.

And Marta was right, about everything. I am what I am. And now I'm dead, probably rightly so.

JULY 2019

TONIGHT

They followed Nadja into the forest, but at some point got separated. She lost Gero, who in this environment was quicker and more agile than her, and now she's stumbling around aimlessly. Until quite recently the crack of a twig has given her the occasional clue to his position, but no matter where she points the flashlight now, the beam of light only picks out the night and black trees. And all of a sudden it's quiet, oddly and menacingly quiet. Laura van Hoven is crying. Everything has gone wrong, for fuck's sake, it's gone fucking wrong and taken on a dynamic of its own. She wishes she could turn back time to the night of Aron's death and simply call the police and an ambulance. After all, wasn't there legal mitigation for crimes of passion? And there were certainly unwritten laws of morality and conscience. Instead they'd forged their plan and were going to send an innocent woman to the gallows.

"What are we going to do with her when we've sorted out everything in the house?" she whispered to Gero the night before, while Nadja was sleeping unsuspectingly in their guest room. Laura feared the answer. Gero, who was getting dressed to drive to Nadja's flat and plant Aron's things and Laura's red dress there, gave her a puzzled look.

"What do you mean?"

Laura merely looked at her hands, which she was squeezing in her lap as she sat on their marital bed, the bed in which she and Aron had made love not twenty-four hours earlier. Only afterward did he tell her that this was the last time and he wanted to break up with her.

"You don't think I'm planning on killing her, do you?" Gero put his hoodie to one side, squatted beside the bed and took her shaking hands. "Why should she die, Laura? It's enough that nobody will believe her. In fact, it's even better, much better. She'll tell them her absurd story about what supposedly happened in the Spreewald house." A sympathetic smile flickers on his lips. "I can already see myself having a drink with Fred Mertens, shaking our heads and feeling quite upset. What a cruel system, we'll say, which, after her mother's murder, didn't pick up on how vulnerable Nadja was and give her the help she needed. But it wouldn't be the first time the system had failed, would it?"

"The police will still have to follow up on her statement," Laura insisted. "She'll send them to our house. They'll spray that—what's it called?—luminol everywhere, then wiggle their black light around and find traces of Aron's blood in our living room."

Gero shook his head.

"I bet that doesn't happen. She's just a murderer who's committed another murder. Who's also been in therapy for years.

No, Laura, believe me. Nobody will be surprised by what she's done, according to our plan. Especially not when you consider that after her mother's murder she tried to exonerate herself with the story she concocted about the last, evil punter. In vain, as we all know." He smiled again and held her hands even more tightly. "Maybe she'll be lucky and this time instead of going to prison they'll put her straight in a mental institution. Think about it—perhaps it'll even be good for her. Finally, she'd have her peace and wouldn't have to torment herself anymore trying to lead a normal life, which she'll never be able to do anyway."

Laura nodded and persuaded herself again that it was the best for everyone concerned. But now, as she's stumbling through the forest, in the knowledge that Gero has already changed the plan once, organized that dreadful courtroom charade and also brought the gun to the Spreewald house—and after Nadja's attack, which showed that she's not going to let herself be the victim that easily—Laura can only see this ending one way: if Gero finds Nadja, he's going to kill her. Why else would he have fetched the gun from the living room before pursuing her?

"Nadja!" she calls out vaguely into the darkness. "We just want to talk!" In truth these words are more a reminder to Gero: *You promised me to sort this out without using the gun. Just talking, Gero*, she implores him silently from a distance. *Encourage her to keep quiet, offer her money. Let her go home.*

Her stomach cramps with every step. This fear. Aron's death was one thing, she thinks. Stabbing him was a rash act committed in the heat of the moment. And that last thrust of the knife was sheer desperation, to avoid losing Gero too. But this here, the thing with Nadja, is premeditated, planned. Malicious through and through. And Laura suspects they've crossed a boundary. This is why she tried to escape in Aron's Land Rover after Nadja whacked Gero with the spade.

Don't kid yourself, her conscience butts in. *You wanted to leave because you were afraid for yourself. Afraid that Nadja might have killed Gero and that you'd be next. What sort of a person are you, Laura van Hoven?*

Is this how it begins? What Nadja predicted earlier at the kitchen table? *That's how guilt works, Laura. You'll carry it within you like an incurable disease, like a tumor growing inside you until one day it's eaten you up completely.*

Laura shakes her head and stumbles on.

Finally she finds Nadja and Gero, as he's explaining that her death was never part of his plan. Instead, Nadja would call Gero after killing Aron Bruckstätt and ask for help. He would race to the Spreewald, persuade her to notify the police and give her assurances that he'd stand by her. The police officers would come and arrest a mentally deranged Nadja. No, she didn't have to die—he laughs—her untrustworthiness would suffice. The untrustworthiness of a convicted killer. In the beam of her flashlight Laura sees the satisfaction on her husband's face and Nadja, who falls to the ground, crying. Maybe she's just realized that it would have been simpler to fight for her life than her reputation. Which isn't a good one. As Gero says, she's a murderer, who nobody will believe. She'll go back to prison and there's nothing she can do about it. No, not her.

"That's enough," Laura says, pointing the beam of the flashlight directly at Gero's eyes.

"Quite right, that's enough, Nadja," Gero agrees, pushing Laura's flashlight away with his hand. "Now you can decide whether you're going to call the police yourself and report your crime, or if you'd prefer me to do it for you."

"No, Gero." Laura blinds him again. "That's enough. I already told you we've gone too far."

"And I told you—"

"No," she interrupts him. "You don't understand me. I don't want to go along with this anymore. If I have to, I'll back up Nadja's absurd story."

"Laura . . ."

She shakes her head firmly, moves away from Gero and sits on the forest floor beside Nadja, who flinches when Laura takes her hand.

"Either we call the police and tell them what really happened, or you'll have to kill both of us—Nadja and me—here and now." How assured she sounds at a moment when everything seems uncertain. It's true: Gero has never broken a promise he's made to her before, and he promised not to use the gun. But now, as his face is swallowed up by the darkness and she can't make out his features, she has her doubts.

Time passes, pulling strings. He must be weighing things up in his mind. *We've got to get away*, is all Laura thinks. *We've got to get away from here before he makes his decision.* So she pulls Nadja to her feet.

"Come on, let's go."

She has to say it again before Nadja seems to understand that Laura is being serious. Guided by her flashlight, they wander hand in hand back through the forest, continually turning their heads over their shoulders in the expectation of seeing a livid

Gero storming after them, furious that Laura has come down on Nadja's side and ruined his plan. Tugging on Nadja's hand, Laura pants, "Faster!" every few meters, until they're finally running.

"Laura!" It's him. It evidently took him a while to rally, but now he is after them. The cracking of twigs beneath his rapid footsteps sounds like shots, shots that seem to come from everywhere, flying over their heads, hitting their backs. They run faster. Soon it'll be a real shot from behind that will knock them to the ground, one after the other. *Nadja*, Laura thinks. *Nadja first*. He'll want Laura to see what he's capable of. Nadja first, then her.

"Laura!" His booming voice echoes through the forest, scaring off some birds.

She trips. Nadja's grip on her hand tightens, but she tumbles, she falls. And screams. Nadja throws herself on top of her, puts her arms around her shoulders. Laura was wrong. She was the first. Not a quick death, but a painful grazing shot, to knock her down yet keep her alive so she can see what he has in store for Nadja.

Oh Gero . . . how did it come to this? What became of us and the most important promise of all?

She blinks and sees Nadja being grabbed from behind, then hurled from her field of view. Gero sinks to his knees and takes Laura in his arms.

"Laura! Oh God. Are you all right?"

Only now does she realize that it wasn't his gun which injured her, but a tree root she tripped over, and judging by the pain she's injured a rib.

She's crying. All three of them are crying. They're exhausted, almost relieved and possibly united in the thought that everything's finally over. It's come to a good end. Just for a moment they're all desperate to believe this, even though Laura knows—all of them do—that the moment won't last. For nothing is good, nothing is over. Aron Bruckstätt's corpse is still lying in the bathtub of the Spreewald house.

"Help me, please, Nadja," Laura hears Gero say as he slides his hands beneath her armpits and carefully tries to pull her up. Nadja complies with his request; at once she's there, helping him drag the injured Laura back to the house. Laura sees flashes of light explode on her retina and the pain in her ribs is relentless, causing her to gasp with every step. Her left arm is around Nadja's shoulder, her right around Gero's.

"So, what do we do now?" Nadja's quivering voice asks. Laura doesn't hear Gero's reply as the pain makes her pass out. She feels her body go limp and then nothing more.

NADJA

Laura is lying on the sofa in the living room of the Spreewald house, her eyes closed. She's not moving; it's like she's dead. I'm sitting on the armrest by her feet, unable to take my eyes off her, and I'm oddly grateful each time I see her chest move, rising and falling again at intervals that seem unbearably long. Herr van Hoven is standing with his back to me, by the bookcase, next to the compartment with Aron Bruckstätt's photo book. It's as if the room has been filled by a cold vacuum that permits no sound and swallows every feeling. I'm utterly empty too, save for the relief that washes over me when I see Laura breathe.

So, what do we do now? I asked Herr van Hoven. He still owes me an answer. I see a broken man with limp shoulders and lowered eyes. Someone who's expended all his energy on putting together a complicated thousand-piece puzzle and now, shortly before laying the final piece, I—I of all people, the piece of the puzzle that seemed to fit better than any other in his picture—have swept the entire thing from the table. Now they're scattered on the floor, all the thousand pieces, and everything has been in vain.

"Herr van Hoven . . ." I begin. My voice only slightly penetrates the vacuum, and it almost sounds as if I'm ashamed. *Of what?* my defiant mind asks. *Of having ruined his plan? Of refusing to take the blame for their crime? Of standing up for yourself for the first time ever? You are mad, Nadja Kulka. Mad and stupid.* I should get up from the sofa. Stride resolutely out of this house with my head held high. Fetch my mobile from Aron's car, call the police and an ambulance for Laura. And yet I do nothing. Nothing at all. "Laura's going to be in pain when she wakes up." I can't think of anything else to say.

Herr van Hoven turns around to me. Nods, as if he's taken a decision. I feel queasy. "I've one last job for you," he says, making it sound as if this is just a normal working day at the office, and he the man I knew as my boss for many years. As for me, I don't ask any questions. I listen to his request and at the end say, "Okay," like I used to do.

"Really?" As confident as he just sounded, now he looks surprised. "After everything . . . ?" He spares himself the rest of the sentence.

"Yes," I say. *After everything* there *is* some feeling now when I look at him, the feverish glimmer in his eyes, the faintly quivering lower lip and the hands that look stiff when he squeezes them in front of his chest. At first I think it's pity. But I'm mistaken. I can't feel pity for someone who's tried to destroy my life. It's something else, perhaps worse. It's . . . a bond. Understanding. Just as I understood Laura for being prepared to do everything to avoid losing Vivi, I now understand her husband. He wouldn't be the first person to try to sacrifice somebody else for his own crimes, or those of his wife.

Laura doesn't regain consciousness until I'm driving her Mini back into town. For most of the journey I've had to keep wiping my face, somehow overcome the tears blurring the road before my eyes.

"What's going on?" she says in shock once she's got her bearings and realized she's sitting in her car with me driving and her husband nowhere to be seen. Before I can reply, she lets out a sound that's racked with pain.

"Does it really hurt?" I ask stupidly.

Laura shakes her head insistently.

"Tell me what's going on!" Her attempt to grab the steering wheel fails because it's too painful. Or at least that's how it seems to me, because halfway across she takes her hand back and groans again.

"Calm down," I say when I realize she might think we've resumed the game, now with the twist that I'm abducting her or doing something else as part of my revenge. "I'm merely following your husband's instructions."

"What?"

I nod.

"What's happened to him? What's happened to Gero?"

"He stayed in the Spreewald house. He said . . ."

. . . Do you know what, Nadja? Even when I was a child I knew that if I were ever blessed with a proper family of my own I'd do everything I possibly could to protect them. I never wanted to be like my father, and I never wanted a wife like my mother—both of them so painfully fickle and ignorant. Instead I vowed to Laura on our wedding day to stand by her for better or for worse, and when Vivi was born I swore to her that for the rest of my life I'd be the father I'd always wanted. Doing everything I had to do, even if it cost me my own life . . .

"No! No, no, no!" Laura starts to panic and wriggle in the passenger seat. I hear the click of her belt.

"Laura," I say. My voice is carried by a peculiar serenity that fills my insides. I wonder whether I really have put all of it behind me, this day and everything before it. But I suspect that can't be true. That I'm probably just too exhausted for a spectacular outburst. Or perhaps it's that feeling. *The bond*. I steer the Mini to the side of the road and reach across Laura's trembling chest for the seat belt to secure her in again. "I had to promise him that we'd do everything exactly as he told me to . . ."

. . . I'm a lawyer. For almost twenty years now, my life has consisted of talking. I talk to judges and public prosecutors, I talk to clients, talk through things with them, talk them out of things or talk them into things. And even the promises I gave to my family are ultimately just words. Meaningless words if they're not followed up by deeds. The right deeds. But for that I need your help. Take Laura home and call an ambulance. Pretend to be Laura and tell them you tripped on one of the living room steps and injured your ribs. It's important you've gone by the time the ambulance gets there. Just go home and have a nice long sleep . . .

Laura is crying the silent tears that I'd run out of during the last stretch of the journey. Herr van Hoven decided to stay behind at the Spreewald house. In Aron Bruckstätt's house, with his body in the bathtub. Outside the house is Aron's Land Rover, and somewhere nearby Herr van Hoven's Porsche. It might look as if Herr van Hoven had paid a visit to his wife's lover. A visit with consequences.

We say nothing. We don't speculate as to what he's planning. All we know is that this time he's not going to sacrifice a third party. This time he's going to make the greatest sacrifice possible—he's going to give himself up. Nonetheless I wonder what's happening in the Spreewald. Whether he's calling the police. Whether the police will possibly find two dead bodies in the house. Two bodies and a suicide letter with a false confession. From the corner of my eye I see Laura shake her head and I know she's contemplating the same scenario.

"Did he say anything else?" she gasps after a while.

I nod feebly.

. . . Tell my wife that I forgive her.

Now Laura falls silent. Occasionally I hear a faint sobbing. I fulfill my task and take her home. I park the Mini in the garage, help Laura out of the car and into the house. Then I call for an ambulance.

"I need help, I've had a fall . . ." I give them Laura's name and the van Hovens' address. I hang up. Leave the house without saying goodbye, without a final glance. We used to be friends, in a past life.

AUGUST 2019

TWO WEEKS LATER

"Vivi . . ."

Laura van Hoven sucks air through her teeth; the pain in her rib cage is a permanent reminder. In half an hour she's got a checkup. Her doctor is satisfied with the healing process, but she herself can feel her injury with every movement and she's still taking the painkillers she was prescribed after the night in the forest. Vivi is also tugging at her hand, which makes the stabbing pain in her ribs even worse. Laura switches her daughter to the other hand and asks her to walk a little more slowly as they make their way to the subway station. Vivi doesn't like the crowds in the subway, but with her injury Laura is still unable to drive.

It's shortly after eight o'clock in the morning, the fourteenth morning after the night in the forest, the sixteenth after the night when she killed Aron Bruckstätt. Sometimes she wonders if it'll go on like this forever and she'll count the rest of her days in this fashion: the sixteenth morning after. The twenty-third. The five hundred and thirteenth. At the same time life keeps going somehow. The world keeps turning relentlessly and the sun keeps coming up. Laura doesn't know if this is a comforting feeling or sheer irony. On the other hand, she'll never have to ask herself again if Gero really was the right man for her. She thinks back to those lie-ins and days in baggy T-shirts and comfy leggings, the endless waiting when he came home late yet again from work, postponed holidays and all the things that at some point made her doubt it was a great love. Now she knows it was the greatest. It still is and so it will remain. Gero kept his promise. He did everything for her and made the ultimate sacrifice. Laura still can't think about this without the tears welling up. She hastily wipes her eyes; she doesn't want Vivi to see her crying.

"Hurry up, Mummy!" her sweet, naïve daughter calls out when the subway station comes into view, tearing herself away from Laura. "Or we'll miss the train!"

Jan Sprenger laughs when a little girl comes leaping past him. She doesn't want to miss the train.

"Good morning," he says to the woman who's making a miserable attempt to keep up with her little one. She doesn't say anything back and Jan shrugs. He winds out the green-and-white awning, already slightly bleached from the rain and sun, to protect the produce he brought here early in his van from the farmer. The morning sky above Charlottenburg is temporarily clear after last night's downpour and the damp pavement is steaming. Jan squints at the sun, which is still peeping coyly across the façades opposite, then he turns the sign on his shop door to "OPEN" and goes in.

He took over the small grocery from his father; he's never known anything else. His friends are engineers, doctors, artists, all of whom call Jan "the vegetable man," and he likes this, it makes him proud. Even as a child he used to come here straight after school and do his homework between the boxes of potatoes and giant melons, marveling at his father. How friendly he was to customers, how much laughter there was, and how wonderfully slow time passed in the little shop where the goods were still weighed with old-fashioned market scales and prices were often approximated, in comparison with the rest of the big hectic city— something that Jan has increasingly come to appreciate the older he gets. He's happy. He was lucky. If Uncle Adwo hadn't sorted out his adoption back then, he wouldn't be in his little shop now, but in a Polish steelworks. His asthma might even have worsened and he wouldn't be alive now.

"Good morning, Frau Kaiser," he says to the elderly lady who, as ever, is the first customer on a Saturday. He asks about her husband's aches and pains as he fills brown paper bags with half a kilo of beans, a head of broccoli and a handful of cherries. "Oh, Fräulein Müller!" he calls out, laughing, to the next regular who enters the shop, followed by Herr Jasper. Every Saturday the latter comes with his little son Mats to get a sumptuous breakfast for the family. Fräulein Müller buys a cauliflower, a grapefruit, a few apples and some mirabelles. As he's totting up her bill, Herr Jasper is already waiting behind her with his items. With one hand Jan gives Fräulein Müller her change, with the other he passes the whining Mats a nectarine across the counter.

"Didn't you sleep well, my little friend?"

"Well? More like not at all." Herr Jasper laughs. "It must be the excitement, we're off on holiday tomorrow."

"Oh, great," Jan says to Mats. "Where are you going?"

"Baltic," the young boy says, chewing, as nectarine juice dribbles down his little chin.

"Are you excited?"

Mats nods so eagerly that his hair flops down over his face. Jan smiles. He always loved the seaside. He still does. Just as his parents used to take him to the sea, so he always goes there with his wife every year. In two weeks they're going to Italy: the three of them, for the first time. His little girl is now four months old, old enough for the sea, the most beautiful place in the world.

"I was six when I went to the Baltic for the first time," Jan says, to which a grinning Mats replies that he was four. "That's good," Jan says. "You can't start going to the sea early enough."

Only when Mats and his father have left the shop does Jan notice something on his counter that shouldn't be there. It's a letter. Fräulein Müller left it.

NADJA

A panic attack is like standing on the edge of white cliffs. Above me the lavender sky is clouding over. One false step, just a little nudge and I'll fall. I peer down into the depths, expect to see Marta floating on her back in the red salt lake of Aigues-Mortes, in a white dress that the water has made almost transparent and now shimmers pink. I know she'll open her blue eyes and stare at me. I take a breath and a step backward. It's still dangerous where I am, but today I'm standing in safety. I've survived. I'm free. I made it back home and I know that this is a chance I'm desperate to take advantage of.

I'm not standing on the cliff edge.

I'm standing outside a five-story apartment block in Charlottenburg and my finger is hovering above the bell beside the name "SPRENGER."

Dear Janek,
I come into your shop every Saturday to see how you are. I didn't dare to begin with. Although you were very young back in Zabrew, just five, I wasn't sure how sharp your memory was, how well you recalled our mother's face and whether you might recognize her

features in mine. So I hung around the display outside, picked up an apple and looked at it. At that moment you came out of the shop and asked if you could help. For a few seconds I forgot how to breathe.

You.

My little brother who's turned into a big man. How good-looking you were, how your eyes shone, how friendly your voice was. I looked at the ground, expecting you to recognize me and chase me away. Not long after I went to prison, Uncle Adwo came and told me he'd found good parents for you and that you'd soon be moving to Berlin. Later, I learned that your new parents' place was lovely, that they treated you like their own son and you'd settled in without difficulty. You were doing excellently at school, you liked playing football in your spare time and you had a few nice friends. I think he told me all of this to motivate me, to make me get a grip on my own life. He only succeeded to an extent.

You must know that after I was released from the youth detention center I went back to Zabrew. I looked after Aunt Evelyn, who'd become very ill. In part this must have been down to me and all the worry I'd caused her. After her death Uncle Adwo persuaded me to move to Berlin and he gave me your address. "Go and see him," he told me. "Talk to him." But I was frightened. I know you never went back to Zabrew after your adoption and there will have been good reasons for this, the most important one no doubt being me.

But you didn't recognize me that day outside your shop, and for the most part I was glad about this. Now I could shop at your place every Saturday. As Frau Schmidt, Fräulein Wagner or Müller, under all those other names you laughingly made up for me, oblivious to the truth. I could see you. Get to know you. Listen to your conversations with customers. I found out that you were married and a father. I found out where you were going on holiday. I found out so much that made me glad. You're leading a perfectly normal, happy life, just as I always hoped you would.

Recently I had a devastating experience which made me realize that I owe you something else: the truth about what happened on June 17, 1999 and the man who killed our mother. Even though you never returned to Zabrew, I know from my own experience how much the past haunts you. You can suppress it, but at certain moments it comes back to get you and tear you to shreds. I'd just like to give you the opportunity, Janek. If you've drawn a line under the past and feel free from it, then I don't wish to impose myself on you. But if in certain moments you do feel you'd like to know what really happened, rest assured that I'm here to answer your questions. I promise to stay away from your shop in the future, but I'll leave you my mobile number. Feel free to call any time, no matter what you want to say.

I love you, my angel.

Your sister, Nadja

PS: Did you know that my name—Nadja—means "hope?"

You just sent me a text message with an address and a time: *Sunday, 3 p.m.*

My finger presses the bell. As I wait for the buzzing of the door opener I nervously rearrange my hair. It took three washes to get rid of the wig glue. The symptoms of my concussion are now milder and the wound on my forehead is just a bright-pink streak. The *devastating experience* I referred to in my letter has left me very thoughtful. I still think about her often, my former friend who was involved in this experience, and her husband. I think I can forgive them, because I know myself what people are capable of doing, out of love or fear. But I'll never see her again. Instead I rang my neighbor's doorbell yesterday evening to introduce myself. Although she had a few friends over, she invited me in. It was a lovely evening.

There is an ugly buzzing sound; I push the door open and enter a hallway with black-and-white tiles. Beneath the stairs is a pram. I wonder if it's yours. As I overheard from a conversation in your shop, the little one is four months old now. I've got a present for her. The fluffy pink dog I originally bought for the daughter of my former friend. I don't want it lying around pointlessly in my chest of drawers anymore. I go up the old stairs, which creak beneath my feet, to the third floor. Your wife is standing in the doorway. She's got long, blond braids and is smiling uncertainly.

"Nadja?"

"Yes," I say, giving her an equally uncertain smile.

"I'm Kati, Jan's wife." She shakes my hand and invites me in. Everything is colorful in your hallway; a mass of coats bulges out from a green wall. Beneath a chain of lights, photographs of you, Kati and the baby hang in different frames. A lovely sight and it also makes me realize what I'm doing here. That I *am* here, with you, twenty years too late. For a moment the ground beneath my feet swells like red water; I want to turn around and run away. But then you appear from one of the rooms and I'm rooted to the spot. I stare at you like you stare at me. I sense you looking for something familiar. Something to connect this thirty-five-year-old stranger to your fifteen-year-old sister. I don't know if you find anything or what it could be. Your expression is inscrutable.

"Come in," you say and go ahead into the living room. I

follow you. Behind me Kati says, "If you need anything, I'm in the kitchen, okay?" She doesn't get an answer.

You sit on a green corduroy sofa; I unintentionally sink into a leather armchair opposite you. For a while we say nothing, just gaze at each other. Then you clear your throat.

"June 17, 1999."

I nod. Squeeze the plastic bag with the fluffy pink dog in my lap. It makes crunching sounds.

"Nadja?" you continue. "Why did Marta's last guest do what he did?"

I nod again. I'd prepared these words specially; now I rummage around in my mind for them, but I've forgotten. It doesn't matter; the truth doesn't need anything prefabricated. I just begin.

"When I was as old as you were back then, I could never get to sleep, you know? It got on Marta's nerves, but she would sit on the edge of the bed, tell me good-night stories and sing me *chansons* until her patience ran out. Then she'd say, *Go to sleep now, for God's sake*, and somehow that worked. She never sang for you, even though you found it more difficult to get to sleep than I did. She was forever complaining. How was she to explain to her guests that in the room next door a child was crying and whining? How could they relax and how could she do her job?" I sniff. "In the end it was the straw that broke the camel's back, as they say. That morning we were so tired, you and I. We'd slept through the alarm several times and could hardly get out of bed. I told you we had to hurry. You said you had a headache and wanted to stay at home, but I wasn't taking no for an answer. I got you dressed and sent you over to Aunt Evelyn so she could take you to kindergarten. When you left I went back into our room and fell on the bed. I reached for the cola, which was on the floor on your side of the bed, and rinsed my mouth out with it. I then noticed the strange white bits that had settled at the bottom of the bottle. I knew immediately. A few days earlier I'd seen the pack of sleeping pills lying around in the kitchen, but thought nothing of it. Marta wasn't taking them, however. She'd mixed some in the cola she'd given you the previous evening. Coincidentally I'd drunk some too. I sat on the bed for ages, in shock—everything rolled past me. The way we lived, how much was wrong, how often we'd resolved to change something and yet nothing had happened. Not even after Aunt Evelyn had put the woman from the child welfare office onto us and we could no longer hide the seriousness of the situation. How you looked at me every day, with your gorgeous, hopeful eyes, and believed me when I said that everything would get better. How I lied to you again every day. I heard sounds coming from the bathroom. Marta had got up and was running a bath. I sat on the bed, sobbing. I heard her get into the tub and the water sloshing as she moved. I heard her humming *"Retiens la nuit"* cheerfully to herself. I took the bottle of cola into the bathroom and screamed at her. *Isn't it bad enough that he's already got asthma from your smoking? And now you're giving a five-year-old sleeping pills so he doesn't disturb you when you're fucking!* She didn't react, she just looked at me and asked why I wasn't at school. She called me a lazy bitch and a sponger, and said I shouldn't have any pretensions. *You are what you are, Nadja.* Most important, I wasn't any better than her— she'd looked through me when I was a child and noticed my slate-gray interior, and one day, when I had my own kid I didn't want, I'd appreciate little tricks like the sleeping pill in the cola.

I left the bathroom, slammed the door shut and didn't intend on coming back, really I didn't. But she wouldn't keep quiet, she kept going on and on. I was now in the kitchen, fetching a glass of tap water. Through the closed bathroom door I heard her start banging on about France. About how she could have been a dancer in Paris. At that moment my eyes caught sight of the bronze ballerina on the windowsill. I put the glass down, took it from its place as if on autopilot, went into the bathroom and screamed, *You're not a fucking ballerina anymore, you're a mother!*

"And then it happened. An outstretched arm taking a backswing. Then striking. *Thud-thud-thud-thud.* Four times in succession I heard the hollow sound. The blows to Marta's head." I look up at your deadpan face. "It wasn't a guest; it was a slate-gray girl. I'm the monster, Janek."

"I know," you reply. "I always did, even as a five-year-old." You lean forward, your forearms on your knees, your hands clasped. "Why did you make up the story about the man?"

I shake my head.

"It's very complicated, Janek. I mean, I loved her too, despite everything. She wasn't all bad. Sometimes . . . quite the opposite. Do you remember how beautiful she was when she danced with us to Johnny Hallyday? Or when, on one of her good days, she got on the stepladder and started ripping the old wallpaper from the wall? Her throaty laugh when she said, *Bugger it. They can all go and get stuffed. We're a family, aren't we?* And how about when she took us in her arms. The three of us against the rest of the world." I wipe the tears from my face. "I didn't consciously lie. First I had no recollection of what had happened in the bathroom. My mind must have simply shut down. I believed what I was saying. That

I thought Marta was ill. That I saw the man. Maybe that way it was simpler for me to deal with what I'd done."

"So when did you remember it again?"

"When I was in custody in Zabrew and scratching the paint off the wall. It was as if I were uncovering the layers of my memory. When Uncle Adwo came, explained the status of the investigation and finally let the cement dust trickle through his fingers, I suddenly knew for certain that I'd never get to the sea. And I also knew why. I didn't deserve to go. Marta was dead and I, her daughter, clearly the only other person in our flat at the time, and ground down for all those years by the situation at home, must have killed her in a knee-jerk reaction. But was it always really that simple? Yes, Janek. It was that simple. It was just as they put it in the charge against me. That's why I deserved to be in prison rather than by the sea. I killed our mother." I utter these words for the first time. They weigh heavily on my lips, they taste of bile and make my tongue swell. And yet they're right. It's the truth. What Uncle Adwo, my therapist, the police and everyone always suspected, what they thought and figured out, but had never heard coming from me so clearly. *I killed our mother.*

"But you never corrected the lie about the last guest."

"Possibly not . . . I'm ashamed to say it, but . . . perhaps I harbored the tiniest, silliest hope that they would believe me after all and let me go. Then I'd have looked after you and that way tried to make everything better again. Very few people, I think, are prepared to stand by what they've done when it comes to such a terrible deed. Instead they try to get off. It's simply human nature."

You breathe audibly.

"I think that's what disappointed me most, Nadja. That you were a coward. For me you were the brave big sister. Who beat up the strongest boys to protect us. Who would have been prepared to make it to the sea with me if we hadn't been caught."

I can't help laughing.

"With the jar of mirabelles from Aunt Evelyn's windowsill."

"Thieving vermin!" you say, imitating her voice and laughing too. It almost sounds relaxed.

I laugh more loudly. Not because there really is something to laugh about. Not because we've finished telling our stories, or because with one laugh everything that happened suddenly has no meaning anymore. I don't know if the grown man sitting opposite me will ever be my little brother again. Perhaps you'll throw me out of your flat the moment we've stopped laughing and yell after me that I'm never to show my face around here again. I laugh all the same, even though this moment may only remain a moment. I laugh all the same and so do you. It sounds so lovely when you laugh.

"Hey!" Kati steps into the doorway of the living room with a finger to her lips and a stony face. "The baby!"

"Yes, sorry," you say to Kati and gesture to me with outstretched hands that we've got to turn down the volume. "Marta's sleeping."

At once I fall silent and raise my eyebrows at you.

You called your daughter Marta.

You nod and say with a smile, "It's a new beginning."

BERLIN STAR LAWYER ATTACKED
BY FELLOW INMATE

Yesterday, a bloody incident took place in Tegel prison. The former Berlin star lawyer, Gero van Hoven (47), currently serving a six-year sentence, was seriously injured in a knife attack by fellow inmate Paul H. (46). Responding to questions, the governor of Tegel prison, Dietmar Jungblut, stated that H. stabbed van Hoven with a knife, narrowly missing his heart.

In July, van Hoven confessed to killing his friend and tennis partner, the photographer Aron B. (39), and pleaded voluntary manslaughter. Van Hoven said he had lent B. money for an art project, but the loan had never been paid back as per their agreement. In 2015 H. became known as the "motorway monster from Zervenwald" and is serving an eight-year sentence for the manslaughter of his young lover Nelly S. (22), which is said to have been the background to the attack. Van Hoven represented H. at his trial and H., who has always insisted on his innocence, blamed van Hoven for his imprisonment. According to the management of Tegel prison, it is still unknown where the knife came from that was used in the altercation.

As van Hoven's lawyer, Tabea Lenggries, stated yesterday morning, her client was in a stable condition. "Herr van Hoven bears no grudge against Herr H., and has no intention of pursuing the matter any further. He hopes that he can spend the rest of his time in Tegel prison peacefully and is looking forward to returning to his family afterward." As a number of sources have disclosed, Lenggries is currently in negotiations with the public prosecutor about a possible reduction in her client's sentence. When asked about this, however, Lenggries refused to comment.

Van Hoven's wife has also spoken about yesterday's incident in Tegel prison. She said, "I'm so relieved that Gero survived the assault. He is the best husband and father you could wish for. I will always stand by him as he has done for me. That's what we profoundly believe makes a good marriage: for better or for worse."

EPILOGUE

Everything's slipping. Inside I'm falling.

It's like going out the jump door. Hold your breath and just let go.

I do it, I close my eyes. And fall—right into you. Now I'm part of you, forever. Just like you always wanted, but in a different way, one that you will curse as soon as you understand what you've done. What it really means is that from now on I'm going to be with you for the rest of your life.

"Do you believe that someone out of the past, someone dead, can enter and take possession of a living being?" Tom Helmore, alias Gavin Elster, asks his old friend Scottie.

"No," Scottie replies, but that's unimportant for he's not the killer.

What matters is what *you* believe, Hannes.

Do you believe that you'll ever be able to look up at a blue sky without thinking of me? Do you really believe you'll ever take a walk in the woods again without me being your shadow, without hearing my voice in the whispering of the trees, in the slightest rustle, in the gentlest breath of wind? Can you walk down the streets of our village without being reminded of how we once wandered down them together? Can you look at my parents and cope with their faces etched deeply with pain?

Oh, Hannes.

At the end, just before the fall, I hear you sobbing. *Forgive me, Nelly. Please forgive me*. I did, I have forgiven you—of course, why not? Why should I have felt hatred in the last few seconds of my life when I could just as easily feel happy? Happy with my love for Paul, with the warm voice of my grandfather in my ears, with the thoughts of my favorite films and one last glance up at an enchantingly blue sky.

No, Hannes, I don't hate you. And I forgive you, even though it won't do you any good and my forgiveness won't protect you from what will happen from this moment on. You would have to forgive yourself—that would be your cure—only you won't manage it.

No, I don't hate you. I feel sorry for you; I always did. For "guilt" is just another synonym for "death"—a crueler, more agonizing death. *Poor Hannes.*

THANKS!

You'd probably laugh if you knew how long this book had been finished before I finally managed to write the acknowledgments. I kept procrastinating. Not because I wasn't grateful. On the contrary, "thanks" is such a small and sadly overused word, and I doubt it can even begin to express my amazement and awe at what has happened over the past two years.

So first I'd like to thank you, Claudia Baumhöver. In dtv you found me the best publishing house I could have wished for (and here I'd like to officially upgrade the rating from "good" to "best"). I'd also like to thank you, Bianca Dombrowa. Not only are you my wonderful, savvy editor, you're also my ever-vigilant "big sister" and such a special person that I always feel deeply touched. Now I come to you, Andrea Seibert and team. You send my stories around the world, thus making something happen that I'd never have dreamed was possible. And all the rest of you at dtv: you don't just do your job, you live and breathe books, and really understand the people behind them. I hope you know how amazing—and extraordinary—that is.

Likewise, thank you, Caterina Karsten, over and over again, not just for representing me as my agent and giving me such valuable support in my writing, but also for saying the right things (or sending chocolate) in the right situation.

Lala: thanks for your friendship and all those good, painful, necessary kicks.

Tim: "If you stop now you'll never know how close you were," I once read in an article of yours, long before I began writing for *myMONK* myself, and I've never forgotten it. Working with you has often given me the courage to keep going and trust what's inside me.

Christian: I tell you far too seldom how happy I am that we found each other—but I am and it's a great gift for me.

Mama and Papa: it's in difficult times that you see just how deep the roots are. Thanks for the most precious thing of all: being unconditional.

Karl: this book is dedicated to you as a reminder that without you nothing would be of any significance. I want you to know that whatever this strange, beautiful and sometimes mean life has in store for you, there will always be someone on hand to give you the lightsaber for your battles: your old mum.

Finally I have to thank you, dear readers, bloggers, booksellers, promoters, my loyal "gang" on social media, who read me, publicize me, invite me and take an interest. Where would I be without you? Thanks for accompanying me on this exciting journey and giving me daily reminders that no dream is futile or—on the contrary—too crazy to dream it.

Romy Hausmann, February 2020

ABOUT THE AUTHOR

Romy Hausmann lives with her family in a remote house in the woods in Stuttgart, Germany. *Dear Child*, her English debut, was a #1 international bestseller, a *BookPage* Top Ten Mystery & Suspense of the Year, and a *New York Times* Group Text pick. *Sleepless* is her second English novel.